Further Acclaim for *Eat Me*

"*EAT ME* caused such a sensation that U.S. publishers have flocked to women's erotica." —*Entertainment Weekly* (who named Linda in their list of the top 100 most creative people in entertainment, 6/27/97)

". . . witty, sophisticated . . . charms as few examples of the genre ever have." —*Kirkus Review*

". . . a vigorous book. . . . There is nothing I can quote directly in the entire book, except a conjunctive clause or two, but one learns a great deal about the uses of fruit, the technical skills required of a dominatrix, the frustrations of voyeurism, and the etiquette of sex with complete and total strangers." —*New York Sunday Newsday,* Currents and Books

"Everybody's talking about *EAT ME*." —*Playboy*

". . . a great chick read." —*Bust*

"Strap on a bib and a pair of stilettos—the feast is about to begin. From the opening lines . . . the reader is in for a rollicking, racy romp . . ." —*Columbus Dispatch*

". . . a racy and entertaining romp . . . settle in for some well-written erotica. You may even pick up some tips." —*Salon*

"I laughed out loud at a kiss that goes on for six pages while the participants ponder each other's intentions . . . very funny stuff." —*Washington Post Book World*

Eat Me
was a Summer's Best Bet Beach Read
in *marie claire* magazine.

Also by Linda Jaivin

Rock 'n' Roll Babes from Outer Space

Eat Me

LINDA JAIVIN

Broadway Books   New York

BROADWAY

A hardcover edition of this book was published in 1997 by
Broadway Books.

EAT ME. Copyright © 1997 by Linda Jaivin. All rights reserved.
Printed in the United States of America. No part of this book may
be reproduced or transmitted in any form or by any means,
electronic or mechanical, including photocopying, recording, or by
any information storage and retrieval system, without written
permission from the publisher. For information address Broadway
Books, a division of Bantam Doubleday Dell Publishing Group, Inc.,
1540 Broadway, New York, NY 10036.

Broadway Books titles may be purchased for business or promotional
use or for special sales. For information, please write to: Special
Markets Department, Bantam Doubleday Dell Publishing Group,
Inc., 1540 Broadway, New York, NY 10036.

BROADWAY BOOKS and its logo, a letter B bisected on the
diagonal, are trademarks of Broadway Books, a division of Bantam
Doubleday Dell Publishing Group, Inc.

First trade paperback edition published 1998.

Book design by Terry Karydes
Cover design by Roberto de Vicq de Cumptich

The Library of Congress has catalogued the hardcover edition as:
Jaivin, Linda.
Eat me / Linda Jaivin.
p.   cm.
ISBN 0-553-06697-8 (hc)
I. Title. PR9619.3.J247E28   1997
823—dc21   96-47517   CIP

ISBN 0-7679-0159-2

98 99 00 01 02 10 9 8 7 6 5 4 3 2 1

For David

Contents

Eat Me

CHAPTER ONE

"Eat Me"

She ran her fingers over the fresh figs. Surprising little sacs they were. Funny, dark, and wrinkled, yet so exquisite on the tongue. Mother Nature had surely been thinking of Father Nature when she invented figs.

Ava looked up, tossing back her long black hair and glancing around with ice blue eyes. It seemed she had the whole supermarket to herself. Sarah, the one cashier on late-night duty, had just checked out the only other customer and was absorbed once more in her Harlequin romance. All that could be heard was the hum of the refrigerators and the uninvasive beat of the Muzak. The artificial chill of the heavy-duty air-conditioning took the edge off what might otherwise have been an almost unbearably lusty cornucopia of smells, from the sweet ripeness of the bananas to the citron pungency of the lemons and limes. Everything was cold in supermarkets—the shiny mop-polished floors, the gelid steel of the shelves, the polar fluorescence of the lighting.

Ava picked up a fig from the pile and sniffed it. She stuck out her tongue and licked it. If milk is for pussies, why not figs? Slowly, she hiked her short black skirt up above the lace tops of her stockings. She wore no underwear. She never wore underwear. What was the point? She touched herself and found that she was warm and wet. With her other hand, she brought the fig down between her legs. She teased the mouth of her cunt with it, gently at first and then with vigor. She could feel the skin of the fig burst. Some of the sticky seed spilled out, adhering to the lips of her cunt and the secret places on the inside of her thighs. She put the fig back in her mouth. Salty sweet. She sucked it dry.

Ava dropped the spent fruit back onto the shelf, and advanced upon the strawberries. Large, red, and firm, they knew exactly where they belonged. High inside her. She took a few tight steps, placing one stilettoed foot in front of the other, concentrating on the sensation the strawberries created as they slipped and crushed against each other. She thought she could distinguish each ticklish green stem. Then she stopped, leaned back against the shelves, closed her eyes, and pulped.

Adam, the store detective, swallowed hard. He tried to get a better view of Ava from behind the piled-up bags of chips where he'd concealed himself. The lump in his throat traveled down his thick neck and into the top of his tightly buttoned shirt. He had been standing there, behind the snack foods, when she strode into the fruit and vegetable section. He'd seen everything. He knew he ought to have apprehended her when she performed that act with the fig, but he found himself paralyzed with . . . what? A shudder went through him now. He hitched up his khaki trousers and ran an awkward hand over his crewcut. His movements were clumsy. A shiny packet of low-cholesterol, all-natural, blue corn chips crunched to the floor with a clamor that made his heart skip a beat.

If Ava noticed, she didn't let on. Her expression hadn't changed. It was rapturous. She hitched her skirt higher, up above her garter belt. Thrusting two fingers deep into her own soft fruit, she plumped and prodded, soaking them in juices fresh and tangy. She pulled them out slowly and placed them in her mouth, sucking on them between pursed lips. A dollop of strawberry-colored cream adhered to her chin. She fished in her purse for her pocket mirror. Bending down, with her ass pointed in Adam's direction, she held the mirror between her legs and, parting her labia with her fingers, studied herself with intense concentration.

Grapes. This was the thought that struck Ava now.

She selected carefully. Firm fruit in a tight bunch. Large, round, purple ones. She turned around so that she was facing, once again, in Adam's direction and leaned back on the shelf. Opening her legs wide, tracing little circles on her clitoris with one hand, she pushed the grapes up herself with the other, a little at a time, pulling back a bit before each new thrust. The stems scratched and tickled, and she liked that.

Without warning, Ava lifted her head to look straight into the eyes of the man who'd been spying on her all this time. A smile played on her bloodred lips. Of course, she knew he was there. Smirking, she extracted a single, dripping grape and offered it to him. Adam stood frozen as a TV dinner. She shrugged. Puckering her lips, she ingested the grape with a great slurping sound and put the rest of the bunch back on the shelf. Never once releasing his gaze from hers, she felt around behind her until she located a ripe kiwifruit. She held it up in front of her face, still looking hard into his eyes, and dug her fingernails into the gooseberry flesh, rupturing the skin. Green liquid ran down her fingers. Her eyes bored into his. She inserted the ragged fruit into the still-hungry maw between her legs, now running with juices of every description.

Adam took a single, tremulous step in her direction. She pretended not to notice. Calmly, she extracted the kiwifruit and proceeded to eat half. Ava held out the other half to the detective and arched an eyebrow. He was striding toward her now. Taking the fruit. Eating with rapture. Dropping to his knees in front of her.

She widened her stance. In one swift movement, she reached out and, grabbing him by the back of his head, brought his mouth up to her cunt. He gasped.

"Eat me," she commanded.

"No, I . . ." he mumbled, panic in his voice.

"Eat me, you filthy spud," she repeated, threateningly this time.

"I . . ."

Ava fumbled in her bag with her free hand until she found her whip. The compact one she always kept in her purse. She cracked it against the floor next to Adam.

He shook his head, but his thick short hair only excited her as it brushed back and forth against her sensitive and swollen sex. The stubble on his chin grated engagingly on her inner thighs.

"Eat me, you coffee stain. You slice of moldy cheese. You slab of five-day-old horsemeat," she taunted, teasing the back of his neck with the handle of the whip.

"No!" he protested. "No, I won't! And you can't make me! I'm a good boy!"

"Naughty boy," Ava contradicted. "Naughty as extra-large French fries with vinegar and salt. Naughty as Heavenly Chocolate Cake." She yanked him closer.

"Not true!" he gasped, clutching onto her legs with both hands. "I'm as unsullied as Sara Lee, as pure as buckwheat pasta. I won't—*ouch!*—participate in your disgusting little game." She tugged his ear, hard. He whimpered and stopped his struggle.

"All right," he whispered inside her. "All right then. I will eat you. I will. You will be my pâté, my calamari, my pumpkin risotto, my roast and three veg." He ate now, ate like a man who was starving. He devoured her with his tongue, his lips, his teeth, and his hands. He ate every last trace of fig and strawberry and grape and kiwifruit, transformed by her love blender into a warm and salty tropical fruit yogurt.

Ava dropped the whip. Her hand closed on a bunch of bananas as she slid down to the floor. Adam was kneeling between her legs now, still feeding at her goluptious trough. He reached out, grabbed her hands, and pinned them to the floor with his own, forcing her to release the bananas. She raised her head and glared at him. Struggled, but to no avail. He was smirking now. At his own, torturously slow pace, he returned his attention to her cunt. Moaning, she came in his mouth, kicking hard with one foot and sending a high-heeled shoe skimming down the aisle in the direction of the breakfast cereals. Still lapping, he released her hands, which lay limp by her side. He fumbled for the bananas and peeled one. She drew in her breath as he pushed it inside her. He scrambled to his feet, and watched out of the corner of his eye as, with well-timed thrusts, she brought herself to orgasm again. She didn't stop until the banana disintegrated into pap.

"You disgusting bitch," Adam spat, walking toward the vegetables. He returned with an English cucumber. She'd stood up and picked up her whip again.

"What did you say?" Her tone was imperious, if a little shaky. "You little piece of rat-trap salami," she spat huskily.

"You disgusting bitch," he repeated, with slightly less conviction, his eyes on her whip hand. "I despise you more than tinned minestrone, more than, than . . . more than angel food cake mix, more than sliced cheese."

"Take off your trousers, Chiko face," she said, fondling the leather.

"No way, cod feet."

"Take off your trousers, I said, full-fat."

"Bitch. Cunt. Soup bones."

Ava snapped the whip with a sudden movement. The end licked Adam's thigh.

His nostrils flared. He pulled down his trousers, revealing that he wasn't wearing any underwear either. He had a massive erection. Ava gently flicked at it with the whip. She sneered. "So curd cheeks. You've been enjoying this all along."

Adam refused to meet her gaze.

"Bend down."

"No."

"Don't make me angry."

He scowled as he bent down, ass to her, balancing with his hands against the shelf with the fruit.

"Give me that cucumber."

Turning his head, he watched as Ava lubricated it in her vagina. Slowly, she insinuated it up his ass. He groaned and twisted with pain and pleasure.

Suddenly, there was a silence. Someone had turned off the Muzak. Ava and Adam froze, as with a slight electronic crackle and a clearing of throat, Sarah's voice came over the PA system. "Attention, shoppers. The store is about to close. Please make your final selections and pay for them at the counter. Thank you for your cooperation. Please shop with us again."

7

Ava removed the cucumber from Adam's anus and tossed it back over into the vegetable section. It landed right next to all the other cucumbers.

"Good toss, cupcake."

"Thanks." They laughed, a little harshly, and quickly straightened their clothing. Ava retrieved her shoe and folded up her whip, putting it back in her purse. "I'd better buy something," she whispered, thinking randomly of coconut milk and small packets of tarragon.

"See you next week, honey pot?" asked Adam. "Usual time, usual place?"

"You bet, sweetpea."

"Bye for now."

"Bye." Adam watched as Ava sauntered down the aisle to the cashier. Sarah looked up at her, wondering how one of Ava's stockings had fallen to her ankle. Hadn't she noticed?

"Good book?" Ava asked Sarah as she handed over her purchases.

"Yes, very," sighed Sarah, her eyes on Ava's bare thigh. "I love romances. Do you?"

"Of course," Ava answered, winking. "Have them all the time."

CHAPTER TWO

Veal

"Delicious," purred Chantal, narrowing her dramatic green eyes and running her tongue suggestively over bee-sting lips. A man striding past their café table came to such a sudden halt at the sight that he nearly fell over his own feet. Even in the smorgasbord of Darlinghurst, Chantal stood out like a designer entrée: elegant, color coordinated, piquant. She looked every inch the fashion editor she was. If she noticed the man, she gave no sign, and he quickly moved on in embarrassment.

To Chantal's left sat Julia, her small pointed chin balanced on folded hands. Her dark eyes were closed and a dreamy smile curved her soft mouth. Her warm olive skin glowed in the sunlight, and her long raven hair cascaded in a frozen flow down her back. So still was she sitting that not a single item of her abundant silver jewelry jangled.

To Chantal's right perched Helen, a whole-grain loaf of a woman in beige and brown, seeded with freckles. Behind tortoiseshell spectacles, her eyes were a dark mustard. Helen glanced down at the manuscript, the pages of which lay scattered on the table in front of them. She shook her head appreciatively. "Chantal's right, Phippa," she enthused to the fourth member of their little group, who was seated opposite Chantal. "*Delicious* is the word."

"Yeah, they're, uh, supposed to be pretty good for you too," Philippa replied, deadpan, holding up half an apple-and-walnut muffin and pretending to study it. "No sugar, no animal fats, no artificial ingredients."

"No shit, Phippa," Helen cut in, rolling her eyes. "We're not talking about the muffins. We're talking about your story. And you know it. It was wonderful finally hearing you read some of your work to us."

"Did you really like it?" Philippa grinned shyly, looking down, sweeping the pages into a pile. She shook them out for crumbs, and then fed them into the mouth of her cavernous shoulder bag, which she replaced on the back of the chair.

The four were having breakfast at Café Da Vida on Victoria Street, their favorite hangout. It was a gorgeous Sydney spring morning, all the more perfect for being a late Saturday morning at that. The native fauna of Darlinghurst, dressed to thrill, were sloping through the urban jungle toward their favorite coffee holes. Actors, artists, sex workers, junkies, nurses, actors who were also junkies, artists who were also sex workers, sex workers who pretended to be nurses, gays, straights, bis, straight-acting gays, gay-acting straights, immigrants with Hungarian accents, young English and German and French backpackers. In pairs and packs they came. There were loners, too. Though some carried just the big black bags underneath their eyes, others toted much-thumbed journals, the weekend papers, or slim books by fashionable authors.

Philippa wanted, more than anything else, to be one of those fashionable authors. There were two things about the publishing industry that she knew favored her chances. One, sex sells; two, she'd look great in the photograph on the dustcover jacket. In real life, she was afflicted by a kind of physical awkwardness born of shyness about her tall, big-boned frame. But in photographs she looked a sultry vamp, the quintessential femme fatale. She had thick black hair, which fell to her shoulders, gray eyes, and creamy skin. She tended toward black turtlenecks worn with dark jeans. She secured the jeans with wide black belts and anchored them with heavy black boots. It was a look that drew inviting glances from dykes in the leather scene as well as a certain kind of neurotic male artist. Glances she returned. But rarely—so far as her friends could tell, anyway—followed up. Philippa appeared to be single-mindedly devoted to her writing. She worked part-time as a journalist in a government department and full-time on her erotic fiction. I am, she would declare, mistress of the V-words: vicariousness and voyeurism. I have, she would insist, an excellent and satisfying sex life, but it's in my head, not my bed.

"Helen." Philippa suddenly looked anxious. "You're up on these things. What's the latest line on pornography among feminists? I'm a bit worried. Think they'll take a dim view of the story?"

"Oh, look, it's not that clear, really," Helen answered. "Some feminists still maintain that all pornography is representational violence against women. But I think that kind of line can hardly apply to women's erotica. Particularly when it involves a woman stuffing an English cucumber up a man's ass. No, I thought the story was fabulous," she affirmed. "Really. I found it, uh"—she raised her eyes to Heaven and paused, as though interrogating God as to how She would have put it—"both erotic and empowering." Helen liked words like *empowering*. She was a feminist academic and film critic, and terms like that came with the turf. She paused, primly smoothing her longish skirt over her knees, and added, "I think you could've done more with the whip, though."

Chantal pursed her lips and lashed at the pavement with an imaginary whip, startling a skater on Rollerblades. An older European at the next table stared, utterly rapt, over the rim of his espresso.

Philippa nudged Helen and pointed at Julia with her chin. Chantal looked over at her too. "Wonder what she's thinking about?" Philippa mouthed to the others.

Sex. That was what Julia was thinking about.

Julia had recently had one heaven of a night. As much as she'd tried to concentrate on Philippa's story, her own steamy little narrative insisted on replaying itself in her head, and she was having trouble finding the "off" button. She was up to the scene where she was watching Jake spoon up the final morsels of beef chili khadi with the last of the naan. She smiled to herself. She was glad she'd taken a punt and called him.

Jake was on the dole, a struggling musician with a clapped-out car that was about to be repossessed and a troublesome band so beset with internal strife that he referred to it as "Bosnia." He lived in a grungy share-house in Newtown and called his dreadlocks his only accomplishment in life. Julia had met him at a party she and Philippa had attended last weekend in Glebe.

At the party, she and Jake had danced. Afterward, he'd gone into the kitchen to fetch some beer. He'd pressed the cool can against her neck before handing it to her and suggested they find somewhere to talk. Snuggling into a sofa in one of the less populated rooms, they'd asked each other most of the usual questions and a few unusual ones as well. He told her about his band; she told him about her photography. She mentioned her fascination for China; he said he'd once thought of learning Mandarin. Their legs just touched. His seemed to go on forever under his gray Levi 501s; he was almost improbably long limbed. Jake had smooth, honey-colored skin; warm brown eyes; a small, neat nose; a wide mouth; and a dry, laconic wit. He seemed sincere when he said he'd like to see her photography. When Julia had laughed loudly at something and rocked forward in her mirth, causing her long black hair to fall in front of her face, Jake had reached out and flipped it back over her shoulder in a surprisingly intimate gesture. He sent her Latin blood racing.

In the style of his generation, which, depending on how you counted, was one or two behind hers, he was so laid back that she wasn't sure what his intentions were or if he had any intentions at all. When an old acquaintance of hers approached with an endless list of have-you-seen-so-and-so-lately's, Jake excused himself and slipped off into another room. Julia hid her disappointment but felt consoled by the fact that—at her instigation—they'd already exchanged phone numbers. She caught sight of him later, but he was deep in a conversational scrum in the kitchen.

Eventually, Philippa approached to ask if Julia wanted to share a taxi home. Philippa lived in the Cross; she could drop Julia off at her warehouse in Surry Hills on the way. In the cab, they talked about the party. Julia neglected to mention her meeting with Jake. It wasn't that she didn't want Philippa to know. But she was superstitious about such things and believed that telling tales too early on might put a jinx on the whole enterprise.

Anyway, there they were, five days later, in a discreet Indian restaurant on a side street in Glebe. After a brief stocktake of the dishes to check that nothing edible remained, Jake suppressed a burp and extended his hand across the table to cover hers. She let her middle finger curl lightly into his palm.

"Glad you're not a vegetarian, Julia," he said after a silence.

"Why's that?" Julia asked.

"Oh, I dunno. It's not really vegetarians I'm afraid of so much as vegans. But maybe I shouldn't tell you. Not now, anyway."

"But you've got me all curious."

"Later."

Oh well. She liked the sound of that word, *later*. "Promise?"

"Promise."

She looked down at his hand now. She often marveled at hands—all nerve endings and capillaries, sensation and blood. And those of younger men could be so beautiful, so tender and supple. With her fingertip, she explored and tickled. He shivered, almost imperceptibly, and leaned forward. She kissed him over the table and, under the table, caressed his leg with her foot. After a minute, he whispered, a little hoarsely, "I have a raging erection." She smiled and caught the attention of a passing waiter. "Could I have the bill, please?" she said.

*C*hantal smirked. "Lights are on. Anyone at home? Oh, Joo-li-ya!" She sang out Julia's name, syllable by syllable, re-re-do.

Julia's eyelids flew open and panic shined briefly in her eyes.

"Well," asked Philippa after a significant pause, "Did you like my story?" Suddenly self-conscious, she mumbled, "Of course, you don't have to, you know, say you did if you didn't."

Julia caught a quick shuttle back to planet Earth. She blinked. "Uh, yes, of course I did," she stuttered. "Put it this way," she continued, slowly, recovering her poise, "I've got the cream. All I need now is another cup of coffee. It was orgasmic."

"You're not faking it?"

"Fake it? Me? Never." Julia smiled charmingly.

"Now I'm really worried." Philippa nibbled at her muffin and frowned. "Do you think 'no animal fat' means no butter? How can you bake with no butter?"

Julia scanned the street as she sipped her latte. "Hey," she alerted the others. "Potential victim." Taking care not to look too obvious, they turned to look in the direction Julia had indicated and performed a quick inventory.

Lightly tanned skin, disheveled brown hair with big blue eyes half-hidden under dense lashes. Late twenties. White Bond T-shirt. Lightly muscled, well-defined arms. Black jeans covering but not concealing lean, muscular legs.

"Clothes horse." Helen approved.

"Maybe, but check out the hooves," observed Philippa. "Think his farrier's made a bit of a mistake there."

Docs. Not the boots but the shoes. With white socks.

"Ee-ew," said Chantal, turning up her beaked nose and patting her champagne blond beehive. She was terribly pleased with the beehive, a new item on her head's endlessly revised agenda. It came courtesy of her best male friend and confidante, Alexi, a hairdresser. Alexi and she shared stories, news, and views about men. They even gave each other the "All Men Are Bastards" desk calendar each year. Chantal hoped, what with her natural style and ab-fab job with *Pulse,* Sydney's bible of style, that she would some-day soon become a camp icon. One of her fantasies was to be plucked from the sidelines at the Mardi Gras parade by a floatilla of gorgeous, half-naked men. They would place her on a throne and thrust and grind and gyrate moistly around her while she waved to the crowds like a prom queen in an American movie or, rather, just a queen. They'd think she was the most divine trannie they'd ever clapped eyes on, even more divine than Terence Stamp in *Priscilla.* Doing nothing to disillusion them, at the postparade party she'd gently push some obliging slave over onto his knees. Steadying herself with one hand on his waist, she would bend over invitingly with her ass in the air. A series of spec-tacularly muscled and shiny gym queens would then take her from behind. "I want *you* now, and then *you,* and then *you* and *you* and *you,*" she'd say, crooking a slender, perfect-ly manicured forefinger at each in turn.

"You've got a milk mustache," Helen informed Julia, who quickly wiped it off with the back of her hand.

"Why do they always put so much froth on lattes?" Julia wondered.

"I'm glad you all think it works, anyway," inserted Philippa, steering the conversation back to her story.

Chantal tapped another cigarette out of her pack.

"What are you calling it?" asked Helen.

"'Forbidden Fruit and Veg,' I think. What do you reckon?"

"Bit obvious," pronounced Julia, after a pause. "You know, Adam, Ava—you might as well call it 'The Market Garden of Eden.'"

Philippa blushed. "You've got a point," she conceded.

Putting her cigarette to lips the color of Courage (from the Poppy collection, of course), Chantal glanced around briefly to see if there was anyone worth bumming a light from. There wasn't. She fished her lighter out of her purse and lit up. She blew a few smoke rings into the air. "How about—thinking of Jule's, uh, reaction—'Crème Fraîche'?" she proposed.

"I'd just call it 'Eat Me,'" suggested Helen.

A rather stunning waiter emerged from the café to deliver another round of coffees—latte for Julia, cappuccino for Helen, short blacks for Chantal and Philippa. As he strode handsomely back inside, Philippa remarked, "Have you ever noticed how all the waiters in Darlinghurst cafés look like supermodels?"

"Yeah, and the ones in Double Bay—or should I say Double Pay—look like bankers and gazumpers," Helen replied. "No kidding. I went book shopping the other day at Nicholas Pounder's and then stopped in a café around the corner. It was seriously weird. They even wear striped ties. You expect their mobiles to start ringing while they're taking your order."

"The waiters carry mobiles?" gasped Julia.

"Julia, for a photographer, you're very literal. I meant, they look like the types who would carry mobiles."

"Oh."

"Have you shown the story to anyone else?" asked Helen.

"Just Richard." Richard was the charismatic man who ran the writing workshop Philippa had been attending as faithfully as any churchgoer, every Sunday for years now. None of the others had ever met him, but they felt they knew him. He was Philippa's guru, her mentor, her confidante, her number one Object of Lust, though, she insisted, she'd never actually Done the Thang with him and probably never would. She wasn't sure how old he was—he could be anything from twenty-eight to thirty-eight. According to Philippa, he adopted different looks according to the characters he was creating in his work. One summer he was a bleached blond surfie with a tan. By winter he was a pale punk. He was widely published in a variety of obscure literary journals under different pen names, one for each persona. He had, she'd discovered one day when all the members of the workshop went for a walk on the sands of Bondi together, *exquisite* feet.

Helen had appreciated the detail about the feet. She quite prided herself on her own feet, which were well arched, plump, and smooth. Her boyfriends had always complimented her on her feet. One, who had a bit of a fetish, had enjoyed worshiping them, though, if the truth be told, Helen had never found it easy to relax with a man licking out what she always imagined were the rather feculent spaces between her toes. When one lover commented about her feet that they looked brand new, like they'd never been used, she wasn't sure how to take it.

"What'd Richard say?"

"He was really nice about it, actually. He encouraged me to get it published. He suggested one of those women's mags where they run pics of men with all the dangly bits, you know, dangling?"

"You mean like *Australian Women's Forum*. Excellent idea, darling." Chantal sipped at her coffee. Alexi and she shared a subscription. "Gonna give it a burl?"

"Why not?" Philippa shrugged. "Though I'm also going to try and develop it into a novel."

"Great," said Helen.

"The next question, of course, is who provided you with the, uh, ingredients for 'Eat Me'? It is 'Eat Me' now, isn't it?" Chantal looked to Philippa for confirmation. "Much to my regret, I know it wasn't me."

"Don't look at me like that, Chantal!" cried Julia.

"Nor me!" squeaked Helen. "Strawberries give me hives."

Philippa smiled. "My writing is purely the product of my imagination," she said.

"Of course it is, darling." Chantal giggled.

"And, of course," Philippa continued, "total attentiveness to the world around me. Speaking of the whirl around me, weren't you supposed to have a hot date with a cool young man the other night, Julia? How'd that go?"

"Oh, I dunno," Julia said, shaking her head. That story, she thought, is not going to get into Philippa's book. She wondered if she was being ungenerous. Philippa wouldn't really just write up their experiences in her fiction, would she? "Eat Me" didn't seem to have anything to do with any of them, and that was all she had to go on. In the past, Philippa had been extraordinarily coy about showing her work to her friends. "Eat Me" was the first story she'd ever let them see. It seemed unfair to be overly suspicious. But she decided to play safe. "It was okay, I guess." Raising the latte to her lips, Julia looked away from the others and slipped back into her reverie.

She'd succumbed to a fit of the giggles as they left the restaurant, for Jake had to bend nearly double in a vain attempt to conceal his condition. He tossed her a doleful look. In the cab, he drew her willing hand to the bulge in his pants and kissed her wetly. He slid his hand into her stretch miniskirt and, as she wriggled encouragingly, into her panties and explored inland with his fingers. He stroked and probed until she was nearly vibrating with pleasure. When she noticed the cabdriver's eyes glued to the rearview mirror, it only heightened the thrill.

"Mmmm," exhaled Julia. "Uh, mmmm, right over there, yes, that's it, yes, oh, yes." The driver pulled up in front of her block of flats. Jake pulled out of her panties.

As she paid the speechless driver, Jake looked away, as if there were some urgent matter demanding his attention in the opposite direction. He'd vagued out in a similar manner when the restaurant bill had arrived. Julia didn't really mind. Being a freelance photographer, she was far from rich, but she did well enough and certainly always had money to wine and dine the sweet young things she fancied.

In the bedroom, Julia yanked off Jake's top and fumbled impatiently with his belt and the buttons of his fly. She was so keen that it caught her a bit off balance when he signaled her to slow down.

He peeled off Julia's clothes as if they were the leaves of a steamed artichoke, savoring each item with his nose, eyes, and skin, cherishing the tender inner leaves most of all. He pushed her gently onto her back on the bed and, holding down her hands at her side, began to move at a languorous pace down her body, devouring her with his eyes. His gaze lingered over her nipples, noting their fine deep coloring, and rested briefly on the smooth Mediterranean caramel of her belly before proceeding down to the most exquisite savories, the tangle of angel's hair garnishing folds of moist gravlax.

Having perused the menu, Jake knew what his choice of appetizer would be that evening. He leaned down to taste the inside of her thighs. Ignoring the pleas of her arched back and raised pelvis, he unhurriedly relished the fine skin with his tongue and lips, and only when he was sated with those, did he move up to position himself just a millimeter or so from her deli door. He breathed deeply of the salty, rich aroma it exuded, exhaling little sighs that felt almost like caresses to her. She tried to push herself down the bed and close that tiny gap that separated her anxious sex from his teasing mouth, but he anticipated her movements and kept himself just that teeny bit farther away, pinioning her still by her wrists against the bed. Just when she thought she'd go mad with desire, he parted the rosy curtains with his tongue and partook of her in earnest, poking, prodding, sucking, and stroking until she was thrashing about and gasping for breath. He covered her with his whole mouth and probed deeply with his tongue, which seemed to expand inside her until it was strumming every one of her secret parts. She could feel her body humming and quivering and dancing and flowing. Now, he withdrew to suckle at her clitoris, pulling and sucking with his lips and teeth and gurgling with her juices. She shuddered uncontrollably, enveloped in pulse after pulse of hot sensation.

Nearly delirious, she picked up her head to see his young face rising over her intimate horizon like a new sun, blond dreads emanating like rays from his orb. Cocking one eyebrow, he looked at her questioningly. His chin was streaked with wet. "You faking it?" he asked with a faint smile.

"Ohhhh," she groaned, collapsing inarticulately back onto the pillow.

He crawled slowly up her body and kissed her deeply. She could taste herself in his mouth. They rolled over until she was on top. "Tell me what you want," she sighed. "Anything."

He considered the offer for a moment before making his request. "Some Chocolate Rock."

Raising herself on her arms, she looked at him with slight alarm.

"It's a kind of ice cream. Homer Hudson's Chocolate Rock," he clarified, insinuating his fingers back into her cunt at the same time. He reached up and took a toffee nipple between his teeth, teased it a bit, and then let it go. "Don't you eat junk food? How old are you anyway, Julia?"

Pretending not to have heard the question and to forestall further interrogation on the subject, Julia quickly slid backward until she could take his dick into her mouth. Soon, the look on his face told her the topic of age was safely buried—for a while, anyway.

Finally, he pulled her head away. "Julia." He didn't say her name so much as breathe it. She smiled, reached into the drawer by her bedside, and took out a condom. Watching her extricate it from its wrapper, he grumbled, "I hate condoms."

"And I hate lingering disease and death," Julia retorted matter-of-factly, popping it into her mouth and bending down again.

"If you're going to put it like that. . . ." Jake sighed, not unhappily, as she rolled it down his stiffened cock with her tongue. Jake relished the main course every bit as much as the appetizer. He proved an inventive and playful lover. And very agile. The Guangdong Acrobatic Troupe had nothing on Jake. She wouldn't have to go to yoga for a week.

At the end of a long and luscious fuck, Jake yawned, looked around, and without pulling out of Julia, reached for the remote control by her bed. He aimed it at the TV. The image that flickered into focus was that of an aging Australian pop star prancing around on stage with a cordless microphone in hand, jowls flapping.

"What a tosser," he commented and surfed to another commercial channel. The old film *Sunset Boulevard* was just beginning.

"That's supposed to be good," said Julia, twisting her neck to look at the screen.

"What's it about?"

"Dunno. I just know it's supposed to be good."

"Well, you should know. It's your era, isn't it?"

Julia gasped. "It is not my era! The 1940s? How old do you think I am!"

"Dunno. I asked but you wouldn't say."

"I'm thirty-two! I was born in 1964, okay? My *mother* was a kid when that movie was made!"

Jake laughed. "Look at you." He chuckled, pinching her flushed cheeks. "Sensitive, aren't we?" He kissed her on the nose, but Julia, only partially placated, pulled away and rolled off him.

"Don't you want to know how old I am then?" he asked.

"Not really," she lied. She'd already checked it on his driver's license when he'd gone to the toilet. He was twenty-two. "Let's just watch the movie, all right?"

He shrugged, peeled off the condom, tied it in a knot, and tossed it over his shoulder. It touched down on the floor with a small plop. Julia made a mental note as to where it had landed and what number it was—she'd counted three so far. She liked the speed with which younger men ripped through her condom supply.

They fluffed up the pillows, and she settled cozily onto his chest to watch the film. As the plot unraveled—down-and-out young writer trying to escape from creditors attempting to repossess his car takes refuge in the home and arms of Norma Desmond, an aging actress with money to burn—she felt her cheeks flush. How mortifying! Of course, Norma was a pathetically vain character and, after all, pushing fifty, but still. She was desperate to know what was running through Jake's mind. Then again, maybe she'd prefer not to know. She lay stiffly in his arms, not daring to meet his eyes. If she had, she'd have seen them occasionally twinkle with mischievous glee. She remained like that even during the commercial breaks, pretending to doze, refusing to look up. After one particularly horrible scene, where the young man, played by William Holden, goes out to a "young people's party" only to return in the end to Norma's tomblike mansion, she glanced furtively up at Jake. She was appalled to discover that he was grinning down at her. "Norma," he cooed, nuzzling her neck. "Oh, Norma."

She flung herself off him and dove headfirst into her pillow.

"Piss off."

"Oh, Norma, don't be like that." He stuck his tongue in her ear and poked her gently in the ribs with his fingers at the same time. He tickled her ass with his dreadlocks. She reached back to flick them away with an irritated gesture. He nibbled on the back of her thighs. She was furious, humiliated, but most of all—though she was determined not to admit it to him, at least not right away—terribly amused despite herself. She tried to wriggle out of his grasp, but he pursued her.

"I said piss off!"

"Look at her." Helen shook her head and laughed. "She's a million miles away."

Julia snapped to. "No I'm not. I was just, uh, thinking."

"Why did you say the date was just 'okay'?" Chantal persisted. "What happened? Didn't things work out?" Chantal loved her friends and wanted things to go well for them always. On the other hand, she was convinced that all relationships were like the *Titanic*—no matter how splendid they appeared to be, they would unerringly find an iceberg and sink. And when they did, she wanted to know every detail of the disaster.

"Oh, yes and no. I think I'm going to give up on younger men," sighed Julia. "Unstable creatures. More trouble than they're worth. I'm going to look for a mature specimen next. But I'm thinking of trying radical celibacy for a while first."

The other three widened their eyes and looked at Julia with disbelief.

She and Jake didn't get out of bed until three that afternoon. She lost track of the condoms. Jake went to the local shop to buy them some lunch—with her money, of course

—and came back with strawberries and Homer Hudson's Chocolate Rock ice cream. They ate nearly the whole container. "Well, I'd better be going," he said through lips limned with black chocolate. He probed his chin for pimples. "I've got to go home and break out."

Just as he was walking out the door, Julia suddenly remembered something. "What was that thing about vegetarians?" she asked.

"Vegetarians? Oh, I used to see this girl who was a vegan."

"Yeah?" said Julia. "And?"

"Well, she refused to have oral sex."

"Silly girl. But what does that have to do with her being a vegan?"

"She didn't, you know, believe in swallowing animal proteins."

Julia snorted with laughter as she shoved him out the door. They were seeing each other again in a few days. But he was to stop calling her Norma, she'd told him, or he'd be in big trouble.

"Yes, celibacy. Really," said Julia, straight faced. "I mean it. Besides, why do I have to be the one who has to give a blow-by-blow account—so to speak—of my love life? Philippa's allowed to be mysterious about hers, Chantie's allowed to be mysterious about hers. Helen's mysterious about hers."

"I am not mysterious," Helen objected. "I don't have a love life."

"Neither do I," chimed Philippa.

Chantal arched an eyebrow. "Nor I."

"Yeah, sure," said Julia with a sigh, tipping her cup and studying the dregs of coffee in the bottom. Looking up, she suddenly brightened. "Check this one out," she whispered. "Looks like Jerry Seinfeld."

"I know him," said Chantal. "He's a VJ for the Green Channel."

"Cool," commented Julia. "A star."

"A star's a star," Chantal shrugged. "But he's the wrong sexual orientation for you, darling."

While the others launched into a discussion of why the prettiest boys were always gay, a name bounced around, just out of sight, in the murky regions of Philippa's brain. Each time she tried to shine her mental torch on it, it hid itself behind another tree. Jason? Jonathan? Justin? Julian? Jeremy? Jay? Suddenly, it popped out and waved. "It's me, Jake! It's Jake!" *That* was the name of the boy she'd met at that party in Glebe, the name that went with the phone number on that scrap of paper she'd found in her pocket a day or two later. She wondered if she should call him.

"And what are you smiling about, Philippa?" Chantal queried.

"Oh, nothing," she replied.

CHAPTER THREE

Roast Lamb

"Do you fancy *Seinfeld* then?" Chantal had taken Julia's glass and was refilling it from a bottle of shiraz.

"Ta," said Julia. "Not as much as Kramer. I suspect Kramer's hair isn't the only thing that's kinky about him."

Over a week had passed since their meeting at Café Da Vida. and the girls were having a TV veg-out evening at Chantal's place in Potts Point. Seinfeld had just delivered his closing monologue. Julia sat curled up on Chantal's prize Norman & Quaine zebra-striped armchair. All in black from her T-shirt to her leather mini and opaque stockings, she looked like a panther relaxing on its quarry. Philippa, who was sitting on the floor and leaning against Julia's chair, had picked up the remote and was channel surfing.

Helen picked distractedly at a spot of tomato sauce on her favorite beige skirt where she'd dropped a bit of gourmet pizza. Wood-fired, half smoked trout, half Moroccan lamb—and it still left exactly the same sort of spots on your clothing as pepperoni and mushrooms. "*So* unfair," she commented to the others. "Whatever happened to value for money?" She sighed. "You might say it's the perfect end to a bad hair day."

"Why?" asked Philippa. "What happened today?"

"You know the class I teach at the university on feminist theory?"

"Not personally," Julia chuckled. "Not in the biblical sense."

"Oh, hardi har har, darling." Chantal rolled her eyes.

"Anyway," continued Helen, ignoring them, "we were discussing Naomi Wolf's *The Beauty Myth*. There's this boy in the class, Marc. He's one of those politically correct and attractive male students who always pop up in women's studies courses—you can imagine the type. Anyway, we were talking about how society typically rewards women who conform to standards set by the beauty industry. He raised his hand and said, 'Ms. Nicholls, I think you're a great example of how women can avoid being trapped by the beauty myth.'"

"He *didn't,* darling." Chantal was shocked.

"He did," Helen replied, mournfully. Helen could be a bit sensitive about body issues. On the one hand, she was an intelligent being, a feminist, and a woman of the nineties. On the other, she hated her ankles; worried about her thighs; and when no one was looking, made small but despairing fistfuls out of the soft flesh that had settled, apparently for the long-term, around her waist and hips. "He even said if I'd written the book instead of the naturally glamorous Naomi Wolf, it'd probably have a lot more credibility."

"Bastard!" cried Julia.

"No, I know he meant it as a compliment," Helen defended. "He really did. He's not malicious or anything. But it certainly knocked me for a loop. What he'd done, of course, was invite all my deepest insecurities to come out and play. You know: I'm fat, I'm unattractive, I'm unfashionable. I'm a dag."

"Hellie, you idiot," Julia objected, scrambling to sit up straight in the big chair, "you are not fat, ugly, or unfashionable. Or a dag. You've got great boobs, sweet looks, and your own sense of style. Anyway, *I* think you're gorgeous."

"Yeah, but you're my friend." Helen moped. "And you can't be gorgeous when your eyebrows are this close to your eyes"—she pinched her eyebrows farther down onto her eyes for dramatic effect—"and when you've got thin lips. C'mon Jules. You read fashion magazines. You know that's true. And you, Chantal, you edit *Pulse* for Chrissake. When was the last time you ran a fashion spread featuring models with figures even approaching mine in size? I'll never be a waif or a gamin," she moaned.

Chantal wore the guilty expression of a little girl caught with her hand in the cookie jar.

"Oh, Chantie," Helen said. "I know it's not your fault. We've talked about it before. The advertisers would never let you use 'normal' women on the fashion pages. I know. Don't mind me. I'm just having a stupid fat attack."

"But Helen, surely you should be the last person to be carrying on like this," Philippa protested. "You're a feminist, for Christ's sake. You don't accept commercially enforced notions of female beauty. You are appalled by anorexia. You are outraged at the fashion industry's manipulation of women's sense of self-esteem and confidence. Remember?"

"Yeah, yeah. I know. It's indefensible. I'd never admit it in public. But, truth is, for the rest of the day I was obsessed by the thought that I really ought to at least update my wardrobe and buy a new lipstick."

"Oh, darling, I'll go with you," gushed Chantal, relieved. "There are some *fantastic* sales on at the moment."

"That'd be great, actually." Helen forced a smile. "You know, the funny thing is, and I don't want to sound too bitchy about it, but Marc goes to a fair amount of trouble himself with his clothes and his looks. He shaves his head —well, a 'number two,' he calls it—leaving only two baby pigtails above either temple." Helen put her hands up to her head and wiggled her forefingers to indicate their position. "And he's dyed these lime green. He secures them with little clips—today they were pink ones in the shape of elephants. And he wears things like retro nylon shirts over baggy black trousers and black-and-white sneakers. Sometimes he wears dresses. He talks about 'gender-free' dressing. I mean, *he's* clearly allowed to buy into a beauty myth of one kind or another."

"Typical man." Julia shook her head. "Double-standards R Us."

Helen grimaced. "Yeah, no, maybe I'm being unfair. He's really quite likable, a bit of a honey, really; and he's smart; and he actually does all of the reading for the course. Which is more than I can say for some of my women students."

"Then again," Chantal noted, "if you were a man taking women's studies, you'd look like a real fraud if you weren't putting in *any* effort."

The same aging pop star to whom Jake had taken exception that night with Julia appeared on the tube again. "Oh, puh-leeese," Chantal exclaimed, "remove that boofhead from my sight. Now." She grabbed the remote control and switched to another channel. "I simply won't have him in my living room," she declared. A current affairs program was just wrapping up a report from the Paris fashion shows.

"Do you know what your problem is, Helen darling?" Chantal opined as the catwalk faded from view. "To misquote that mortal pop song, you're just too sexy for your skirt."

Helen looked down at her lap and remembered the stain. "Oh God, that tomato is going to be murder to get out."

"I'll get a wet cloth," Philippa volunteered, rising and heading into the kitchen.

Helen studied her whole outfit, seeing it as if for the first time: conservative white blouse, beige pleated skirt of about knee length, brown cardigan, brown leather belt. Maybe the pizza stain was a sign from God. After all, if She created women in her own image, She'd be pretty concerned about what they were doing with it. But hold on, weren't beige and brown supposed to be coming in again? Chantal had complimented her on her brown leather tie-up ankle boots with the little heels, after all.

Philippa emerged with a cloth and a glass of water. "Here," she said, passing them to Helen. "Pat, don't rub. By the way, did you know that tomatoes were once called 'love apples'? They were believed to have aphrodisiac powers."

"Surely not in the form of pulp on clothing," Helen replied.

Philippa shrugged. Helen worried the spot with the damp cloth. "Thanks. That's a bit better."

Chantal, having refilled glasses of red all round, now sprawled decoratively on the sofa beside Helen. "I didn't exactly have a drama-free day either, if you really want to know," she announced, hoping they would.

They did.

"We were doing a photo shoot with Jessa at Circular Quay. Do you know Jessa, that model with the shaved head and tattooed neck who can usually be spotted mainlining short blacks at Tropicana's?"

"I'm sure I've seen her," Philippa said.

"Anyway, she's what you might call a cerebro-atmospheric individual."

"A what?" Helen asked.

"Airhead. And she happens to be a paranoid coke addict as well. Charming to work with under the most ideal circumstances, as you might imagine. Anyway, we were planning on posing her with two Dalmatians down at Circular Quay for a series of photos with ferries, the Opera House, and whatnot in the background. She was wearing a series of black-and-white vinyl minidresses. You can imagine the crowd that gathered. It's not like shooting anywhere else in the city where people actually have lives. You know, where they stop for a minute to look, glance at their watch, and move on? At the quay it's all either tourists or people killing time waiting for a ferry; and within seconds we had a crowd of, oh, maybe a hundred people watching us set up. Well, I don't know what that girl douches with, but as soon as those dogs were handed over to her, they both immediately dove for her crotch. I swear, it took both their handlers to pull them out of her skirt. The crowd roared with laughter. She, of course, had a breakdown on the spot. She even accused me and the photographer of trying to humiliate her, of planning it all. It took ages to repair her makeup after all those tears."

"Have you ever had a dog lick you out?" Julia asked the others.

"No!" Helen looked at Julia with intense curiosity. "Have you?"

"Uh, no, no, of course not," Julia responded. "Just wondering if any of you had."

"Joo-li-ya," coaxed Philippa. "Tell the truth."

"Leave me alone," Julia protested, blushing. "If you want to know the truth," she said, changing the subject, "I haven't exactly had a model revolutionary opera of a day either." She sighed dramatically and took a sip of her wine.

"What happened?"

"Well, I was racing to finish up some photos for a magazine story on Chinese artists in Sydney."

"You're getting obsessed with China, aren't you, Julia?" Philippa interrupted. "When is it you're going on that cultural exchange program?"

"January. Can't wait. Anyway, would you believe, I dashed into the magazine offices at four fifty only to learn that the editor was canceling the story because some idiot had told him that Vietnamese were the new multiculti flavor of the month?"

"Bummer," Philippa sympathized. "But don't they have to pay for the photos anyway?"

"So you'd think," Julia said, nodding. "But no, the bastard sleazed out of paying me a kill fee. He claimed he hadn't actually commissioned them, that he'd just said he'd probably be able to use them."

"Asshole!" Now Helen was outraged.

"Quite. And then he fobbed me off, saying he had to get the magazine to bed, and that he'd talk to me some other time. I exploded at him."

"Good on you!" Philippa approved.

"Yeah, but I was really unprofessional. I called him a fuckwit, a shit-for-brains, a sleazebag, and worse. Then I burst into tears and stormed out of his office."

"Oh, darling, you poor thing," commiserated Chantal.

"So I raced home." The Surry Hills warehouse where Julia lived was a low-rent, high-status place with poor plumbing; worse lighting; a few sweatshops; and a resident tribe of artists, photographers, and designers who wore nothing but black. "I waited for ages for the lift. It never fucking comes when you want it to." It was one of those old-fashioned industrial lifts, a large cage in the center of the stairwell. "To top it off, Sarah, that pretentious performance artist, artiste, whatever she calls herself—I know for a fact that the only real job she's had for ages has been checkout chick at a Kings Cross supermarket and that she's addicted to romance novels—opens her door and this acid jazz floods out of her space. I *hate* acid jazz! I don't give a stuff how sophisticated or trendy it's supposed to be! Well, I started to sob all over again, and I decided not to wait for the lift. I pelted up the stairs to my studio.

"Slamming the door behind me, I flung myself down on the bed. Chocolate, I thought, I must have chocolate. I got up and did a search and destroy in the kitchen. You know, opening cupboard doors and banging them shut again, trying to find just a morsel of chocolate. Then I remembered I had some Chocolate Rock ice cream in the freezer. Wouldn't you know it, the container was caught in the jaws of this major stalagmite-stalactite situation, and I had to chip it out from the ice. There were only about two scoops of ice cream left, and I was spooning them out and cursing and about to burst into tears again when the penny dropped."

"Don't tell me . . ." Helen had guessed.

"Oh yes. PMS. Isn't that terrible? I'm so embarrassed about what I did with that editor. I mean, I was right and he was wrong, but still. I'll never be able to work for them again, I'm sure. Do you think I should go back and admit I was suffering from premenstrual stress?"

"Don't be stupid, Julia." Chantal shook her head. Her bobbed red hair—it was now bobbed and red—swung like something out of a mousse ad. "Never *ever*,

ever admit to a man that your bad behavior was caused by PMS. It only reinforces stereotypes. Which isn't a good thing even if they happen to be true. Besides, it confirms their sense of superiority."

"I agree," Philippa had chipped in. Philippa was sitting back down on the floor, nibbling contentedly from the bowl of roasted peanuts on the floor beside her. She listened sympathetically to the others, but had no tragic stories of her own to contribute. If the truth be told, she'd actually had an excellent day. But she didn't want to spoil the general mood by saying so. She'd done an entire draft of the second chapter of her novel. And she'd called Jake.

A commercial came on for lamb. Julia turned to the others. "Remember that old advert where the girl passes up a date with Tom Cruise for a roast lamb dinner?"

"Certainly do," said Chantal. "Could you believe that?"

"Actually, I could." Philippa wrinkled her nose. "I'd take lamb over Tom Cruise any day. He doesn't appeal to me at all. That's because he looks so stupid."

"I thought he sort of redeemed himself in *Interview with the Vampire,*" Helen commented.

"I refused to see that film. I'd read the books, and no matter how much blond dye he put in his hair, Tom Cruise is *not* Lestat—and I don't care what sort of sucky things Anne Rice said in the *New York Times,*" Philippa remarked testily. Then she smiled. "When they make the film of my book, of course, they can have Tom Cruise in it so long as they pay me enough. But I won't ever say I'm happy about it."

"How is your book going, by the way?" Chantal couldn't wait to read it.

"Two chapters down. Heaps to go. But back to the Tom Cruise issue. This stupidity thing really is a problem with me. I'm not saying he really is stupid. He might be a rocket scientist for all I know. But he looks dumb. I have the same problem with Richard Gere and Keanu Reeves, actually. I wouldn't sleep with either of them. Even if they begged. On their hands and knees. In tight black leather chaps with their bare asses sticking high in air. While licking my boots." She popped a handful of peanuts into her mouth and chewed thoughtfully. Well, maybe if they licked her boots really, really hard.

"Me neither," Helen jumped in. "I think we all have to stare into the void at one time or another in our lives, but I'd rather not do it while looking into a man's eyes. In my opinion, there's no sexier attribute than intelligence."

"Oh, you intellectuals." Chantal laughed, rolling her eyes and blowing a smoke ring into the air. "A man doesn't need a Ph.D. to be a good lover. Besides, dumb men tend to have better muscles. You don't develop excellent pecs reaching for library books. Anyway, you don't really want him coming up for air long enough to be able to say more than a few words at a time anyway, and those don't have to be in Sanskrit. 'Me Tarzan' is good enough for me."

"I remember quite distinctly when you had a thing for weedy poets, Chantal," Philippa smirked.

"Don't remind me. That was a very long time ago. And I did learn my lesson." Chantal took another puff on her cigarette. "God, old friends are a pain. Especially ones with good memories. If you don't watch it, I'm going to trade you lot in for new ones with no knowledge of my previous life."

"Never mind. We'll take the new friends aside and fill them in," Julia promised cheerfully.

Chantal took the remote control from Philippa and idly flicked through the channels, stopping briefly to flake out over the Mr. Muscle commercial for a household cleaner that masquerades as a young spunk. "Wouldn't mind having him in my kitchen cabinet. I wouldn't even make him do the chores. Well, not those chores anyway."

"You know, on this brain versus brawn thing, I'm with Chantal," Julia commented. "What were the words to that old song by Shakespear's Sister? You know, something about needing a 'primitive lover,' a 'Stone Age romance'? That's me all over. Except, on second thought, I also tend to go for young artistic types. Do you think there's such a thing as an artsy caveman?"

"I can see it now," said Philippa. "Conan the Expressionist, fresh out of art school, thwacks Julia on the head with his easel and drags her by the hair into his studio."

"Mmmm," Julia purred. "I'd like that."

"Why can't a man have both muscles and brains?" Helen mused, pushing her glasses up on her nose. "Conan the Barbarian becomes Conan the Librarian. Still, Arnold Schwarzenegger's not really my type. Although, I must admit, *Terminator I* was a very postmodern sort of film."

"Postmodern, shmost-modern," replied Julia. "I'd just like to glide up and down all of Arnie's luscious, shiny hillocks and buttocks."

Chantal switched channels again. *Beverly Hills Cop III* was playing on one of the commercial stations. "Stop!" cried Julia. "That's my man! I would suck Eddie Murphy's toes after his feet had been in basketball high-tops all day. That's how much I love him."

"I don't know about the toes," rejoined Chantal, wrinkling her nose. "But I'd put my mouth anywhere else on that man. He's scrumptious. Hot chocolate."

"Not for me, thanks," said Helen. "I'm uncomfortable with the treatment of women in his films. I suppose *Boomerang* was sort of interesting, but overall, I think the image that comes across of women in his movies is negative."

"Helen, darling." Chantal shook her head. "We're not talking deep and meaningful relationships here. We're talking sex. Keep your mind in the gutter. And pass the peanuts."

Chantal aimed the remote control at the TV. Some male journalist was fronting a documentary on the bar girls of Southeast Asia. *Click.* A public service announcement about safe sex. *Click.* Eddie Murphy again. *Click.* The leader of the Labor Party nattering on about budget deficits.

"What are you stopping there for?" Julia asked in an anguished voice. "The economy is such a turn-off."

"He isn't exactly Mr. Sex Appeal in the best of circumstances," Philippa observed.

"Hey," cried Helen. "You don't prefer the other mob, do you?"

All four opened their mouths and, pointing fingers at tonsils, made little retching noises.

"So," Helen persisted. "If you had to take one . . ."

"I'd take the prime minister," said Chantal, her voice heavy with sacrifice, "close my eyes, and think of Australia."

Julia reached over and snatched the remote control from Chantal. The Bush Tucker Man appeared, promoting some product in an advertisement. "Now that's what I call a fetish object," she squealed.

"The man or his funny bush hat?" Philippa asked.

"Both. I really got off watching him range over the outback eating bizarre leaves and crunchy insects. I loved the way he'd never admit it when something didn't taste very nice. His face would scrunch up into a kind of pained, heroic smile. Reminded me of the expression on some men's faces when they're giving you head."

They all laughed. They knew exactly which expression Julia was talking about.

"Do you remember the episode where he consumed honey ants?" Helen sighed at the memory.

"Absolutely. One of my favorites. I've always had this mad fantasy about making love to the Bush Tucker Man in some wild corner of Australia. He'd be wearing his hat and nothing else, and an echidna would be licking wild berry jam off our bodies. And, of course, there'd be an entire film crew standing by, just out of sight, to capture the action. But I think it's time for you two"—she looked at Helen and Philippa—"to fess up. Who do you fancy, media-star-wise?"

Philippa narrowed her eyes, tilted her head back, and smiled. "John Travolta. Uma Thurman. Flacco. Ernie Dingo. Linda Hunt. Dale from *Twin Peaks* dressed in his FBI jacket and nothing else. And that wonderful little fellow who played the out-of-work circus clown in *Delicatessen*. All at the same time. With a bowl of chocolate cake mix, a feather duster, a snap-on bow tie, some olive oil, and five silk scarves for props. Richard, the head of the writing workshop, would be there too, of course, watching."

"You're really weird, Philippa," said Chantal appreciatively. "I can't figure out for the life of me what the fifth scarf is for. But I'm sure you've got your reasons for everything."

"How 'bout you, Helen? Tell all. Lay the object of your fantasy on the table, so to speak."

Helen took a long while in answering. Then, a trifle unconvincingly, she mumbled, "I was going to say Flacco or Ernie Dingo, but Philippa's got them."

"We can share. I don't mind."

"No, look," Helen blurted out after another pause. "I'll come clean." She took a deep breath. "But I think I need a touch more wine first."

"Get the girl some more wine!" Chantal commanded. She recovered the remote control from Julia and switched off the TV. Philippa shuffled to her feet and filled everyone's glasses. She sat down again on the floor but this time in front of the set, hugging her knees, facing Helen.

"This is so hard to admit." Helen smoothed her skirt. The stain was still visible. "And I know it goes against everything I said earlier." Taking a fortifying swig of her drink, Helen set her glass down on the coffee table and, in a tiny voice, declared the object of her affections: "Rambo."

"Really?" Julia was dumbfounded.

"Rambo?!" Chantal laughed. "But darling, I thought you didn't like musclemen!"

"And," Helen continued, "I know exactly what I'd do with him."

Encouraged by the expectant looks of her friends, Helen leaned back, closed her eyes, and began. "I'm walking along the beach in Manly. I think an encounter with someone who looks like Rambo has to occur in a place called Manly, don't you think? Anyway, I'm looking out to sea, wriggling my toes in the cool, wet sand close to the water when this enormous wave comes crashing onto shore, depositing at my feet a very wet, very disoriented Rambo. I extend a hand to try to pull him up. He is very heavy, and I end up falling down on top of him instead.

"I wriggle around a little bit to get comfortable. I'm feeling very comfortable. Our faces are about three inches apart, and we are gazing into each other's eyes.

"'Uh, where am I?' he asks.

"'Australia,' I reply. 'G'day, Bo.'

"'Australia? Is that in Europe? Isn't that what used to be called Germany?'

"'No, Bo, it's not. But don't worry your little head about it.' I slide off him slowly, careful to drag my sensitive bits over his. I give his nipples a tweak as I go. His big, round eyes grow rounder. 'Now, just come with Helen,' I say, slipping a pair of handcuffs around his wrist and attaching it to mine.

"'Uh, okay,' he says.

"We get up and stroll along the beach like that, various bits and pieces of his muscled body bumping into my side, as I deliver a detailed critique of the images of women and femininity in his films. I use lots of postmodern terminology that flies over his head. I'm getting very turned on. He fixes me with a bovine stare and says, 'Gee, Helen, are all the women in Austria as intelligent and beautiful as you?'

"'It's Australia, Bo,' I reply, smiling and patting his cheek. 'But don't talk. And let me help you out of those wet things.' I uncuff him now, and then slowly strip him, starting by taking away his machine gun and cartridge belt. I quickly slip out of my T-shirt and shorts and they join the jumble of clothing on the sand. 'Give me a hand with the bra, will you?' I ask.

"He fumbles around but can't get it. 'Never mind,' I say, and unhook it myself.

"'I thought women's libbers didn't wear bras,' he says. He's serious.

"'We're called feminists these days, Bo,' I say, slipping out of my panties. 'Third-wave feminists, if you want to be very precise about it. Now just lie there on the sand for me, will you? No, no, no, on your back, thanks.'

"'Like this?'

"'That's right.'

"By this time, a small crowd has gathered. It's the middle of the day, after all. They arrange themselves in a circle. Among the faces, I recognize a small clutch of nuns from a nearby convent; Murphy Brown; a couple of my colleagues from the uni; Harold Holt, wearing a Soviet swimming costume and looking rather waterlogged; Batman and Robin; and David Letterman. Letterman is standing with the nuns, all of whom are so tall they could eat peanuts off the top of his head. I beckon to Murphy, Letterman, and one of the tall nuns and ask them each to take a wrist or an ankle and help hold him down. Not that he's putting up a struggle. I straddle his body and sit down on his face. 'Kiss me on the lips, Bo,' I command."

Julia, who'd been sipping her wine as Helen spoke this last line, choked and spluttered. Philippa leaned over and patted her on the back. "Sorry," said Julia. "That came as a bit of a shock. But do go on."

"'I'd like that, Helen,' he says, and does.

"Did you know the tongue is a muscle too? Anyway, about forty-five minutes later, I finally tire of this and move back a little to sit on his stomach. It's as hard as a park bench. I look at him, panting a bit and considering my next move. He is licking his lips. So is David Letterman. One of the nuns has her hand up the skirt of another, who has her head thrown back and is saying her Hail Mary. Murphy is rubbing up against Harold Holt. Batman is rubbing up against Robin.

"'Show me your gun, Rambo baby,' I say. He points to the machine gun on the sand a few feet away.

"'No, I mean the really big one.' I turn around. 'Oooh,' I say, 'I think I've found it.' It's very hard and erect, and pre-cum glistens on the tip. 'What do you think, Bo, does it need cleaning?'

"He is still licking his lips. He seems to find it difficult to speak.

"'If I put the barrel in my mouth, can you promise not to fire?'

"He nods and closes his eyes. I play the pink oboe. Each time I look up, I am staring into the face of the nun who is holding down Bo's ankle. Shifting my body slightly so that Bo-burger gets a good view, I alternate giving him head and tongue kissing the nun."

"I thought you were a *lapsed* Catholic, Helen."

"Shut up, Chantal. Let her continue."

"Rambo, meanwhile, has inserted a finger as big as any other man's dick into my extremely moist cunt and is moving it around vigorously. He asks the onlookers where the clit-er-us (a word he pronounces very slowly but carefully) is, and a very nice elderly man shuffles over and stoops down to show him not only where it is, but what to do with it. With a shudder and a yelp, I come all over their hands.

"'Are you ready for engulfment, Bo?' I gasp.

"'Engulfment?' He's sounding a bit overwhelmed. 'Isn't that war over already?'

"'We're not talking war, Rambo-pambo,' I say. 'You know, engulfment. It's what is referred to as penetration in masculist language.'

"'Uh, I guess so.'

"I signal to the four helpers to move away and to the crowd to leave us a path to the ocean. Slowly, I lower myself down onto him. It feels like I'm being fisted."

"You've been fisted? You never told us that!"

"Shut *up*, Chantal. Go on, Helen." Philippa was rapt.

"Locked together we hump to the rhythm of the waves, if waves had a rhythm that grew faster and faster, that is. Finally, we roll together toward the sea, and I come for the last time as a great wave breaks over our bodies. He comes too, and as he comes, he cries out, 'I know! I know! Australia's where they made *Crocodile Dundee!*' I embrace him and pant, 'Yes, Bo, yes. Oh yes!'

"He is still smiling when an undertow catches him and pulls him off to sea. As he waves good-bye, one of the onlookers tosses his clothes, gun, and cartridge belt at him; and he catches them in his outstretched hand. Just as he disappears, he shouts, 'Thank you, Helen. I'll never forget this day. By the way, how do I get back to Hollywood?'

"'You're headed in the right direction, Bo,' I shout. 'Just keep on swimming.'

"The crowd applauds, and then disperses. I sit on the sand, at the edge of the water with my arms around my calves, licking the salt off my knees."

The room was so quiet you could have heard a condom wrapper drop.

"Well, that's it." Helen shrugged. She looked around. No one moved or said a word. They looked as though they'd been snap-dried. Chantal was breathing a little unevenly.

"I'll never," Julia said after a long silence, "be able to think of David Letterman the same way again."

CHAPTER FOUR

The Road to Gundagai

Dearest Fiona,

How's life in Darwin? Is the work with Aboriginal women going well? Let me know if you crave anything from Sydney. I can't send you the cafés of Victoria Street or fireworks over the Opera House, but anything else your heart desires that can fit in a postpak, just let me know.

It's been an age since I've written. Can you forgive me? I've been flat out, what with exams to mark and preparing a paper called "Like Chocolate for Water: Food and the Femme Fatale in Contemporary Cinema" for a womyn's studies conference in Canberra last week. I know I should probably tell you all about the conference, and the papers, and all that, but I can't resist jumping straight to a little adventure I had on the road.

It was funny because, just the night before, I'd been talking with Chantal, Julia, and Philippa about fantasies (they all send their best, by the way), and I'd admitted that, as ideologically suspect as it may sound, I rather fancy the odd macho muscleman. But I'm getting ahead of myself.

Don't you love driving long distances by yourself? I bet you do a lot of it up there. Of course, there are times you do crave company. Like when you see that sign that says "Injured Wildlife, phone XXXX" and you just want to turn to someone and quip, "If they're injured, how are they going to get to the phone?" But I digress.

I left Canberra to drive back on Thursday evening, getting on the road a bit later than I'd intended. I hadn't been driving for very long when my engine started making these wretched clunking noises. Soon, steam was pouring out of the hood. Luckily, I was almost at Goulburn. I took the turnoff and kept going till I reached the Big Merino. You know the Big Merino—it's that huge concrete sheep that squats on a souvenir shop, one of those places selling heaps of eye-glazing generic Australiana like Akubra hats and flyswatters in the shape of the map. The merino has little red eyes that light up at night. (The locals say that once it had testicles too, but that they were sawn off—an urban, sorry, rural myth?) There's a restaurant and a service station just next door. I was praying that the service station, which is the biggest in the area, would still be open and a mechanic on duty. It wasn't. I was beginning to panic. Thinking the car was about to blow up, I pulled into the parking lot there anyway.

There was hardly anyone around. They were just shutting down the souvenir shop for the night when I got there, and the last of the staff were locking up, getting into their cars, and driving off. I opened the hood and stared in despair at my smoking engine. Do you remember when we vowed that we would learn about our cars so that we would never be intimidated by male mechanics again, and we could fix them ourselves? I don't think we ever got much beyond changing the tires. Well, I could've kicked myself for not taking it all more seriously. I was trying not to panic. I was thinking, now that's the fan belt, and those are the spark plugs, and that's the carburetor—isn't that pathetic? You're probably wondering why I didn't just call a tow truck. Well, there's no logical reason at all. I just didn't think of it. I didn't get my Ph.D. in common sense, after all, I got it in film theory. As you know, they are completely unrelated fields. I'm sure it would probably have occurred to me to call them before much more time had passed. As you'll see, fate intervened first.

A huge rig pulled in to the parking lot and began to circle me. Slowly. My heart jumped into my throat. I was thinking *Thelma and Louise.* I was thinking trouble. The driver stared out the window of his cab at me. I glared back, trying to look fierce and potentially armed.

"G'day," he called out, in a friendly tone of voice. "Bit of strife with the vehicle?"

I nodded cautiously, still suspicious. He asked if he could help and, before I had time to consider my answer, hopped out.

It was a warm night. He was just wearing a T-shirt and jeans. He was probably in his fifties, and as he bent over the hood, I got a good look at him. I was still thinking along the lines of how I would describe him to the police. His face was suntanned and deeply etched with lines. He had well-defined, thick eyebrows and attractive blue eyes, from which fanned a bold network of smile lines. He had light brown hair sprinkled with gray. It was cut short and probably for just ten dollars in some country town, you know the look. He didn't seem like a bad sort. I began to relax.

He fetched his toolbox from his truck and set to work. Every so often, he'd look up at me and explain, in his deep rumbly voice and really broad Ocker accent, what he was doing. I wasn't taking in a word of it.

I was noticing how hard the muscles of his arm were, how they rippled and bulged as he fiddled with the engine. His hands were large and callused. Each fingernail was outlined in black with dirt and engine oil. He had a tattoo on his right arm of a bunch of red roses, and there was a blue-and-gold oriental dragon on the left. The hair on his arms was thick and blond, his skin browned and freckled from the sun. The back of his neck had the look of tan leather. He was solid around the waist, which only increased his very manly attractiveness. His legs appeared strong and powerful through his jeans.

There I was, Ph.D.; lecturer in women's studies; big, noisy critic of even most educated males as having questionable, not wholly reconstructed attitudes toward gender politics; sort-of wannabe lesbian (we've discussed this, haven't we? how you never quite feel accepted within the hard core of feminist circles if you're not a lesbian?) who in all my thirty-three years has never even slept with a guy who had less than a master's, and there I was being rescued like a classic damsel in distress by this big brawny bear of a man—and absolutely wetting my pants over him at the same time.

"Thanks so much for this," I finally managed to croak. My voice had inexplicably gone all husky.

He grinned. "No worries."

"See this?" He pointed to something or other near the, you know, big bumpy thing in the middle where the spark plugs go. "That was where your problem was. She'll be right now."

"Mmmm," I replied, vagueing out. Leaning closer to him, I breathed in his pungent male odor, all sweat and motor oil. My heart was beating. Without really thinking about it, I shifted my position slightly, so that our arms touched, and it was, literally, like a jolt of electricity. A great big shiver ran down my back.

"Cold?" he asked, the hint of a smile playing around his lips.

Then, can you believe it—I still can hardly credit it myself—I replied, in my new, Mae West voice, "No. I'm hot, actually." Insinuating my body against his, I pressed my lips against the crinkly brown sausage of his neck. Honestly, Fiona, I've never ever done anything like this before in my life. I've hardly even had any one-night stands!

And you know I've had my eye on this very nice, sensitive, and intelligent fellow in the Asian studies department, Sam, for months now. I think he might be interested in me too, but the political correctness vibe on campus makes it very hard for anyone to make a move. It's not like either of us really fears the other would jump up and scream "sexual harassment" or anything, I mean, I'm not his boss and he's not mine, we're just colleagues, and not even in the same department; but the mood on campus surrounding all this sort of thing has left everyone a bit edgy. Maybe it's just me. Maybe I've forgotten how to flirt. Well, I thought I'd forgotten how to flirt.

"Struth," chuckled my truckie. "You are hot, aren't you?" He put down his tools. He leaned over and kissed me, not at all tentatively or gently like those M.A.s and Ph.D.s have always tended to do, but with a kind of rough urgency that, well, if I'm admitting everything else I can admit this too, I really liked. He grabbed my breast and squeezed my nipple hard, through my shirt. Cars whizzed past on the road. We were shielded by the hood of my car, which was still propped up. But when someone drove into the parking lot to turn around, we found ourselves suddenly bathed in the beam of headlights and jumped apart, a little self-consciously.

Glancing around, he said, "Come on," took my hand, and led me over to behind the Big Merino. There are some picnic tables there. He sat down on a bench and pulled me onto his lap. Fumbling with the buttons on my blouse, he finally just ripped it open. He grappled my breasts out of my bra and rubbed them and pinched the nipples. I threw my head back and closed my eyes. He nibbled and sucked, occasionally biting my nipples so hard it hurt, but I liked that too, the wild intensity of it all. I was straddling him by now, my skirt riding up high on my hips, and he was kneading my ass with those strong hands. (You should see the grease and oil stains on the blouse and the skirt —they're practically fingerprints! And half the buttons are torn off the blouse. It's funny, but I was just thinking about disposing of those old things the other day and getting some new clothes. Now I have to!) I could feel his dick straining hard against his jeans, and I was riding up and down on it.

Is this too pornographic? Are you shocked? I can't really stop here, though, can I? Besides, if it's pornographic, do you think it proves or disproves Robin Morgan's thesis that if rape is the practice, pornography is the theory? What happens when we women write the pornography? Can we rape ourselves? I've been thinking about this issue a lot lately. The other day, Philippa shared one of her erotic stories with us and asked about the latest line on pornography. I've never quite understood the difference between erotica and pornography, have you? I mean, is erotica merely porn with literary pretensions? Or is something pornography if written by a man but erotica if penned by a woman?

Anyway, there we were, writhing away. I was really digging his gamey smell. I don't think I'm going to give up on intellectuals after this by any means, but they do tend to have a bad habit of wanting to shower before going to bed, and I think I'm just not going to allow that any more.

He took my hand and placed it on his crotch. Then he unbuckled his belt and unzipped his fly, and took my hand right down into his jocks. His dick felt hard and hot under my touch, and I swear I could even feel the pulsing of his veins. He squirmed around a bit so that I could pull down his trousers and his underpants. "Hold on a tic," he said. He wrapped my legs around his back (my arms were already around his neck) and stood up. Hobbling along (his trousers had fallen down to his ankles), he carried me over to the back wall of the Merino, his tongue down my throat the whole time.

As I slid down his body and onto my feet again, I became aware of music playing. You know those tapes they play in souvenir shops? Songs of the bush, that sort of thing? It seems when they'd locked up the shop, the attendants had forgotten to turn off the tape.

Anyway, he now put one of those big paws on the back of my head and pushed me down to my knees, urging my mouth down on to his ginormous cock (certainly the biggest I've ever seen!). He leaned over sideways. I could hear the sound of leather sliding along cloth—he was slipping his belt out of his trousers. Without pulling out of my mouth he leaned over me and yanked my hands behind me and strapped them together, behind my waist, with the belt. I could tell he wasn't fastening the belt very tightly. I'm pretty sure I could have gotten my hands out if I'd wanted to. It was frightening and thrilling at the same time. He used his hands now to control the rhythm by pushing down on my head. We both responded to the Muzak coming out of the store, so I ended up sucking to the beat of "Waltzing Matilda." After a long while—but I don't want to seem like I'm complaining because I was enjoying every minute of it—I could feel his balls begin to tighten. He groaned. Lifting my head off his knob, he unfastened the belt and helped me to my feet. My knees were raw from the pavement and my stockings were in shreds, but I didn't care.

Now, he pushed me against the wall, where the stucco strip between the windows dug into my back. He dropped to his knees, clawed down my undies and my torn pantyhose and, well, he gave as good as he got. I remember having one, oddly lucid thought, and that was of registering that directly above me was a round window exactly where the sheep's asshole should have been. I don't remember much else except that he took me right over the edge, and then immediately did it again, and I could hardly stand by the time he finished.

He had a cheeky grin on his face as he stood up again, wiping his mouth and chin with the back of his hand, and saying, "I love a wet woman." He took a condom from his wallet and gave it to me. My hands were shaking, and I could hardly rip the little package open. Then I couldn't tell which end was up. Don't you hate that? Trying to roll it down and it won't go because the teat's facing in and it's upside down? Anyway I worked it out. Would you believe, and I'm not exaggerating, his dick was so big that, in fact, I actually couldn't roll on the condom—he had to show me how to stretch it out with my fingers and pull it on that way. He whirled me around now, so that my back was to him and shoved me up against the wall. I vaguely made a note to interrogate myself thoroughly —at a later, more convenient date—on why I found this rough, dominating sort of sex such a turn-on. It really is a worry, ideologically speaking. Anyway, it was. A turn-on, I mean. Now I was bent over, ass up, head down, hands flattened on the windowpane to steady myself. "The Road to Gundagai" was playing now, and he entered me in energetic thrusts perfectly timed to the music while gripping my hips with his hands. The sensation of that massive rod sliding in and filling me up was both agonizing and exquisite. When he really began to slam it in, I orgasmed again while staring through the glass at rows of stuffed koala bears waving little Australian flags. He came too, with a powerful, animal grunt. We just rested there for a few minutes, his arms now wrapped around my waist, his hot, sweaty, prickly chin resting on the back of my neck. Then we straightened up and got our clothing back in order and headed to our vehicles, arms around each other's waist.

I could hardly walk.

He removed his toolbox from my engine, closed the hood, and said, "You shouldn't have any trouble getting that going again now." He added that I should have it checked by a mechanic when I got back to Sydney, and said he'd wait and see that I was able to get off okay.

"By the way," he said, in a tone that was almost paternal, "I wouldn't let strange men tie you up like that. That was shocking. Someone could really do you harm, you know."

Still a little unsteady on my feet, I thanked him, for everything, including the advice, and got into my car. Everything was purring, including me. I waved good-bye and got on the road. And that was that! We never even asked each other's names. My leg muscles are still sore, and everything else is tender, and all the clothes I was wearing that day are wrecked (I stopped at another petrol station outside of Mittagong to change) so I know it wasn't just a hallucination. Besides, I've still got the Wide Load condom wrapper ("maximum head room") that I picked up from the ground as we left.

I wonder what Sam would have thought of it. He'll never find out, of course, but I'd love to know whether he'd be turned on by the idea, or repulsed. Part of me would like him to be turned on, and the other part, maybe the good Catholic girl in me, would prefer it if he were horrified. As if that were somehow a guarantee that Sam was a higher life form, more capable of caring and commitment or something. I think I'm getting in touch with my inner pagan. I must reread Camille Paglia.

I really did mean to tell you all about the conference, but maybe I'll do that in another letter.

Do tell me what you've been up to. You owe me a vicarious adventure.

Much love,
Helen

P.S. Please, please do me a favor and not mention any of this to anyone. As you know, I'm not really the confessional type. Then again, there's usually not much for me to confess!

Helen pressed "Control P." The department's laser printer whirred into action. She glanced at her watch. It was getting on to evening and she'd told Julia that she'd meet her for dinner. She wanted to go home and change first. But there was still time to do a few more things before leaving the office. She quickly tapped out two letters to colleagues, one at the Australian National University and another at Melbourne University, requesting copies of the papers they'd given at the conference. She then composed a cover letter to send with a copy of her own paper to a prestigious women's studies journal in the United States, printed all of these out, and started a note to her parents, who lived in Perth. She went to the photocopy machine and made a few copies of an article she thought would interest her colleagues, and of some of her own writing for her parents.

Dear Mum and Dad,
Hope this finds you both well. I'm so glad Dad has recovered. You've got to be so careful with heart conditions. Remember what the doctor said—no stress and no undue excitement.

Sorry I haven't written for a while. I've been working long hours. Last week I presented a paper at a conference in Canberra on food, women, and film. It caused quite a bit of discussion, so I suppose from that standpoint it was a success; and I've just finished revising it (partly on the basis of the comments at the conference) to submit to a journal in the States.

Other than that, I haven't been doing much of interest to report. I see a fair bit of the girls, of course; and they all said to send their best to Dad and to say they're glad he's doing so well. Julia's heading off to China in January on a three-week cultural exchange. She's very excited.

I'm enclosing photocopies of the paper I gave at the ANU. Let me know what you think. I'll write again soon. Take care.

Love,
Hellie

Helen swept the sheets of paper off the top of the laser printer and glanced at her watch. Damn! She'd be late if she didn't hurry now. She closed all the files, saving the work-related ones and dragging the others into the little trash bin on the bottom right hand corner of the computer screen. She told the computer to empty the trash. While shutting the machine down, she fumbled in her desk drawer for business-size university envelopes. Hastily, she addressed them and shoved the letters into the envelopes together with the photocopies. She tossed the envelopes, all of which were quite fat, into the outgoing mail sack. After a quick trip to the toilet, she returned to her office to grab her bag, turned off the lights, locked the door, and headed out of the building. She was nearly at the front door when she turned around. She half-ran back to the mail sack and, rummaging through its contents, retrieved the letter to Fiona. Maybe, she thought, I should just have another look at this before mailing it. Maybe, she thought, I won't mail it at all.

Helen arrived ten minutes late at the new Thai restaurant where she was meeting Julia, but Julia wasn't there yet. Chantal had recommended the place to them. The interior had been featured in *Pulse*. While she waited for Julia, Helen looked around at walls painted to look like the outside of a decaying building, complete with graffiti; she gaped at the wildly tilted and outsize chandelier illuminating the galley where busy chefs tossed colorful dishes in flaming woks, and squirmed to get comfortable in the aesthetically impeccable but ergonomically impossible metal seat. Julia bounced in about five minutes after Helen, swung her bag onto the floor beside the table, and apologized for being late.

The waiters were the crème de la crème of the Thai gym queen crowd. One sashayed over to their table. He presented the menu with a gestural flourish that would not have been out of place in the court of Louis XIV.

"No wonder Chantal likes this place." Julia giggled after the waiter had taken their drink orders. "Gay boy heaven."

Over the entrées, fat parcels of banana leaves wrapped around microscopic chunks of chicken, Julia told Helen that she had decided to do a series of photographs on the theme of PMS as a way of creatively processing the outburst of the other day. They talked about the kind of images that she might try to capture, of female rage and despair, that would convey the full weirdness of being in the thrall to one's hormones and yet not demean women in any way or imply that they were, well, in thrall to their hormones.

As their dishes arrived—chicken with cashews, stir-fried beef with coconut milk and green vegetable curry—Helen silently debated whether or not to tell Julia about her own encounter of a different hormonal kind. Before she had a chance to say anything, Julia confided that the boy she'd been out with the other night was really turning out to be something special. They had seen each other twice since then, she said, and the sex was fantastic.

"Sounds like a relationship to me," Helen marveled.

"Oh, I wouldn't go that far," countered Julia. "Or rather, I'd go that far, but I'm not so sure he would. He's young and doesn't like the idea of being tied down. Once, I brought up the subject of commitment. He yawned and said, 'Isn't that a movie about an Irish rock band?' I didn't feel like pursuing it after that. He doesn't even like to make plans more than three days ahead of time. Never mind. He's a major babe. And it's the nineties after all. I feel lucky to have found a man who actually wants to have sex. You know, sperm counts are falling all around the globe. It's a real worry."

"It's often said that another reason people aren't having sex is for fear of catching AIDS," Helen said. "Personally I think it's also for fear of catching a relationship. I think a lot of people, men in particular, look on relationships as potentially fatal conditions as well. But back to your spunkrat. He sounds great. And he's not bothered by the age difference?"

"Doesn't seem to be," Julia answered. She had neglected to mention the *Sunset Boulevard* episode. After all, when she read him the riot act over his ongoing Norma Desmond jokes, he'd finally dropped the subject.

"Super," Helen approved. Julia asked if there was any romance on her horizon, and how things were going with Sam.

"Oh, things aren't really 'going' at all. I don't know."

"I reckon you should make a move, Hellie. Jump his bones."

"I don't think so, Jules. Not Sam. If it works out at all, it's going to be one of those relationships like risotto, that needs a long cooking time and just a trickle of emotional stock poured in at a time."

"I suppose I've always been a fast-food girl myself." Julia chuckled. "But you must give me your risotto recipe someday."

A young executive type with an Armani suit and a gold earring entered the restaurant. He stood just inside the door surveying the scene. When he was satisfied that he had been noticed by everyone, he sat down at the table next to Julia and Helen. He pulled his mobile phone out of his pocket. Removing it from its fake tiger-skin case, he dialed a number and loudly instructed whoever was on the other end to "e-mail me the proposal." He put the phone on the table; stretched his pinstriped legs arrogantly in the direction of the girls; and ran his fingers through his pony-tail-length, slicked-back hair.

"Wanker," Julia whispered to Helen.

Helen rolled her eyes in agreement.

The man then snapped his fingers at the waiter.

"That's rude," Helen observed, sotto voce. The hand-some waiter clearly thought so as well. He approached the man's table. The waiter tilted his head back so that he was looking, literally, down his nose at the man. "Takes more than two fingers to make me come," he hissed. With that, he turned on his heels and strode back to the kitchen.

Julia and Helen snorted with laughter. The man, who had gone red as a chili pepper, pushed up his jacket sleeve to look at his watch, shook his head as though he'd been waiting for ages for someone who had failed to show, got up, and walked out.

Helen decided against mentioning her Goulburn adventure for now. It was already quite late. She had a class to teach first thing in the morning and needed to prepare for it. Besides, now that she'd written that letter, she was beginning to have second thoughts. The analytical bit of her brain, the part that had its hair pinned up in a stern bun and wore suits and black-framed glasses, was back from its holiday and wasn't at all pleased about the mess on her desk. Ms. Analytical interrogated Helen mercilessly:

What was she doing having that sort of blatantly submissive sex, and with a total stranger at that? What on earth had she been thinking of? He'd handled her so roughly. And she'd liked and encouraged it. But there was another voice in Helen's head. The chick with the short, short skirt; long, long legs; and big attitude sitting on that desk, the one who'd piled up the cigarette butts in the ashtray and was swilling lemon Stoli. She pointed out to Ms. Analytical that in fact Helen had taken the lead, and that they had just been playing at rough sex. It had been exciting and consensual and no one had got hurt. And it was safe—they'd used a condom. So what was her problem? Longlegs blew smoke in Analytical's face. The upshot was: Helen didn't think she was ready to talk about it quite yet. She wouldn't mail that letter after all. She'd write another one to Fiona, concentrating on the conference this time, tomorrow at the latest.

"Do you want coffee or shall we get the bill?" Julia glanced at her Swatch.

"No coffee for me," Helen replied. "I've got a big day tomorrow. I'd better get going soon."

"Me too."

After classes the following afternoon, Helen stepped off the train, and hurried through the sad sleaze of Kings Cross to her tidy flat on Bayswater Road. Throwing her bag and the mail she'd picked up from her mailbox down on her kitchen counter, she set the kettle to boil. She fetched the container of freshly ground coffee out of the freezer and savored its aroma before scooping out a few spoonfuls into her plunger.

The phone rang. It was Marc, the student with the lime green pigtails, with a query about the final paper for the course. His voice triggered a replay in her mind of the day in class when he'd made that comment about the "beauty myth," and how she'd reacted. If she hadn't been so distracted, she might have realized that his question now sounded suspiciously like an excuse just to speak to her. She balanced the receiver on her shoulder while making her coffee. It was only after he said, "I think you're a really cool teacher, Helen," and hung up rather quickly did it occur to her there might have been, as they liked to say in film studies, a subversive subtext.

She pushed the thought to the back of her mind and sat down to open her mail. Nothing wildly exciting: a telephone bill, a catalog from DJs, a letter from her parents, and a postcard from Fiona in Darwin. The last reminded her of her own letter, and she fished it out of her bag. She tore open the envelope. That missive would go no further than a discreet file in her desk drawer. What she saw caused her face to pale and her heart to skip a beat. She dropped it to the floor and put her hands over her mouth, which, behind her stretched fingers, had formed a large "O." She double-checked the envelope. Yes, it was clearly made out to Fiona in Darwin. But the letter inside began:

Dear Bronwyn,
It was nice to see you again in Canberra and catch up with what you are doing. I was very intrigued by your thesis on the valorization of gender identity in contemporary Aboriginal theater and dance . . .

CHAPTER FIVE

The Fifth Scarf

The woman in the red corset smooths on her elbow-length black kid leather gloves. Her dark hair flows like warm chocolate over the plump vanilla scoops of her shoulders. The corset pushes up her breasts, exposing them nearly to the nipples. Turning with a coquettish flounce of her tutu, she bends at the waist to study herself in the mirror that is propped up on the floor. She reaches for lipstick the color of raspberries and freshens the bow of her lips. She is aware that she is displaying her firm round buttocks to advantage. Red garters stripe the immaculate white flesh, and sheer black stockings encircle the pale fullness of her thighs. Her stilettos further elongate her legs, heightening the dramatic effect. Her sex is barely covered by the black lace g-string. Widening her stance, she lowers her head to look back from between her legs. Her hair hangs down in a lustrous curtain to the floor. Yes. Just as she had expected. Those big green eyes, with their thick fringe of lashes, are welded to her. They say, come to me, love me, tease me, fuck me now.

Beg me, darling. I'd like that.

A white lace curtain flutters in the cool mountain breeze. The silk fringe on the lampshade undulates in the draft. The dusky rouge lampshade is pure Victorian, like everything else in this history-encrusted room. Although it is only midafternoon, the room seems to exist in a perpetual gloaming. The densely forested slopes outside the window glow a soft eucalyptus blue. Shafts of slanting light play sensuously with the patterns of the lacy bedspread and warm the threadbare colors of the woven rugs scattered over the wooden floor. A fire glows and crackles in the small fireplace, licking even more intricate rivulets of light and shade over the scene.

Wait a minute. If it's cold enough to have a fire going, then it's too cold to open the window. One or the other. Let's take the fire. Forget the breeze.

Drawing herself up again, she inspects the fire. With a poker she gently stirs the logs; under her precise touch, the flames leap up with the alacrity of desire. Concealing her emotion, she shifts her gaze to the naked slave on the bed. She's been there a while now and has been very good, too. She hasn't even needed to be gagged.

Sashaying over to the bed, she spreadeagles the willing, wide-eyed creature and ties her by her beautiful hands and perfect feet to the bedposts with silk scarves. Placing a gloved hand on her slave's instep, she notes with satisfaction how her whole body jumps as though jolted by an electric current. Then, moving her hand up to encircle the slave's ankle with her fingers, the mistress lowers her lips down onto the big toe, which still smells faintly of ylang-ylang and sandalwood oil from the bath. She flicks the top of the toe with the tip of her tongue and then takes it into her mouth and sucks on it. Planting rows of tiny kisses all the way down the foot, she continues up the leg to the knee, where she rests her head. Her right hand lies casually on her slave's stomach; the left traces baroque patterns on the inside of the opposite thigh. A train rumbles past. She feels the vibrations from the walls and floor through the bed frame, through her slave's warm and silky leg.

She places her mouth on the inside of her slave's thigh and pulls long and hard on the creamy skin. Pinching it between her teeth, she draws the blood to just below the surface where it remains in the form of a love bite. The slave moans. The mistress raises her head and looks at her sharply. "Did I say you could make any noise?"

"No, mistress," she breathes.

"Good girl," she says, stroking the other lightly from the tip of her toes to just below her sex, which, the mistress notes with satisfaction, is already glistening with dew. She lightly tousles her slave's pubic hairs. Standing up straight now, she thoughtfully surveys her domain.

Philippa stares at the words in front of her. She stands up again and walks thoughtfully over to the bed. Holding onto one of the bedposts, she leans on it, pensive. The bed creaks. "Sshhh," she says. "I'm trying to think."

*H*ow I long for her touch! I should have known. It never pays to be too eager, too greedy when you're the bottom. Now, I turn my head to look at her. She is shaking her head with disapproval. She reminds me that I am not to look at her without permission. I'm a naughty girl, and I'm going to be punished now. I hear the sharp click of her heels on the floor, and my heart beats fast. I resist the temptation to look and see where she is going. I hear the crisp sound of an unlocking clasp. I know what's coming next. I stare hard at the molded ceiling. My gaze madly strokes the intricate details of the plaster roses and latticework. I try to stay calm. A log explodes in the fireplace and, outside the window, a child calls to his mother. Outside, I know, the Blue Mountains sky is a cold and emotionless blue. The wind is whipping through the gum trees. The child is probably rugged up snugly in a thick woolen sweater and jacket, with the strings of the hood tied in a bow under a chin still padded with baby fat. He has mittens knitted by Grandma on his little hands. There are apples on his cheeks, and the neglected half of a Violet Crumble in his pocket that will melt when he gets indoors, and lead, upon discovery by his mother, to a spanking. A very vigorous spanking too, I imagine! A spanking would be nice. I hear her walk to the window. She must have noticed the child too. At last, she's coming back to me. I can't resist looking at her. She is a vision in red and black. Her voluptuousness strains against the criss-crossed laces of her bodice and her beautiful breasts form two mounds as mysterious as any of the sensuous peaks of the mountains sprawling around this town. I want to worship those breasts. Will she let me?

She is frowning again. She spills a handful of tiny instruments onto the bed beside me. They fall onto the lace of the bedspread with a soft metallic whisper. She is reaching behind her now, to the bedside table. She has a scarf in both hands and it's coming down over my eyes. Don't blindfold me! I want to see you, I want to devour you with my eyes. Ohhh. Now I am in darkness. I close my eyes and surrender to it. Every nerve in my body is quivering.

And Chantal couldn't figure out what the fifth scarf was for! Silly girl.

I can hear the whalebone in her corset rasping ever so faintly and the rustle of the tutu as she shifts position. What's she doing?

It can't really be whalebone, can it? People would find that so offensive. Unless it's an antique corset, of course, in which case, no new whales were killed. I think they still call it whalebone these days when it's not, really. It's plastic. Maybe she should just say she could hear the bones in her corset rasping—they do call the plastic in corsets "bones," I believe. I should double-check that with Chantal. Doesn't have quite the same ring, though. Sounds like she might have some osteological disease. Philippa reaches for a box on the desk. Studying the contents, she extracts a chocolate in the shape of a miniature conch shell. Putting it into her mouth, she sucks on it till it begins to melt, running thickly over her tongue and down the back of her throat. Concentrate. Concentrate.

I can feel her face close to mine now. The ripples of heat off her skin and low, sweet breathing caress me. Her breath has the odor of chocolate and mint; her skin is a more subtle musk. She's pulling away again. My cheeks are cool. I pout. A soft, leather-clad finger traces my lips, top and bottom. I throw kisses up at it. The smell of leather, the scent of her perfume, these are driving me insane. I open my mouth and take the finger between my lips. I suck on the finger, and now it's two, and three fingers. The animal taste of leather fills my senses and makes me tingle all over. Another rustle of the tutu and creak of bone and her other hand is resting lightly—so lightly!—on my sex. My clitoris swells and aches for her touch. She knows me too well. She strokes it once, twice . . . please, please, keep going . . . but she won't, not now anyway. I know her too well also. The hand slips away. I hear another jangle of metal, as her lips, warm and oily with lipstick, close around my nipple. She is flicking my nipple with her tongue; it stands up stiffly between her teeth, eager to please. I want her hand back on my pussy. I strain my hips toward her. I hear her straighten up and laugh. "And what are you trying to do, you naughty girl?"

"Nothing," I gasp.

"Nothing, Madam," she says, a severe tone coming into that lush and husky voice.

"Nothing, Madam," I repeat, chastened, trying to quell the rebellion in my hips.

"That's better," she says, and rewards me with a kiss. A long, wet kiss that teases me and vibrates through my soul, making me want her even more. And then, suddenly, I feel a sharp pain in my right nipple as she attaches the clamp. My body arches. There is another sharp pain, in my left nipple, and I hear the minute clicks of the chain that she attaches to each clamp. The weight of the chain dragging on the clamps intensifies the agony. Is she pulling on it? Sensation billows through me; I am a surfer on the swells of my own torment. I try to breathe more slowly, more deeply, but my breath comes fast and shallow. I am trying desperately to center myself, to find a quiet place outside the pain. OhmyGod, she's got her fingers on my thighs. She's drawing her nose up the inside of my thighs . . . She's planting chaste, maddening little kisses up and down the outside of my pussy, separating its folds with her tongue. And now—clamps on my labia. There are two of me. There's one that's riding up and down on the bucking pain like a rodeo star, and there's another who has dissolved into pulses of pure, floating sensuality. They meet and fall away, rush together, and are torn apart. What's this now? Cool metal insistent against my lips. The chain, of course, that's it. I take it obediently between my teeth, though the pull of the chain reignites the fire in my nipples.

She is kissing my neck. Her warm lips travel down over my collarbone to my breasts, as her hands rove my stomach.

I hear her strike a match and a delicious burst of sulfur fills my nostrils. She is picking up a candle, I am guessing. A new layer of sensation—slender loops and crosses of shivery anticipation—covers me like tulle. The first hit of wax, just above my navel, makes me jump. By the third and fourth, on my breasts and thighs, I am writhing, out of control. As though from a distant place, I hear her voice and feel her soothing touch on my arm. She is asking if I am all right. Tears of mortification and of gratitude come to my blindfolded eyes, and I nod. Her mouth closes over mine and I pull on it as hard as I can. Our tongues intertwine and her hand moves down to my pussy. She spreads it open with her fingers, pushing on the clamps, and now, pulling away from my kiss, she bends over my hips and breathes into that hot, wet, yearning crevice. I move closer to the edge of insanity. Touch me, lick me, bury your face in me! My head twists from side to side. I beat the pillow with my cheeks. At last, her tongue enters me, swift and probing, and I am fractured and whole, all at once, a lit and sizzling fuse.

I think she's really enjoying this. Philippa smiles to herself.

I know the rhythms of her body well. I can feel that she's on the edge of explosion. But it's too soon. Reluctantly, I remove my mouth from that sweet, salty cavern and stand back. I love to watch her writhe and moan and strain against her silken bonds.

There's that child again. How long has he been looking for his mother? How much time has passed? It feels like a nanosecond and a century. What shall I do to her now? I walk over to the fire and put in a fresh log. A burst of new warmth ripples across the room as it ignites. It is getting dark outside. I light another candle and place it by the bedside. Perhaps it's time for the riding crop.

Removing the labial clamps, she strokes her slave hard now, to a point just short of orgasm. As the slave arches her back, teetering on the edge of the threshold, the mistress bends over and kisses her deeply. At the same time she slides the head of a large dildo into the slave's widened sex. The slave thrusts her hips violently in a vain attempt to swallow it. Constrained by her silken ties, she succeeds only in pushing the tool out by a millimeter or two. Panicking, she tries to stay still, but she so desperately wants it in her to the hilt, to pump on it, to have it fill her up, that she is frantic. Her mistress removes the blindfold. The slave blinks, though the light is low. She can just see the heavy pink toy extending out of her. The head of its Siamese twin nods in the air. This only doubles her desire, if it's possible to double something that is infinite, and she longs for her mistress to mount the dildo's other head. Her carnal craving is so strong she forgets momentarily the pain that continues, a bit more dully now, to emanate from her nipples. Then her mistress gives her nipple clamps a gentle squeeze, and waves of pain cascade over the shores of her consciousness once more. But it is the dildo, with its tantalizing presence inside her and yet not enough inside her, that is really driving her mad. The mistress, seeing her misery and her yearning, smiles again, and places a light kiss on her cheek. With a slow, sexy gait, she ambles over to the closet and removes a hooded velvet cape, which she puts on. Her slave's eyes widen. You're not leaving me like this? Her lips tremble. She has not even had a chance to give voice to her question when her mistress exits in a lush swish of fabric. The door shuts and she hears the click of high-heeled shoes echo and fade down the corridor.

*H*elen stood anxiously in the queue at the business counter of the post office, compulsively twirling the strap of her purse around the fingers of one hand, unwinding it and doing it again. Her no-nonsense eyebrows knitted together on a face that forecast imminent rain. The old man who is always standing in front of you in bank queues with bags of coins to be counted, a worn passbook to be replaced, and a complicated answer to the teller's innocent question, "And how are you today, Mr Green?" was now just ahead of her arranging for a postal money order and trying to figure out whether to send his package air or economy air and, if air, whether he should take out the box of chocolates to bring the weight down to five hundred grams. His wife's brother had always loved chocolate but wasn't supposed to have them anymore. But he did, sometimes, anyway. Not that these were for him. Oh no. But you had to sympathize.

Helen began to hyperventilate. She was so stressed that when she heard her name ring out from behind, she jumped.

"Gee, you're edgy, aren't you?" Philippa observed. "What's wrong? You look terrible."

"Oh God, Philippa, you wouldn't believe it if I told you."

"Next, please."

Helen grimaced apologetically to Philippa and bounded toward the counter. "How do I go about getting some letters back that were posted yesterday?"

The clerk patiently explained that they could put out a search, if she could provide the time and place of posting, but that there was no guarantee that they could retrieve them. Especially so late in the piece. Completely destroying Helen's cozy view of the postal service as a lumbering wombat, incapable of high speeds, he described how in all probability her letters were whizzing off to their destinations at that very moment. He did say he would try to find out what the chances were and asked her to fill out a form. He then disappeared into the back room with it.

"What's happening, Helen?" Philippa was most curious by now.

Helen outlined the problem. "And so," she concluded tensely, "it could be in any of those envelopes. I will die no matter which person gets it, but I will die a thousand deaths if it goes to my parents. Especially with my father's heart condition. But the worst of it is, I won't know whom it's gone to until it gets there."

"Could you ask your mum not to open the next letter she gets, to just send it back?"

"Oh, sure," replied Helen. "Would your mum not open the letter under those circumstances?"

"Hmmm," Philippa reflected. Her mum would definitely open the letter. "You've got a point."

"Miss Nicholls?" At the booming sound of the postal clerk's voice, Helen spun back to face the counter.

"Ms.," Helen automatically corrected.

"Ms. Nicholls, sorry. They'll check for you. Don't want you to get your hopes up, though, given that the letters are probably already at the central sorting place. If we do find them, there'll be a fee of twenty dollars for each one recovered. In any case, there's no point waiting here any longer. We've got your phone number. We'll call you if we find any of them. About the twenty dollars, is that all right then?"

Helen stared at him dumbly. Philippa intervened: "I'm sure she'd pay two hundred dollars under the circumstances. Come on, Helen, let's go get a cup of coffee." Philippa wanted every detail.

About an hour later, at Café Da Vida, Philippa was sitting back appreciatively and Helen was chasing crumbs of carrot cake around her plate with her finger, pressing them into the white plate and licking them off her fingertip.

"What are you doing off work on a Tuesday anyway?" Helen suddenly asked. She'd just noticed what looked suspiciously like a lipstick smudge on Philippa's neck.

"Flexitime. I saved up enough for a whole day off."

"Great. What have you been doing?"

"Oh, you know, the usual."

"Writing?"

"You could call it that."

"What do you call it?"

"Playing. Working. Sex. Whatever."

"Interesting way of looking at it," Helen smiled. She was debating whether or not to raise the subject of the lipstick when a passerby caught her attention, and she looked up. She cocked her head to one side. "I could swear," she said, "that that was the poet, you know, whatsisname, the punk that Chantal had a fling with ages ago."

"Bram?" Philippa twisted her neck round to look, but he'd turned a corner. "Missed him. But wasn't he supposed to have moved to LA? Or ODed or something?"

"I'd heard he'd gone into advertising in New York. That was probably a malicious rumor, though. Anyway, he certainly hasn't been spotted round these parts in ages. He was such a waster. I certainly never liked him. It's always been a mystery to me how our gorgeous Chantie ever ended up with such a character."

"Love moves in mysterious ways."

"So I hear," Helen said. "So, have you shown any more of your novel to anyone?"

"Just Richard."

"His reaction?"

"Whisky a go go."

"Meaning?"

"Meaning, he seems to like it." Philippa changed the subject. "Have you seen Chantal or Julia recently? I haven't caught up with either of them for a week or so."

Helen told Philippa about her dinner with Julia. "She's off to China soon. She's really psyched. She's just a bit nervous about leaving the new boy so early in the game. Seems totally rapt with him." Helen leaned toward Philippa over the table. "Apparently," she revealed, "the sex is mega-hot."

"Excellent," Philippa smiled. "What's his name?"

Helen slapped her forehead with her hand. "I'm so bad with names," she said after a pause. "Jason, I think. Yeah, Jason." She wiped a bead of sweat off her forehead. "It's like summer already," she commented. "I'm so nervous about that letter. I need to keep distracted. Do you want to go to Nielsen Park? Have a quick dip?"

"Sounds tempting. But I really have to be getting home," Philippa apologized. "I've a friend waiting for me there." She added, after a pause, "I'll probably be tied up for the rest of the day."

CHAPTER SIX

Alchemy

"No, you never can tell," echoed Alexi. "Not these days. But I do suspect he's straight. In which case, gorgeous, he's all yours."

"Oh God, darling, I couldn't possibly. Not this morning anyway," Chantal moaned.

Alexi glanced at his watch. "Arvo, darling," he corrected.

Chantal rolled her eyes. "Do me a very big favor, sweetheart, and get me some Alka-Seltzer. In a champagne glass. No one will notice."

"Of course, Fabulous One. We'll be most discreet." Alexi leaned over to give Chantal a peck on the cheek and wove his way through the other guests to the back door of the house. They were at a Sunday afternoon garden party in Paddington, at the large terrace house of a wildly successful painter who signed his paintings "∞" and was known as Finn—short for "infinity"—to his friends. Finn's sculptor wife, Myrna, occupied the fourth floor; and his gay lover, Craig (who doubled as Myrna's live model), ruled over the third. Finn's work, with its kitsch retro themes and vivid Day-Glo colors, had recently formed the backdrop to a fashion shoot for Chantal's magazine ("Nothing More Today Than Yesterday!"). The backyard of the terrace was lushly planted with trees and flowers and dotted with bird baths into which stone angels pissed copious streams of water. A gay boy in a floral frock chatted animatedly with a seventy-year-old matron in an electric blue suit, the author of a hot collection of gothic-erotic fiction currently climbing the best-seller list. Well-dressed art dealers sipped champagne cocktails and complained about the gallery scene in London or Paris or New York or wherever they'd just flown back from. Artists in ripped T-shirts concentrated on heaping their plates with salmon, caviar, and other luxury tucker from the buffet.

Like a gaunt bird, Chantal perched on a wrought-iron bench in the shelter of a pergola canopied with flowering wisteria. Her silver satin slip dress—latest look this season, silver being even more trendy than mere color —shimmered wherever the afternoon sun pierced the thin shade of the wisteria to lick the fabric. Alexi had dyed her hair blond again, keeping the roots dark, to give it a fashionably trashy appearance. Before they'd come out, he'd artfully messed it up for her and then gelled the tangle into place. But Chantal was uncharacteristically in no condition to luxuriate in her own appearance or its impact on others. Something about her aura and the subtly defensive posture she had adopted warned strangers off impulsive approaches.

She felt absolutely shocking. Behind her Ray•Bans, her dry eyes ached; she thought she could trace the thudding pulse of her optic nerve all the way down to her queasy stomach. Her head pounded like a track from that wretched Nine Inch Nails CD her last boyfriend had insisted on playing when they made love—he hadn't lasted very long. She had had to apply a ton of concealer to mask the bags under her eyes. Too much alcohol, too little sleep, and most of all, the shock of—how would you describe exactly what had happened last night?—the shock of the old, yes, that was it. Where the hell was Alexi with her Alka-Seltzer?

He was in the kitchen flirting with the Thai caterer's assistant.

Why hadn't she also remembered to ask him for an aspirin? Why had she let him talk her into coming? Having heard what had happened the night before, he insisted she come. He said it would be good for her. It would get her mind off etcetera. Besides, he really wanted to come himself and it was she who'd been invited in the first place.

Chantal squinted through her sunnies. Sydney had the most appalling excess of sunshine. It was obscene, all this bright light. Why didn't they just filter most of it off into solar heating systems, leaving just a few gentle beams for general use? Why didn't she live in Melbourne? That's right. She remembered now. Too many poets in Melbourne. She pushed the glasses farther up on her nose and wondered if she was passing for mysterious or if she looked as tragic as she felt.

Bernard, a handsome Burmese cat that had scrupulously avoided all previous offers from party-goers keen to pet and pose with him, slunk over to her feet and fixed her with a calculating blue stare. He hoicked his backside up into the air, stretched his front legs, and spread his claws, digging them into the ground. Bernard liked the woman he saw in front of him and, like so many other of his gender, didn't really see the need for formalities before making his move. He crouched and pounced and landed squarely on her lap.

"Puh-leese," Chantal hissed as the cat hooked the claws of one brown paw and then the other into the lace trim on her frock and pulled at it with precise and self-satisfied little gestures. "That's a Richard Tyler original, you bloody feline!" she snapped. "Piss off!" Extricating claws from fabric, she hoisted Bernard by the scruff of his neck, and chucked him off to the side. Shaking her head, she minutely inspected her frock for damage. Bernard, meanwhile, had landed up to his pretty ankles in the moist dark mud of the well-watered and fertilized garden. Mewing with annoyance, he reviewed his options, and pounced again. When Chantal reached for him this time, Bernard swung his head around swiftly to sink his fangs into her hand. Then he bounded off before Chantal had time to retaliate, leaving her to contemplate the smarting red marks on her hand and muddy paw prints on her skirt. Bernard, at a safe distance, turned his back on her and licked his paws clean. Women! He was sticking with birds and mice from now on.

"Chantal!" Chantal looked up to see Philippa loping across the lawn toward her with her vaguely awkward gait, shoulder bag bouncing off her hips, big grin on her face. "I didn't expect to see you here!"

Chantal managed a wan smile. "Hello, darling," she said. "Nor I, you."

Philippa sat down. They brushed lips over cheeks.

"So how do you know this lot of vile bodies?" Philippa asked.

"They are pretty appalling, aren't they?" Chantal grimaced, glancing around. "Work," she answered. "And you?"

"Oh, Myrna was going to my writing workshop for a while. We hit it off and used to go out for coffee afterward. Later she said that words weren't 'plastic' enough for her and dropped out. But we've kept in touch." She looked up. "Say, isn't that Alexi?"

"Oh, thank God! He's got my, uh, drink."

"G'day, Alexi," Philippa greeted him cheerfully.

"Hi there, gorgeous," replied Alexi, handing Chantal a champagne glass and air-kissing Philippa.

"Champers. I might go get some of that too," said Philippa. "Be right back."

Alone with Alexi, Chantal pouted. "Where have you been?" she whined, gulping down the bubbly liquid. She put a hand over her mouth to screen the burp that welled up as the frothy antacid did its work.

"Nice," Alexi commented. "Very ladylike."

"Shut up, Alvin," she replied with a smirk, feeling better already.

"Shhh!" He looked around quickly. No one had heard. He frowned and pouted. "Never, never call me that in public, darling! You know how sensitive I am!" Chantal was one of only three or four people in the entire universe, including his parents, who knew Alexi's real name. "I shouldn't really tell you, I suppose," he sniffed, "that I also thought to get you aspirin. I should just let you suffer." He waved his closed hand in front of her. Chantal grabbed the fist, unclenched it, and holding his hand up to her face, licked the pill off his palm. A waiter passed by with champagne, and she held out her empty glass. A touch of Moët, and the aspirin was on its way. She was regaining form.

Philippa returned with a flute of champagne and a plate of canapés, which she held out to Chantal and Alexi. "You'll never guess, Chantie, who Helen thought she saw on Victoria Street the other day," she said, watching Chantal carefully for her reaction. "A real blast from the past. Bram. Back in town."

Chantal suddenly didn't feel so good again. She replaced the wedge of baked brie she'd taken from the plate, untouched. "I know," she moaned.

"Really?" Philippa asked, surprised. "Have you seen him then?"

"I've already heard this story." Alexi rolled his eyes sympathetically. "It's too, too tragic. I'll leave you fabulous creatures to it." He had wanted to head back to the kitchen and his meaningful eye-alogue with the caterer's assistant at the earliest opportunity anyway.

"When did you have that thing with Bram?" Philippa mused. "Seems like a lifetime ago."

Chantal expelled a little puff of air. "Ten, eleven years ago? We were third-year students at uni. I was in my black hair phase."

"Black everything. You had the most incredible collection of lace and velvet frocks. You took on the whole gothic look."

"I know. I always was such a fashion victim."

Philippa laughed. "You even changed your name, remember?"

"Ooooh, darling," Chantal mewled. "Don't remind me. 'Natasha.' Talk about walking clichés." She sculled the champagne and held out her glass to a passing waiter. "Yes, please."

"So, tell me already. When did you see him? What happened?" Philippa prodded.

Putting her glass down on the bench beside her, Chantal took her forehead in both hands and shook it, as if to dislodge the memory. "I don't know if I can bear talking about it, actually."

"Surely, he doesn't mean anything to you now, does he?" Philippa persisted, incredulous. "He was only a punk poet with an interesting haircut."

Funny, that, Chantal thought to herself. She actually mistook him for a god at the time. Twelve years older than Chantal, Bram had the kind of tough, wry character etched into his face that the apple-cheeked boys her age tried to affect but could never achieve. He encased his small, thin body in tight black jeans and tattered T-shirts, and cut his thick black hair himself, chopping it back till it stuck out in short uneven spikes from his handsome, angular face. She'd been dead impressed by the fact that not only had he been to London, but he'd hung out at the Batcave, home of the original goths.

"Of course," Chantal said, "I was a bit of a punk too."

Philippa shook her head, observing her fondly. "Chantal, correct me if I'm wrong, but your razor blade earrings were boutique-purchased trompe l'oeil."

Chantal shrugged.

"Do you remember"—Philippa giggled—"how we used to read *Les Fleurs du Mal* to each other in the Newtown cemetery? Along with our own adolescent jottings? Isn't that a hoot? We were such romantics."

"That we were," agreed Chantal, tapping a cigarette out of her pack. A memory welled up of the first time she went to hear Bram read. It was at the university. She'd gone early to get a seat up front. When it was over, she felt like she wanted to say something to him, though she wasn't sure what. Silly young thing that she was, however, she found herself intimidated by the cluster of beautiful young women and pale, thin boys who thronged around him. She stood a few paces away as he talked to a blond girl who seemed to Chantal to have reached some plane of desirability that didn't even exist in her personal geometry. At one point he looked over at her and the intensity of his gaze caused her to turn and walk away as fast as she could without actually running.

"You know," said Philippa, "you were always very mysterious about what happened between you and Bram."

"Oh, darling," said Chantal, lighting a cigarette, "it was all a bit sordid, really."

Philippa interrogated Chantal with her eyes. It was hard to read her expression behind the Ray•Bans. Chantal wasn't giving anything away. Philippa motioned to a passing waiter to refill their glasses.

Chantal had gone to all of Bram's readings after that. One evening, as she was heading out the door, she felt a hand on her arm. For some reason, she knew it was him. Turning, she blurted out, "You're my idol," and then blushed to the ears. He smiled.

To cover her embarrassment, she asked about the tattoo on his arm. He explained that it was an alchemic symbol. He asked her if she believed that common metals could be transformed into gold. He didn't pay much attention to her answer. "Come on," he said, taking her hand. It didn't occur to her to ask where they were going.

"So," Philippa broke into Chantal's reverie, "what happened last night? Any reigniting of old flames?"

Chantal rolled her eyes. "More like the final scattering of the ashes." Though she was making light of the whole affair, the memory made her feel momentarily queasy. She put down her refilled glass on the bench beside her, but picked it up again quickly as Bernard pounced, landing precisely where the glass had been.

"What a beautiful cat," Philippa marveled.

Chantal cocked one stylized eyebrow and treated the creature to a look of high disdain. "I suppose. If you like cats."

Before Chantal could react, Bernard jumped onto her lap and picked his way across it to Philippa's, stopping briefly as his front paws reached Philippa's jeans to lift and stretch each back paw in turn, waving them offensively close to Chantal's face and exposing his little asshole to her view. Then he curled happily onto Philippa's lap and began purring loudly. Philippa made clucky noises and tickled Bernard behind his wispy ears. He closed his eyes and arched his neck. You'd almost swear he was smiling.

Some men are like that, reflected Chantal. Complete bastards to you and perfect pets to the next woman. Why did she always seem to catch them on the first half of the cycle?

She recalled that first night with Bram as though it were yesterday. When they'd reached the fringes of Darlinghurst, he had led her without speaking into a side street crammed with ramshackle terraces and then down the narrow steps of one to a cramped basement flat. The lounge had a makeshift kitchen in one corner, a sofa with several springs poking through the upholstery, and messy stacks of books and vinyl records. The other room featured a bed, snail trails of dirty laundry on the floor, and a low table on which sat a makeshift bong and an ashtray overflowing with cigarette butts. The only other furniture was a wooden folding chair. The whole place stank of stale smoke, mold, and sweat. Bram opened the ancient fridge and ferreted in it for two bottles of beer. Opening them with a practiced gesture on the edge of the counter, he handed one to her and ambled without further comment into the bedroom. She noticed he left the bottle caps where they lay on the floor.

"Well?" Philippa scratched Bernard's tummy. The purring rose to a crescendo. "Aren't you going to tell me anything?"

Chantal narrowed her eyes and sighed. "I'm not sure, darling. What do you want to know?"

"All about last night, of course. But I'm also curious about how you and Bram got together in the first place. You've always been most secretive about that."

"Oh, darling, it hardly bears thinking about. He dragged me home to his wretched little hovel after a reading of his that I'd attended. I remember my first reaction was, like, could I live like this? And my second was, Jesus, I haven't even slept with him and I'm already fretting about the housekeeping. Next up I'd be worrying about whether this is really the best place to raise our family. I do so hate it when I discover I'm conforming to stereotype."

Philippa laughed. "Don't we all."

"Mmmm."

Philippa waited patiently for Chantal to continue. But behind her Ray•Bans, Chantal had closed her eyes and was back in memory land.

She'd followed Bram as far as the doorway. He sat down on the bed, cross-legged, and rolled a joint. What am I doing here, she wondered. Is this really what I want? To be seduced without ceremony, or romance, or even the pretense of either? She was nervous, and excited, and a little peeved as well, more with herself than him. Peering at him over her beer, she lingered indecisively, leaning on the door frame.

He took a puff and held it out to her. "Come here, little girl," he said, patting the bed next to him.

"Natasha," she said, her voice coming out in a whisper. She felt humiliated. He hadn't even asked her name. "My name's Natasha. And I'm not that little."

She looked down at her feet. Her face felt flushed.

"Come here, Natasha."

Still she didn't budge. He shrugged and took another puff.

In her fantasies he'd tried a bit harder to win her. In her fantasies, he had pretended to be interested in her own poetry. In her fantasies, he had at least asked her name before he asked her home.

As Philippa studied her friend, an awful thought occurred to her. "You weren't," she said, breaking into Chantal's thoughts, "you know, a virgin or anything, were you?"

"Sorry?" Chantal looked momentarily lost. "Oh, God no. No, no. I'd had several boys by then. Boys our age."

"Oh, of course. I remember now. There was one who used to trail you around like a pageboy to a princess. As a matter of fact, if I remember correctly, they were all a bit like that. Besotted."

"I think," said Chantal, drawing on her fag, "I liked Bram because he was different. He seemed, I don't know, stronger, less malleable, and more defined."

Philippa sucked a few globules of caviar off the top of a cracker and waited for Chantal to continue. "So, did he seduce you or what?"

Chantal considered the question. "I suppose you could say that I seduced him."

Bernard rolled onto his back. Philippa blew on his tummy. His head hung off her lap and almost touched Chantal's silver satin-covered thigh. His eyes closed, and a thin train of saliva dribbled down onto the shiny fabric. Absorbed in her memories once more, Chantal didn't even notice. All she ever needed to do, she was thinking, was turn around and walk out. Bram was still beckoning to her. She shook her head. She nearly did walk out then.

The reason she didn't was because she decided that she would neither give in nor give up. No. She would have him, but on her terms, not his. She drew herself up to her full height. (She'd been stooping slightly so he wouldn't seem shorter than her, which he was.) She looked him straight in the eye. A smile played across his features, but she greeted it with a cold sneer.

"Take your shirt off," she ordered.

He looked surprised.

"Or should I just go home?"

She could see from his eyes that this new game excited him. He put the joint out in the ashtray, pulled his shirt over his head, and leaned back on his elbows. "What next, Natasha-girl?" he asked.

"Trousers. Boots. Socks."

He did as he was told.

"Good boy," she said.

Chantal had noticed candles stuck to saucers or jutting out of candlesticks around the room. She put down her beer, fished her lighter from her purse, and walked around the room, touching the flame to the wicks and watching them sizzle to life. He watched her, trying to appear cool —though it's hard to look cool when you're just wearing little red briefs. She could see he was getting a hard on.

He'd switched on a lamp that rested on a shelf above the bed when he'd come in. She knelt on the bed to turn it off. When she did that, he wrapped his bony fingers around her leg just above the knee. She stared down at his hand. "Off," she said. He relaxed his grip and looked at her with a curious expression on his face.

Men. Treat 'em mean and keep 'em keen. How true it is. Chantal sat down in the chair and crossed her legs. "Take off your jocks."

He took off his jocks.

"Good boy," she repeated. She liked the patronizing sound of it.

He was horny as a toad. Chantal laughed. This seemed to make him even harder.

"Play with yourself," she told him. Her heart was pounding. She was on unmapped territory here. She'd never actually seen a man spank the monkey before. She found herself hypnotized by the rhythm of his hand and the incense of the scented candles. She uncrossed her legs.

Still pulling away, his eyes bulging, he watched riveted as Chantal slowly pulled off her own shirt and then wriggled out of her long skirt, which she let fall to the floor. She then unlaced and toed off her Docs and pulled off her socks. Black socks, of course. She still had on her favorite slip, a black satin number she'd got in an op shop. It had a rip at the hem. Leaving the slip on, she reached up for her panties and snaked out of them as well.

She sat and watched him for a while like that.

Spreading her legs a bit more, she inched her slip up until she was just exposed to him. She was very wet. She inserted her fingers into herself and then pulled them out and sucked them.

"Natasha, please . . ." he moaned.

She ignored him. Taking her time, she stroked herself to orgasm. She felt powerful and attractive and sluttish, a truly wonderful combination. She threw her head back as she came and closed her eyes. She didn't hear him get up but she felt warm lips on her neck and another hand stroking her cunt. Bram was kneeling in front of her, caressing her and kissing her face and eyes and hair.

They stumbled over to the bed and fell on each other with such an intense passion that they were both amazed. He bit her nipples hard, and then she went for his and punished them with her teeth and her nails. She rolled him onto his back. She liked the way she could make him gasp by teasing the head of his dick with the lips of her cunt and then, in one long smooth motion swallowing it whole, squeezing it tight. After a while, she eased herself down onto his chest and they rolled onto their sides, still locked together and humping away, now penetrating each other with their tongues as well. By now they were sliding on mingled sweat, and she couldn't tell the beating of his heart from her own. He moved her body like his poems moved her head. Suddenly, he grabbed her buttocks hard and, with a stuttering moan, came inside her. The sensation of his hot jetting sperm caused her to crest again. As they lay there panting, wrapped in each other's arms, Chantal knew she had just had the best sex of her life. Being a woman of insufficient experience, she naturally confused it with love.

When they reluctantly untangled their limbs for a smoke, he stroked her hair with his hands and kissed her forehead. "Well, well, little Natasha," he chuckled.

They saw each other often after that. The sex was hotter than Parramatta in January. Bram initiated her into vampiric rituals where they'd suck each other's blood and even talked her into shooting up with him a few times, the asshole. God. Chantal remembered when AIDS awareness took hold. She had a sickening vision of herself as one of those human tenpins on the telly. She became the first one of their little group to have an HIV test. Miraculously, it was negative. He called her Little Natasha and declared her his muse. He never did ask to see her poetry.

Because Chantal was in love, she never protested at the fact that he never wanted to stay at her place. Nor did she complain (much) that he had no interest in meeting her friends. Or, for that matter, introducing her to his—except when they ran into them by chance, and then only if one of them asked her name. He didn't ever care if she had an exam or a paper due; they met and mated according to his needs and schedule. But the sex was phenomenal, and she worshiped his genius. She could never admit to anyone how humiliating it was at times.

The worst, of course, was that night she thought they'd had an appointment and went over to his place only to find some blond girl in his bed. With him. He hadn't even tried to conceal what was going on or apologize. Worse, he'd laughed. Not a good look from where she stood. Nor did he run after her when she turned and fled. Later, he told her he needed his space and his freedom and if she "couldn't deal with that" then she should just "find a nice bourgie boy and move to the 'burbs to drop bubs." Later, one of his mates told her that Bram had said to him that he was in danger of really falling for her and had to end it before it became too serious. His mate thought this was a perfectly logical position. Then again, he was male too.

"Hello hello? Earth to Gorgeous. Earth to Gorgeous." Alexi had returned to find Chantal sitting perfectly still with her head thrown back and her eyes closed behind her sunnies. Next to her perched Philippa, Bernard sound asleep in her lap. Philippa, having given up on the conversation, had finished the whole plate of hors d'oeuvres. Mellow with food and champagne, she was absentmindedly stroking Bernard and watching the other guests flit about the garden.

At the sound of Alexi's voice, Chantal's eyes flew open. She blinked. "Oh, dear," she said. "Have I been off with the fairies?"

"No, darling, I have. And I've got a date with a particularly delicious one who's waiting by the front door. I've just come to say too-roo, sweetie."

"Have a good one, darling." Chantal smiled.

"Exactly what I'm planning to do." Alexi puckered and air-kissed both girls good-bye. They watched his lithe form weave through the garden.

"He's a scream," Philippa observed, smiling. "And so are you, Chantie. I don't think I've ever seen you flake out so badly before."

"Oh, darling," Chantal said. "I really am not myself today. Have I been gone long?"

"Nearly filed a missing person's report," Philippa replied. "But no worries. I've been having a good time people watching. You know me. I get a bit shy at these things if I actually have to mingle." She suddenly looked down at the furball in her lap. "Oh, yuk!" she exclaimed.

"What?"

"It just farted," Philippa said, curling her lip and forcefully evicting Bernard from her lap. He landed on his feet, shook himself, and meandered off to see if he could score some of the smoked salmon off the buffet table. He'd had enough of her anyway.

"Where were we?" Chantal frowned and lit a cigarette.

"You said you saw Bram last night," Philippa said.

"Oh, God. I ran into him at a party over at my new neighbors' flat. It was a jungle party. You know the sort of thing. African music, ambient jungle mist from a dry ice machine, drinks in coconuts. Everyone in leopard-skin prints and cat masks."

"What were you wearing?"

"My new zebra-stripe minidress. Leopard skin is so five-minutes-ago. Unless it's white leopard, of course."

"Of course."

"Anyway, Bram just sort of materialized in front of me. Wearing a pith helmet and a safari suit."

"Oh dear." Philippa's hand flew to her mouth. "Not a safari suit. How totally naff."

"Totally. There are few sights more tragic than that of a poet in a pith helmet. But, you know, I didn't recognize him at first. He's aged pretty badly."

"He must be what, forty-three? Forty-four?"

"Forty-four. His eyes were red and puffy, and his lean frame had filled out in all the wrong places. Wrinkles fretted his skin. He even had that awful line that slices from the middle of the eyes straight down the cheek that long-term smack users all seem to get. Not that I know that many of them. But you see it on aging rock stars a lot. And his skin was even more sallow than I'd remembered it. A steady diet of drugs and alcohol doesn't exactly do wonders for the complexion." Chantal gestured ironically with her champagne glass and cigarette. "Not that I'm exactly drug-free. But at least I use mud packs and have a facial whenever I can afford it. And getting enough sleep is very important too, of course."

Philippa didn't want to hear a beauty lecture. "And then?" she prompted.

"Anyway" —Chantal paused to blow a smoke ring— "before I twigged to the fact it was him, I'd said something like 'Dr. Livingstone, I presume?' and he responded by singing that silly Moody Blues song. He was quite drunk and the words came out all slurred: 'Shtepping outta n jungle gloo . . .' Suddenly, there was this shocking moment of mutual recognition. He stopped singing, and gasped, 'Li'l Nas, Natasha!'

"You know, darling, for years I'd held imaginary conversations with Bram in my head in which, with haughty wit and perfect composure, I'd assassinated his character so thoroughly and so devastatingly that he'd died and come back a new man. But now that he was there in front of me, I felt only pity."

"As you would." Philippa nodded.

"I mean, *I've* progressed. The last torn slip I wore was made that way by Comme des Garçons. And I gave up poetry when I met Alexi, which was soon afterward, and he made some comment about it being on the 'whiffy' end of literature."

"That's a bit unfair," Philippa protested.

Chantal shrugged. "Darling, life is unfair. Anyway, we talked about the old times. He made some mumbling apology about what a shit he'd been. Then he talked me into showing him my flat, which, after all, was just next door. By then I'd had quite a few of those violent coconut cocktails and was feeling a little unsteady on my Patric Coxes. If I felt any foreboding, it was coming from some distant, anaesthetized place. I led him inside. 'One for the road, eh, Little Natasha?' he belched. While I was trying to figure out whether he was referring to alcohol or sex— and I was quite horrified by the thought of either at that point—he just stumbled past me and made a beeline for my bedroom."

"How is it," Philippa wondered, "that some men have an unerring instinct for finding the bedroom unaided?"

"By the time I'd followed him in, he'd fallen crosswise over the bed, feet dangling off one side, head off the other. He was mumbling something. I moved closer, a bit apprehensively, to hear what it was. 'A bucket, Nats, gettush a bucket.'" Chantal lay a slender hand against her forehead.

"He didn't." Philippa gasped.

"He did," Chantal affirmed, rolling her eyes. "I got him a bucket, and I can tell you it was not a moment too soon." Chantal didn't have the heart to regurgitate, so to speak, what had transpired after that, although she certainly remembered it in excruciating detail.

She had raced into the bedroom and placed the bucket under his chin. "*Uh-rroooop,*" he ejaculated. A shudder passed through his body as his dinner and drinks passed through his lips. "*Kakakaka,*" he coughed weakly in epilogue. "*Uh-rrrooooooop!*" She turned away, curling her lip and feeling none too salubrious herself. Teetering into the living room, she poured herself a whiskey and stared glumly out the window.

Chantal was not by nature the nurturing type.

"*Uh-rrrooooop! . . . Kakakaka,*" came the chorus and verse from the next room.

"*I* did try at one point to suggest that he remove himself to the toilet," Chantal remarked weakly.

"Would seem like a more appropriate habitat for his species under the circumstances." Philippa shook her head sympathetically.

"By then he was, however, well and truly passed out, his head pointing down into the bucket, his body immovable on my nice new quilt. I returned dispirited to the living room. Around 6 A.M., I finally managed to doze off on the zebra chair. Given the fact I was still wearing my zebra dress, it gave me the comforting illusion of camouflage. Three hours later, I was woken, stiff-necked and stiff-limbed, with whole jungle tribes beating tomtoms in my head, by my mother, just calling to say hello."

"Mothers have the best sense of timing," Philippa commiserated.

"I told her I'd call her back and straggled back into the bedroom. Bram had by now crawled under the covers and arranged himself longitudinally on the bed, arms and legs thrown across its width, sound asleep. I could have woken him, but didn't feel in any state to deal with the consequences. So I went back to my chair and sunk into a miserable half-sleep. I thought I dreamed that I was a little girl and my father was going off to work and then he turned into Bram, holding his shoes in one hand and his forehead in the other, crossing through the living room and out the door. . . . It was only when I heard the click of the lock as the door closed, that I realized it was no dream. I went into my bedroom. Averting my eyes and holding my nose, I picked up the bucket gingerly and carried it into the toilet, where I flushed away its bilious contents. Pouring in half a bottle of disinfectant, I filled the bucket with water and let it rest. I checked my quilt cover for vomit stains, silently praised his aim, and passed out on the side of the bed least touched by the adventures of the night. Two hours later, Alexi called, horrendously chirrupy of voice, to ask me when he should come by to pick me up for the party. And here I am."

"What a postscript to a relationship."

"You know, I have a lot to thank Bram for," Chantal reflected.

"What do you mean?"

"Taught me not to place such a premium on sex. Sex is easy. Relationships are hard. I haven't exactly been a nun since then but honestly, I have no problems with celibacy."

Philippa laughed. "Sure, Chantie."

Truth was, Chantal, stunning, stylish, intelligent, and sexy—a nineties dream girl with a happy career, a disposable income, and an excellent wardrobe—honestly thought sex was a bit overrated as a pursuit. For one thing, she considered most heterosexual men to be a bit too low on the food chain to be worth the effort. In her experience, it was mainly gay men who would go willingly to subtitled films or the opera or hold genuinely interested conversations about hairstyles. They never forgot your birthday and often brought you flowers for no reason at all. Even the most promising of heterosexual men usually had some terribly off-putting element in their character, like a tendency to play air drums when they listened to music or a fondness for televised sports. Much to her regret, she was not sexually attracted to women.

Philippa yawned. She obviously wasn't going to get much more out of Chantal. And in any case, she wanted to get back to her computer. "How long are you going to stick around?"

"Oh, I think I'll just say good-bye to Finn. I really wouldn't mind crawling back into bed, to tell the truth."

"Let's rock," said Philippa, standing up and brushing cat hair off her jeans.

Meanwhile, in another city, in a café, two women were facing each other with expressions composed of equal parts mirth and guilt. The popular George's in Melbourne's trendy St. Kilda filled up fast on Sundays. Bronwyn and Gloria had been lucky to get a table. On it rested two cups of cappuccino, half-drunk; two pastries, half-eaten; and one letter, fully consumed and digested.

"What are you going to do?" chortled Gloria.

"I don't know. But you know my friend in Sydney? Philippa? The one I told you about, who's writing an erotic novel?"

"I remember you telling me about her."

"I reckon she'd get a real kick out of this letter. I might send it to her."

"That's so naughty."

"Naughty is my middle name."

CHAPTER SEVEN

Multiple Choice

The following Saturday found Philippa sitting at the edge of the Boy Charlton pool at Woolloomooloo swirling her feet in the water. She was wearing a black Speedo one-piece. The way she leaned forward onto her hands maximized the dramatic effect of her cleavage. As she knew. Not, she understood, that any of the beef-cakes lying about soaking up January's rays with their Coppertone-marinated fat-free flesh would have noticed. They had eyes only for each other. Where was Jake? She dabbed some more sunblock on her shoulders and squint-ed, for the umpteenth time, toward the entrance.

At last he came, sauntering toward her with a lazy grin as if to say, hey, what's an hour between friends? "Sorry took so long," he said, shuffling off his jeans and T-shirt. He had his bathers on underneath. He tossed his clothes in a heap, slid his long lean body into the water, immersed himself, stood up, and shook out his dreads. "Had to see someone off at the airport." He held out a hand to her. "Aren't you coming in?"

"What's that on your wrist?" Philippa ignored the ges-ture and slipped in to the pool unaided.

"Stamp," he explained. "Went to a gig the other night. I'm a bit of a stamp collector. Do you like hearing bands, Philippa?" He smiled to himself. Nearly called her Norma.

"Sometimes," she answered. Nice smile, she thought.

"What kind of bands do you like?" he asked. He couldn't remember if he'd told her he was in a band him-self. He hoped she wouldn't say she went to cover bands. Cover bands were for suburbanites in boat shoes and peo-ple who had only got around to piercing their navels this year. Anything else, he could pretty much cope with. Except for country and western. Or REM. Or anything associated with aging rock stars with tragic hair. Still, he was a broad-minded kind of guy. He didn't mind Tom Jones's latest album. And while he'd be really pleased if she liked the Nine Inch Nails, he wouldn't really care if she didn't; girls rarely did.

"Good bands," she replied, and kicked off down the lane. He followed behind at a lackadaisical pace. Jake didn't think too much exercise was good for you. He preferred to conserve his energies for other, more important things. Like eating and sex. A few laps later, he rested at the shallow end.

His elbows propped up on the side, he watched her plow along with strong strokes. He liked the defined muscularity of her arms. She pulled up beside him. "Nice freestyle," he complimented.

"What sort of stroke were you doing? I couldn't quite put a name to it."

"My very own stroke," he replied. "The slacker."

Laughing, she reached out to splash him. He slipped down underneath the water and grabbed her ankles, pulling her off balance. "Trying to sweep me off my feet?" she asked when they both surfaced.

"Being a writer, you should know, Philippa, that the pun is the lowest form of humor."

"How do you know I'm a writer?"

"You told me. At that party where we met."

"Oh. I didn't think you were listening, actually." Philippa kicked off and did another two laps.

"So," he addressed her when she came to a halt by his side. "Where are you taking me for dinner?"

Who said I was taking you out for dinner? Philippa thought to herself. "Where do you want to go?" she asked.

He thought, to as nice a place as you can afford. I may look like a slob, but I've got a cultivated palate. He said, "Wherever. Some place not too expensive. I'm easy."

"Do you have a car?"

"Just."

"What do you mean, just?"

"It's about to be repossessed," he explained. "But I don't think they'll come for it tonight. Besides, I neglected to inform the bank where I'd be today."

Philippa thought a moment. She had almost forgotten about Nielsen Park until Helen mentioned it that day they met in the post office. She suggested they have a bite and then go there for a walk.

"A walk? That's something old people do. My parents go for walks. How old are you, anyway, Philippa?"

Philippa raised one eyebrow. "Would you prefer," she countered, deadpan, "that we take our skateboards? How old are *you*, Jake?"

"Is it, like, a cool place, this Nielsen Park?" The best defense, he often reflected, was to change the subject.

"In what sense, exactly, do you mean 'cool'? Being by the water, there's a bit of a breeze, if that's what you mean. But I don't think we're likely to run into Tex Perkins. On the other hand, Hugo Weaving has occasionally been spotted there."

"That guy who was in *Priscilla*?"

"That's the one."

"That's okay then."

They hung out at the pool for a while longer, showered, and dressed. At a Moroccan restaurant in Darlinghurst, Philippa watched Jake clean the plate of mezze with a wedge of Turkish bread and silently marveled at how much food such a thin boy could put away. When the bill came, he excused himself to go to the toilet. Upon his return, he thanked her for paying and put his hand over hers across the table. He's cheeky all right, Philippa thought to herself. Aloud, she said, "My pleasure." She withdrew her hand and suggested they head off to the park. Wandering out across the beach, they found a secluded spot on the rocks that offered an enchanting view of the setting sun and of the city, glowing in the late dusk across the water. Philippa sat down and hugged her knees. Jake lay down, at an almost perpendicular angle to her, ankles crossed, head just touching Philippa's thigh.

"Have you got a boyfriend, Philippa?" he asked after a silence.

"Not really," she answered. Girls didn't count as boyfriends, did they? "Are you seeing anyone?"

"Oh, not really," he dissembled. "Well, I was sort of seeing this other girl. But she's gone away now, and anyway, it was pretty casual." He arched his neck to look at her and gauge her reaction. Philippa was a cool number, compared to the last one, not quite as easy to read, especially upside down. "She was older too. I rather like older women." He returned to his original position and stared intently at the sky.

"Why is that, Jake?"

"Dunno. Guess I can relate better," he told the moon. "I like a woman who's got her shit together."

Not to mention her finances, Philippa thought. "Do you think all older women have their shit together?" she asked.

This was getting difficult. Jake rolled over, hauled himself up to a sitting position, and looked her in the eyes as soulfully as he could manage on such a full stomach.

"No. But I think you do."

Philippa regarded Jake through narrowed eyes. A smile briefly tugged at the corners of her mouth. "Oh really? And what makes you think that?"

Her gray eyes had a steely gaze that he found a little disconcerting. He grew intrigued. Jake was fairly lazy in his habits. It hadn't actually occurred to him before this point to be intrigued by Philippa; the only real thought he'd given to the matter was that she was likely to feed and possibly fuck him as well. Julia had been good fun, but he had never been particularly *intrigued* by her. Besides, with Julia he had begun to smell the unmistakable, yeasty aroma of a relationship rising and ready to be popped into the oven. Not to put too fine a point on it, but he wasn't really into relationships. He was what you might call commitment-challenged. "Cause," he said.

A light breeze blew up and rearranged Jake's dreads so that three momentarily gathered in a single column at the top of his head. Philippa snorted with laughter.

"What?"

"Nothing. I think your head's got a stiffy." Philippa swiveled round to look at the sea, concealing her mirth. Jake patted his head. But the dreadlocks had fallen back down again. He hadn't a clue as to what she was talking about.

Most people had left the beach by now. Except for the sound of the waves breaking below them and a phrase or two of conversation drifting over from the path nearest the rock where they perched, a quiet that seemed almost preternatural for the city had descended on the park.

When Philippa turned to face him again, she noted his slightly bewildered look. He was an operator, all right. But there was an appealing vulnerability there as well.

He leaned toward her. Just a little. Testing the waters. The steel in her eyes seemed to have warmed a degree or two. Everything about her was naturally cool, he thought, from the smooth icing of her alabaster skin to the watermelon gelato of her lips. He lowered his eyes to those lips, wanting a taste, and then raised them to meet her unsettling gaze. He moved a little closer. She did not move away, but neither did she draw in toward him. He looked at her lips again and caught the flickering curl of a smile. Would they melt under his? Or just mock him? He looked up at her eyes again; the steel seemed to have given way to a calm winter sea. Should he dive in? A dreadlock bounced down in front of his left eye. He pushed out his jaw and blew up at it. It was a particularly heavy dread, and it rode his breath playfully, like a kite, but refused to return from whence it came. He decided to ignore it. It's hard to ignore a big blurry stripe dissecting your vision in half. Never mind. He returned his concentration to those lips. They seemed to be halfway to a smile. He looked back into her eyes for a clue. She lowered her lids a little. The sea warmed fractionally. He lowered his eyes, he looked down at her lips. He looked at her eyes, he looked at her lips. Eyes, lips, eyes, lips. With each swing of the vertical pendulum, they seemed more inviting. He thought, now or never, stood on his mental diving platform, bent at the knees, took a deep breath, and flung himself into the water, closing his eyes as he went. His lips came gently to rest upon hers.

No reaction. To be precise, there was no positive reaction, but then again, there was no negative one either. He could have been kissing a statue.

A gull squawked and swooped. Sandshoes crunched the gravelly dirt of the path by the rock. "Mum, what are those people doing?" squeaked a young girl's voice. The footsteps sped up and faded away.

Jake felt sillier and sillier. Time passed. Should he do something else, put his hand on her waist or something, or nibble, or just retreat while he was ahead? For some reason, a picture of his amp popped into his head. It was broken and would need to be fixed before the gig in a couple of weeks at the Sando. That could cost a hundred dollars at least. Such a ripoff. Where was he supposed to come up with that kind of money? Certainly not from anyone else in the band. They were even less solvent than he was, if such a sorry state were possible. He should have borrowed it from Julia. Julia. Philippa. He suddenly remembered where he was and what he was doing.

What *was* he doing? He opened his eyes to see if her face could give him some signal. Her eyes were closed. He considered this a good sign.

He was jumping to conclusions. It was not necessarily a good sign, because, in this case, it meant Philippa was thinking. Philippa was not quite as easily impressed as Julia. She had a slower reaction time with boys. Of course, she wasn't comparing her reaction time to Julia's because she had no idea just how relevant the comparison was. And if she had, her reaction time would have been less than zero: she didn't believe in fooling around with her friend's lovers.

What was running through Philippa's mind, racing, in fact, neck and neck, were the following two thoughts: Thought 1: She fancied Jake. He was a total spunkrat, a sexy boy with a dry and wacky sense of humor. She liked his cheeky presumptuousness and found his slacker style—in and out of the water—highly amusing. Thought 2: He was Big Trouble. Her warning system was going off like a smoke detector in hell. Did she really need Big Trouble in her life, she asked herself.

Just as he was contemplating a tactical withdrawal, Jake felt the slightest twitch of her lips against his. He persevered.

Of course, she didn't have to get too involved. He was ten years younger than her. He probably wasn't into the idea of involvement anyway. She could make it just a one-night stand kind of thing. She didn't mind a touch of discreet, casual sex now and then. But hold on, what if it proved a truly excellent one-night stand? Wouldn't she want a second night? And what if they had a second night, and that was good too, and then it ended? Two-night stands were actually far worse than one-night stands. A one-night stand is just that. You wake up in the morning, you look at each other. You go, hmmm. If you're both thinking, so that's what the cat dragged in last night, the visiting team packs up its gear and exits the stadium. The home team takes a shower and gets on with the day. If you're both thinking, *babe,* you have one for the road. They don't call, or you don't, or you do, or they do, and you discuss it, and then you get over it. But two-night stands, those are the really painful ones. To you it's a relationship, to him it's just a coincidence. You've started to tell your friends, he's already on the prowl for someone new.

Oh dear. Philippa suddenly realized that Jake was holding his breath.

He was beginning to feel faint. Philippa pursed her lips against his. He exhaled through his nose, as calmly as he could, and she felt the tremulous breath tickle the corner of her lip. Trying to breathe normally, he pursed back.

Then there was this younger man–older woman thing. Philippa wasn't too sure about this. Julia was all for it, and swore by the virtues of younger men. Their playfulness, their sweetness, all the free time they had to spend clipping their toenails on your bed and installing games on your PC, their sense of adventure, their reliable erections. You didn't have to spend half your time putting bandages on festering old wounds caused by some other woman, or pretending to sympathize with the jaded, cynical outlook on life of an older man. You could be successful in your career without being perceived as a threat, or competition, Julia had also argued, because the younger man would expect you to be farther down the career path than he was anyway.

Philippa could certainly see the virtues of younger women. But when she went for men, she usually liked them a bit older, a bit kinkier, and a bit more experienced. Still, there was something about Jake, something deeply naughty, which strongly attracted her. It would be foolish to make decisions on some vague principle. She didn't like making rules for herself. When she discovered she'd made some sort of rule, she usually tried to break it.

When Philippa opened her lips slightly to nibble at his, a tremor reading at about 5.6 on the Richter scale erupted in the region of his solar plexus and rippled out through his torso and down his limbs, including the crucial fifth one. Trembling, Jake sighed into her mouth and eagerly nibbled back.

Then again, precisely because she was so attracted to Jake, if it did turn out just to be a one-night stand she'd probably get really depressed. Maybe it wasn't such a good idea after all. She willed her lips to stillness while she reviewed all the options. Why were people in such a rush these days anyway? I mean, how does it happen that if you make a move to see someone you met once before that the question of sex comes up before you're even through the first date? Then again, not only had she asked him out, she'd suggested they come to this park. Everyone knew that couples came to Nielsen Park for one reason: to pash. And she would tell people that she was writing an erotic novel, wouldn't she? She shouldn't be such a hypocrite.

Jake felt pins and needles creeping up his left leg, which was folded under him, and in his right hand, which he was leaning on. He was sure there was a mosquito feeding on his left arm. But he didn't dare make a move to slap it. She still hadn't responded to that last nibble and this worried him. Maybe he was moving too fast. Maybe she wasn't the sort of girl who jumped into bed on the first date. Maybe she'd need a trifle more work, a tad more time. That was cool. He didn't really mind. He was having fun. It was a bit misleading, though, all that stuff about being a writer of erotic fiction. I mean, why would she tell him that straight off if she weren't hinting at something? The thought briefly crossed Jake's mind that he might just be, well, *research*. Something about that actually quite appealed to him. On the other hand, he wondered what her writing was like. He didn't think much of the erotic fiction he'd come across. It was either, oh, wet and over-written or off-puttingly cold and brutal.

Jake momentarily relinquished his position upon her lips. He nuzzled her cheeks with his own and nuddled her chin and rolled his head around on her neck. At the same time he managed to shift that annoying dreadlock from in front of his face. She appeared to like this change in tack; she seemed to be nuzzling and nuddling back.

Or maybe, the thought niggled him, she was just using the opportunity to stretch her neck which, like his, had grown stiff with tension and suspense. He was beginning to wonder if he'd made a mistake. Perhaps she wasn't just equivocating. Maybe she was just passive. He couldn't stand passive women. Jake prided himself in being a sensitive, feminist-reared New Man of the Nineties. He liked a woman who took an active interest in the goings-on.

His dreadlocks felt furry on her skin. She found dreads fascinating. She'd read somewhere that people lose about six thousand hairs a year. Unlike other hairstyles, where the dead, shed hairs ended up clinging to clothing or floating in soup or embedded in computer keyboards or between the teeth of combs or in big wads down the drainpipes, with dreads virtually every hair stayed with you, matted for life.

She liked the concept. It was a bit like having perfect memory, no experience ever slipping away, each strand of the past preserved and densely interwoven with the present. She felt that sexuality was like that. Every sexual act adhered to your sensual consciousness forever. Every time you went to bed with someone, you brought along everyone else you'd ever slept with. Every touch expressed an entire history of caresses.

Practically speaking, however, she had a few doubts. According to her hairdresser, some people with dreadlocks didn't think they were supposed to wash their hair ever again. Several times, when her hairdresser had been asked to cut off dreadlocks, she'd been overwhelmed, almost to the point of fainting, by the pongy perfume of scuzzy scalps. Philippa wondered if Jake washed his hair. She sniffed. His dreads smelt rather nice, actually. And so did he. Sun-toasted flesh with a faint bouquet of young male sweat.

Philippa wondered suddenly why she had been feeling so *reactive* in all this, so passive. Without further ado she brushed her mouth across his face, tasted his cheeks, with their soft down, licked the tip of his nose, rubbed her lips across the clear line of his eyebrows, and sucked gently on his eyelashes. The stilettos in chapter five! Why hadn't it occurred to her before? They wouldn't click on rugs. She'd have to get rid of the throw rugs in that Victorian inn. She made a mental note to do this as soon as she got home, and then, with a great effort of will, she loosened her grasp on philosophical and authorial and other dilemmas and reached out to draw Jake closer. Closer was exactly where Jake wanted to be. The unexpectedly sudden flowering of her desire allowed him to relax and float on the honeyed vibrations that her tongue and lips were setting off all over his face. She buried her face in his hair, tentatively at first, and then boldly, and then focused in on his ear, probing its recesses with her wet tongue, chewing on the octopus flesh of his lobe. From his ear she worked her way slowly down his neck with big soft bites to his Adam's apple.

By the time she worked her way back to his mouth, his lips were parted and waiting for her. By now, there was no danger of rational thought interceding on either side. They drew hungrily on each other's mouths. Philippa felt sensation streaming down the tingling pathway to her sex, which was growing wet, and Jake's erection strained uncomfortably against his jeans. They were inside each other's shirts now, and then pants, and the darkness—it was not a particularly moonlit night—was their cover as they tumbled over the hard rock. They fucked with clothes half off, half on—a sleeve here, a sock there—and it was a wild, animal, bruising romp that took no account of the hard, uneven rock or the possibility of passers-by or anything else except their united, raw desire. Afterward, they lay panting and spent in each other's arms, Philippa stretched out on top of Jake.

Jake reached out for a pair of trousers to fold under his head, and shifted slightly to find a more comfortable place for his hip, which felt as though it were being stabbed. They heard a brief skidding sound and the soft but distinct plop of a medium-size object falling into the sea below.

"What was that?" Philippa wove her fingers possessively into Jake's dreads as she spoke. She really did not want this to be a one-night stand.

"Dunno," answered Jake, who was now concentrating on ignoring a pebble lodged under his shoulder blade. "I think I kicked a rock or something."

"Didn't really sound like a rock," Philippa observed.

"No, it didn't," Jake conceded.

Shortly afterward, they straggled along the darkened path, holding hands. Jake was barefoot. In his free hand he clutched one of his boots.

Far below them his other boot settled on the seabed.

The next morning, Philippa woke up first. She found herself wedged into one corner of the bed by Jake's sprawling limbs. His hair had taken over the pillows. She tried to recover some territory with gentle nudging but couldn't budge him. Funny how heavy such a thin person could be. Giving up on the thought of going back to sleep, she rolled out of bed, threw on a singlet and jeans, and went to the corner shop to get some milk, fresh croissants, and big purple grapes. Back at her place, she undressed again and slipped into a sarong. She parked herself in the living room, which also served as her study, eating grapes and skimming the weekend papers while waiting for Jake to wake up.

When he finally arose, he scratched his head, stretched, and wondered briefly where he was. He looked up at the stack of books by the bed. Oh that's right. Philippa. The writer. He yawned, threw on a towel, and headed into the toilet to have a piss. Then he padded out to find her, by which time Philippa, alerted by the sounds from the bathroom, had arranged herself as alluringly as possible on the sofa. He smiled at the sight. Choosing a Gadflys CD from her collection (Jake approved of her musical tastes after all), he put it on the stereo.

"Now we're heading for the stars and shooting for the sun; it's time to rise and shine," crooned the Gadflys. Perfect morning-after music. Jake cuddled up next to Philippa. He popped a grape into his mouth, leaned over and, positioning his lips just over hers, bit into it and let the sweet juices run from his mouth onto hers, licking the spill off her chin. *"Put on a smile for me and say you are my friend."*

"You my friend, Jake?"

"What do you think?"

She took a grape now, and chewed it to a pulp before kissing him with an open mouth, pushing the pulp and juice from her tongue onto his. They consumed nearly a whole stem of grapes like that. Then Philippa, feeling naughty, took four grapes and, one by one, inserted them into herself. She opened her legs. "Like diving for pearls?" she smiled, lying back against the cushions.

Jake was a very skillful diver. Still chewing on the grapes, he sat back up and reached for one of Philippa's feet. He pulled them up toward his face. Taking the foot into his mouth, he sucked moistly on each toe, licking the spaces in between them with a wet and squishy tongue. Philippa gasped and squealed with the pure sensual pleasure of it.

Jake smiled and licked his lips. "Bit like walking through mud, isn't it?" he said, tucking that foot back down onto the sofa and reaching for the other.

"There's something about you, wherever you go, I call your name out low." Nearly helpless with bliss, Philippa reached out and pulled off Jake's towel. They tumbled off the sofa and onto the rug. As they went, Philippa just managed to snaffle the condom she'd hidden in the bowl of grapes. Pulling her clean-licked feet over his shoulders, he entered her with slow, lazy thrusts timed to the rhythm of the song. *"And there's nothing I can say. You've got to take a chance on me and see what it gets you, and see what it gets you."*

See what it gets you. Philippa's warning system was down. The night before she might have perceived irony in those lyrics. At this moment, however, undulating underneath this charismatic semistranger, love songs in the air, hormones on the brain, she suffered a severe, if temporary, irony deficiency.

Afterward, as they lay cuddling on the rug, Philippa looked up past Jake. Was that a man's face in the window of the building opposite? That's odd, she thought, that flat's been vacant for ages. How long had he been there? What had he seen? She was just maneuvering for a better look when Jake kissed her again. By the time she looked again, the man, if he'd been there at all, was gone.

"What are you looking at?" asked Jake.

"Nothing."

He shrugged. "Can I've a shower?"

"Sure," she replied, following him into the bathroom.

Afterward, they made coffee. Seated side by side on the sofa, they dipped warm croissants in each other's coffee. After consuming two regular and one almond croissant, Jake patted his stomach and put his arm around her shoulders.

"It just occurred to me, Jake," Philippa said, with a touch of trepidation. "When you said you were seeing someone off at the airport yesterday, was that the woman you'd been seeing?"

"Uh, sort of."

"Sort of?"

"Yeah."

"Where'd she go?"

"China."

"Really? She might have been on a flight with a good friend of mine, Julia, a photographer. What a funny coincidence. You might have even seen her in the queue—she's short, thin, dark with long black hair, and usually wears interesting, retro clothing."

Jake choked on his coffee. He coughed rather violently, and Philippa, concerned, patted his back. He had to think fast on this one. "Doesn't strike a bell," he shrugged, thinking, *clang clang clang*. Oh well. He'd have three weeks with Philippa and then he'd say good-bye. Three weeks was plenty, really. Practically a lifetime.

Or maybe this is how it happened:

"Where'd she go?" Philippa asked.

"China."

"Really? What's she doing there?"

"She's a photographer. She's going on some sort of cultural exchange."

"Oh really?" Philippa said, covering up her emotions. "What's her name?"

"Julia. I actually met her at the same party where I met you."

Philippa needed time to digest this.

"Uh, Jake, I don't mean to be rude or anything, but I'm going to have to get to work soon."

"But it's Sunday."

"I know. That's my day for working on my novel."

Perhaps, she thought, it simply went like this:

"Where'd she go?" Philippa asked.

"O.S."

"Is that a place?"

"Yeah," said Jake, stretching himself out and into Philippa's lap. "It's a place." He started to pull up her sarong over her legs, exposing her thighs, which he kissed. He meandered upward. "But I like this place better."

CHAPTER EIGHT

Peking Duck

What a mad, mad place. I wonder if I'll ever be back, if I'll ever see Mister In Your Dreams again, if his snakes made it through the day, if my interpreter will ever recover, if I paid too much for that opera costume, if my films will come out all right, if I'll ever be able to pay off my Visa, if Jake will be waiting at the airport and, if so, what I'll say to him. Mengzhong, "In Your Dreams," what a name. Mengzhong, Mengzhong. I'm sure I never pronounced it correctly. But then, he didn't do so well with *Julia*. Never mind.

I'm sure I should have bought that rug. Sure, it'd have cost a fortune to ship, but where are you going to find one like it in Sydney? I wonder if I'll have to declare my tea? Australian customs are so strict. I can't believe I did what I did with Mengzhong. I can't believe it was just this morning. Seems like another universe. God, I'm wired. Hope the neighbors remembered to water my plants. I wonder if there's any interesting mail waiting for me.

Yes, it was my first trip to China. And you? I know I should have closed my eyes. I hope this guy in the next seat isn't going to talk to me the whole way back to Oz. I'll die. I wish they had a special section on planes for "people who are not in the mood to share feelings or exchange experiences or communicate in any other fashion to the person next to them." Unless, of course, their seat companion happens to be a killer spunk, in which case you could just move straight to the mile-high club lounge. Unfortunately, Mr. 38A is not a killer spunk; in fact, I don't think he'd count as even a mildly threatening spunk. Of course, that's so unfair. Shouldn't judge books by their covers, and I suppose I should consider myself lucky that he's waited this long to start talking. It probably helped that I just stuck my nose in *The Wild Girls Club* all the way from Beijing to the stopover in Guangzhou.

Oh really? You do business there? How interesting. Stop it Julia. Don't encourage him. *Yeah, no, actually, I'm a photographer. On a three-week exchange sponsored by the Australia-China Council.* Why are you telling him all this? It's just going to incite more conversation. *Both black and white and color. . . . Yes. . . . For magazines, mostly.* Here we go. Maybe we can just switch on to automatic pilot. Maybe I should pull out *The Wild Girls Club* again. No. I'll never be able to concentrate.

Uh, Julia. Nice to meet you, Mick.

God, aren't the girls going to die when they hear that Mengzhong was a snake-charmer and sword-swallower, *and* a contortionist. He had the most amazing stories about sneaking across the border to North Korea and being in jail. Jesus, that's what you call turbulence! Hate that! It's so scary! *No, I'm right, thanks, Nick. It's only a little turbulence. . . . Oh, sorry. Mick. I'm so bad with names.*

The interpreter, Mr. Fu, didn't seem highly amused. Still, didn't that woman at the embassy say that in China nothing was as it seemed? I mean, judging from the general picture she painted, Mr. Fu might have been offended politically, or he might just have wanted to be paid off to piss off, or maybe—and I'm no bad judge of body language, especially when it comes to these things—he was just jealous. Wouldn't that have been bizarre!

Tomato juice, no ice, thanks. . . . Oh, I said no ice actually, but never mind. . . . Oh really? Minerals exploration and development? That's interesting. Not. Why do I always use the word interesting when I mean exactly the opposite? I shouldn't be unfair. I'm sure it's fascinating, if you're into that kind of thing. It's just that I'm not. That's all. I wonder where he stands on Aboriginal land rights. Oh, God,

Julia, don't bring that up. He'll either say the wrong thing and you'll be arguing with him all the way home or he'll turn out to be okay and you'll be so relieved that you'll feel obligated to talk to him. Mengzhong. Mengzhong. It's a bit like the peal of a bell, really. I wonder if I am pronouncing it right?

That rug, I really am beginning to regret not getting it. Damn. Never mind, I'm sure I'll be back someday. Thirty-six kilos of luggage is probably outrageous enough for one trip, especially when I went with only fifteen. Bizarre how they didn't even blink at the overweight luggage at Beijing airport, but then, half the people on this flight seemed to be taking forty or fifty kilos, no worries at all. I don't really want to dwell on the safety implications of that. *Yeah, I had a great time. . . . Yeah, it's a fascinating country. . . . Just Beijing and Shanghai. . . . Sure, the women are beautiful.* Pig. Western men in Asia think they're God's gift. I think he's about to treat me to some tale of conquest. Better nip this one in the bud. *The men are pretty dishy as well, of course.* Ha! That surprised him. *Yes, I do find them attractive, actually.* Look at this guy. He still can't get over it. What a sadster. The second the food comes I'm going to clap on my earphones. *Chicken or beef? Chicken please. . . . Oh, you only have beef. Beef then. Thanks.* If they didn't have the chicken, why'd they offer it? Now, on with the headset. Oh dear, what's this channel? Peking opera, I think. Don't think I like this one either. Ah, classical will do. Urgh. Disgusting, even for airline food. Really poxy. Doesn't really matter. I can still taste that Peking duck we had for lunch, or brunch or whatever that was. I'll be back in the land of mesclun salad and real coffee soon.

Can't wait to have a cuppa with the girls and tell them all my stories. I wonder where Mengzhong is now? Is he thinking about me? I can't believe it snowed this morning. Hard to imagine that it'll be summer again when we land in Sydney. The snow was so beautiful. I wonder whether Mr. Fu was spying on us? Is that why he was so stressed out when I caught up with him again back at the car? Wonder how you say, "Chill out, dude," in Chinese? Oh, I should be fair. He was probably worried that, having safely shepherded me for three whole weeks through the hazards of Beijing traffic, indulged nearly all my mad impulses (except, of course, my idea that we could just kind of talk our way into one of the prisons, which he firmly resisted), and put up with my taste in evening entertainment (Beijing punk rock—what a trip), he was going suddenly to lose me to the clutches of some street performer who would cause me to miss my plane, overstay my visa, possibly even disappear forever and completely derail Sino-Australian relations. He'd be stuck with the responsibility —and the snakes. I can imagine Mr. Fu sitting there in the car, watching the bag with its creepy contents slithering against the sides, certain that they were poisonous and going to get him. I mean, you can't blame the man for being such a gloom merchant when you've had the history he has—deprived of education in the Cultural Revolution, brother persecuted to death, scraping by on a meager government salary when everyone else seems to have gone into business and is saving up for their first Ferrari.

What *is* this meat? I'm sure it's not beef. I think I've had enough of it, whatever it is. *Sorry?* I can't believe he's persisting in speaking to me when I've got my headset on.

No, it's not the best meal I've ever had either, but never mind. . . . Yes, I like Chinese food. . . . What? No, I most definitely did not eat dog! Have you eaten dog? But dog is woman's best friend! Dogs lounge on the sofa and watch videos, dogs play Frisbee and eat ham sandwiches! *Really? You did? How did it make you feel?* If only the hostess would come and clear the tray, I could pretend to go to sleep. *Warm? Oh, that's interesting.* Interesting, hah! Bet it was even more interesting for poor Bluey! Let's put the headset on again before he has a chance to continue. God, Julia, you're terrible. He's probably a perfectly nice man who's just a bit lonely and wants a chat. On the other hand, what am I, a chat machine? Besides, how could a perfectly nice man eat dog!

I hope the neighbors managed to keep the big fern in the entranceway alive. I wonder what the girls have been up to. Wonder if any of them have had any little romances? *No, I won't have any coffee. No, no tea either. Thanks.* Seat back, headset on, eyes closed. I'm going to be so trashed when we arrive, I can tell already. My mind is such a jumble of images and smells and sounds. Let's try and focus, why don't we? I know what I want to focus on. I don't want to forget any detail of what happened this morning. It's been such a rush to here from there, packing and checking out. Before I knew it I was saying good-bye to Mr. Fu and Xiao Wang, and I was on the plane—no chance really to savor the events of the morning at all. Let's be disciplined. Start from the beginning.

All right . . . I wake up very early. I look out my hotel window and see it's been snowing all night. I go for a walk with my camera. *Yes, I'm finished, thanks.* Strangely enough, it doesn't feel that cold. The sparkling white of the snow, untrammeled at that time in the morning, and the soft glow of the dawn makes Beijing seem like a new city, one that's more ancient, pure, and calm. I walk to the Forbidden City and thrill to the sight of the snow piled in uneven drifts on the golden tiles and crenellated red walls of the palace. For nearly two hours I stroll around the palace and Tiananmen Square, taking pictures. When I get back to the hotel, I find a fretsome Mr. Fu waiting in the lobby. He tells me there are lots of bad people around in Beijing these days, robbers and thieves and rapists, and that I shouldn't go wandering around like that by myself. I laugh. You would think from the way he was talking that we were in New York! Poor Mr. Fu. He'd see disaster lurking in a well-made bed.

We go to the hotel coffeeshop where I warm my hands and cheeks on a cup of coffee and tell him that I want to make another trip to the Old Summer Palace to see it in the snow. He says it's too far away. He says it's too cold. He asks, didn't I have to do some last-minute shopping and packing? What about our planned Peking duck lunch in that famous restaurant in the center of town? I insist. I say the plane's at four in the afternoon, we'll be right if we leave right now. I don't care about the duck. And I can forget the shopping. My Visa's expiring anyway, so to speak. (He doesn't get this. Never mind.) Please, please, please, Mr. Fu. Please, please, please. Finally he's shaking his head and saying I'm crazy, but telling me to put on more clothes so I don't catch cold. I'm already as rugged up as I can be, so I just grab some more lenses and batteries and film and we're off. In the rental car driven by the ever-amiable Xiao Wang, we traverse the city. All its nonstop clamor—the horns, the shouting, the jackhammers, and pile-drivers—is magically silenced by the blanket of snow.

When we reach Beijing University, tantalizingly close to the old palace, Mr. Fu says something to Xiao Wang in Chinese and Xiao Wang pulls up at the side of the road, in front of a restaurant. Mr. Fu tells me we'll have duck first, then we'll go. It's only ten thirty in the morning, I protest. But I've learned when to give in, and so in we go, all three of us, of course. I really do appreciate the way the Chinese always invite the driver along to meals; from what I can gather, it's one of the few egalitarian customs they've got left these days. Anyway, when the steam fades from Mr. Fu's glasses, he orders our duck.

The restaurant is pretty empty, not surprising given the time. There is an extraordinarily handsome man at the next table. He has the classic single-lidded eyes and strong bone structure of the northern Chinese and an unusual, somewhat hooked nose; but what's most striking is his beautiful, almost waist-length hair. Like a lot of northerners, he's tall and well built too. He's wearing one of those army greatcoats that you used to see in the photographs from China in the seventies and eighties but which almost no one seems to wear any more.

But what catches everyone's attention is his leather case on the floor beside his seat. It's moving. Is that an animal in your bag or are you just happy to see me? Mr. Fu and Xiao Wang are as intrigued as I am, though Mr. Fu is clearly nervous. Xiao Wang leans across his seat and asks, "What's in the bag?" The guy answers. Xiao Wang laughs and Mr. Fu shudders. Of course, I didn't understand what they were saying. Three weeks in China and I'm not much beyond *ni hao!* ("hello") and *xiexie* ("thanks"). "What is it, Mr. Fu?" "Snakes," he tells me, shaking his head. "Terrible. Terrible."

Sorry? Oh, you're right. Can you step over me or shall I get up? No worries. Did he touch my leg on purpose? Creepoid. I'll just get up next time. Anyway, back to the restaurant. I'm totally intrigued. Ask him what the snakes are for, Mr. Fu. By now, this guy is checking me out as well, and I wait impatiently for a translation. He tells Mr. Fu that he is a street performer, snake-charmer, sword-swallower, kung fu master, and contortionist. Cool! He doesn't belong to any official organization, and Mr. Fu tries to explain to me some concept about "rivers and lakes," which I gather refers to people who live outside the system. Mr. Fu clearly doesn't approve.

I'm enthralled. Snake-charmer tells us how he has always wanted to travel, but that he doesn't think he'd ever get a passport, and so, at different times, he's sneaked across the border to North Korea or Vietnam. Each time, he was caught and sent back. Each time, the Chinese police interrogated him and let him go. Apparently, the police think he's a bit of a nut. He doesn't mind. Gives him more freedom to maneuver, he says. North Korea! Of all bizarre places to spend a holiday.

Mr. Fu is lemon-lipped as he translates this story. Our Peking duck arrives. I signal to snake-charmer to join us. He hesitates, looking at Mr. Fu. It's obvious that Mr. Fu is not at all happy. Snake-charmer then looks at Xiao Wang, who just picks up a pancake and concentrates on folding it into a little parcel of duck and shallot and plum sauce. Then he looks at me. I've got a big smile on my face and I'm patting the chair next to me. He shrugs, and smiles and, carrying over his bag of snakes, sits down. I'm Julia, I say. He looks at Mr. Fu for help. Mr. Fu, uncooperative, looks at the duck. I point to my nose—I learned that Chinese people point to their noses when they want to refer to themselves just as we point to our chests—and say, slowly, "Ju-li-a." He smiles, points at his nose and says "Mungjoong." I make Mr. Fu spell it for me: M-e-n-g-z-h-o-n-g.

I lever up some of the crisp duck skin, meat, plum sauce, and sliced shallot with my chopsticks, drop it onto a pancake, and fold it as best I can, following Xiao Wang's model, but when I raise it to my lips, a fat lubricated piece of shallot pushes up through the corner and tries to escape. Mengzhong looks amused. He signs for me to watch and demonstrates how to create the perfect Chinese blintz, and then hands it to me. Our fingers touch and I feel a spark. I'm sure it's not the same kind of spark that I feel even with the funny, bookish Mr. Fu, thanks to the amazing static electricity of the Beijing winter. Speaking of Mr. Fu, he's gone a bit sullen now. But Xiao Wang chats with Mengzhong and I recognize the word *Yuanmingyuan*, which is Chinese for the "Old Summer Palace," so I know he's telling him where we're off to. Impulsively, I point to him and then to us, and with a circling motion somehow make it clear that I'm asking him along. He glances at Mr. Fu, and then mimes a bicycle to me. Ah, he's got a bicycle. He says something to Mr. Fu, who tells me, with an air of triumph, that Mengzhong is worried about keeping his snakes warm. He had been thinking about performing in one of the local parks but changed his mind when the snow continued to fall and was planning to have lunch and go straight home. Xiao Wang says something. Mengzhong says something. Mr. Fu is shaking his head most officiously.

I'm dying to know what's going on. I'm fixated on Mengzhong's hands. They are smooth and totally hairless, with long, fine fingers that throughout the meal agilely continue to fold and proffer Peking duck blintzes to me. We've finished everything by now (Mengzhong's dish of fried tofu and vegies was delivered to our table and shared around) and Mr. Fu pays for the meal, refusing Mengzhong's vigorous attempt to pay for us all himself. We all layer on our sweaters and coats and scarves, and leave the restaurant. The duck is rich and makes me feel warm inside. Mengzhong is talking to Xiao Wang, who shrugs and says that other phrase I picked up, *meiyou guanxi*, which I gather is sort of like "no worries, mate."

Mr. Fu does not look thrilled, and I see why when Xiao Wang opens the back door of the car and Mengzhong puts the bag of snakes on the seat. Mengzhong then collects his bicycle from where it was leaning against the outside of the restaurant, and walks it over. He pats the small shelf over the back wheel that people use to carry everything from groceries to books and parcels, and says something that I gather means, would you like a ride? *Oh, sorry, no I'll get up. No worries. You're right.* Now go to sleep and leave me alone.

I nod enthusiastically, ignoring Mr. Fu's censorious look. Mengzhong starts pedaling slowly. Arranging my camera bag on my shoulder, I jump on and throw my arms around his broad back. The bike wobbles a bit on the packed and slippery snow but Mengzhong quickly finds his balance, and we're off. I wave an enthusiastic good-bye to Mr. Fu and Xiao Wang. Mr. Fu tosses off a gesture that seems closer to "piss off then" than "see you soon," but I'll give him benefit of the cross-cultural doubt. Mr. Fu, Xiao Wang, and the snakes, I assume, are going to meet us at the Old Summer Palace. This is so thrilling! It's just started to snow again, and Mengzhong turns his head and grins at me, a very sexy, self-assured smile; and I grin back and hug him a bit tighter than I really have to. This part of Beijing is still quite nice and relatively undeveloped, and there are fewer people around as well. I bury my face in his back and breathe in the musty, woolly smell of his greatcoat, which, like nearly everything else in Beijing in winter, gives off a faint aura of garlic. We swerve off the main road and I swivel my head just in time to see the car zoom on ahead, Mr. Fu's panicked face following our progress up a lane too small for cars. Mengzhong gestures and says something, and I assume he's just explaining he's taking a shortcut. I'm not worried. We're now riding through this really charming rural lane. We pass small peasant homes made of brick, and cheap local eateries with padded blankets hung in the doorways as extra insulation against the cold. When we reach the edge of a large frozen field, he stops the bike. He asks with words I don't understand and hand gestures I do if I'm comfortable back here. Something in my look tells him it's all right to kiss me, and he does, quickly, almost shyly, just brushing my lips with his.

Oh Jake! But why am I feeling guilty? Jake took pains to make it clear to me before I left that whatever we had between us had been great and all that, but he was making no demands on me to be faithful to him, which, if I know men—and I think, by now, I know men pretty well—meant that he had no intention of being faithful to me. I mean, it was pretty clear that it was over, even if we did sleep together the night before I left. He didn't have to take me to the airport, of course; and that was a really nice gesture, even if I did end up paying for the petrol. And a big breakfast at the airport. I wonder if he'll like the Chinese "punks not dead" T-shirt I got him? We didn't say "it's over." But I can recognize over when I see it. I think. Anyway, even if it's not exactly over, he's not the sort of guy who's going to be fussed if I had a one-night, no, make that a one-morning stand. Anyway, I don't have to tell him about it. It's probably not a great idea to tell him, even if it is over between us. "Even if" —do I believe it's over or don't I? Goodness, what is this movie? I have to check this in the in-flight magazine, it's just too bizarre. Hmmm. *Joyous National Minorities Celebrate the New Harvest*. Right. Where was I? That's right, not far from the Yuanmingyuan.

We get going again along the path skirting the field. We arrive at one of the entrances to the park and from there proceed to the famous ruins. It's so hard to imagine this place once housed thirty imperial pleasure palaces. Now it's a sprawling public park with some dramatically collapsed columns and a few other remnants. Last time we were there, Mr. Fu had told me all about its history, how it had been plundered by the British and the French in 1860 and burned to the ground by allied Western forces again forty years later and how the ruins have been preserved as a symbol of China's humiliation at the hands of the imperialists. We spot him first. Mr. Fu is obviously feeling pretty badly done by. He's stamping his feet impatiently in the snow and blowing out anxious little puffs of steamy breath. I assume Xiao Wang's in the heated car with the snakes. I call out and give Mr. Fu a big wave and a smile. He lifts his chin in a curt greeting. He doesn't take his hands out of his pockets. Never mind. I take out my camera and shoot pictures of the ruins, which look even more desolate and dramatic with their lashings of snow. Children are playing at the base of the old palace, and their bright red cheeks match their red padded coats and knitted caps. I point the lens playfully at Mengzhong, and he signals me to wait a minute. He takes off his coat and hat and before I know what's happening, he's flying through the air in an extraordinary series of loops and spins and somersaults. He lands on one of the columns, nearly loses his balance on the slippery snow there, spreads his arms, and laughs, a big throaty hahahaha laugh that sounds straight out of the Peking Opera we saw the other night. Even Mr. Fu is impressed.

I applaud, and Mengzhong shakes out his hair. My camera is waiting for him as he makes an equally dramatic descent back to where we are, and I use up nearly an entire roll of film. Mengzhong puts his coat back on, says something to Mr. Fu and the next thing I know, I'm on the back of the bike again, and we're off and racing down one of the pathways in the park. We're both in high spirits now, and I laugh and hold on tighter as we strike a patch of ice and zigzag madly, nearly taking a tumble. I have no idea where Mr. Fu is, whether he's following, fuming, or just planning to meet up with us later.

We arrive at the entrance to a giant maze. The emperors always had the best toys. The gray stone walls of the maze are topped with at least a foot of snow, and it's another popular spot with the kiddies. Mengzhong locks his bike and buys us entry tickets. Before I know what's happening, he dashes into the maze and disappears. I bolt after him. I keep hitting dead ends but finally I collide with him rather suddenly as I round a corner, skidding on ice. He catches me, taking my mittened hands in his. He is a very naughty boy. I see this in his eyes. I'm a naughty girl, too, and I stand on tiptoes to kiss him and this time I slip the tongue in. He's not, shall we say, averse. He says something in Chinese. I look at him blankly and laugh, and he laughs and shakes his head, and I say *Meng-joong* and he says *Jyu-Li-Ya,* and now it's me running off through the labyrinth and him chasing after me. When I find myself in a dead end, I quickly scoop up some of the snow and make it into a snowball, which I pelt him with. I try to make a getaway, but he tackles me and we both fall to the ground. We're just about to kiss again when some schoolchildren in lurid red-and-pink outfits pour round the corner and, pointing at us, jump up and down and yell something I guess meant something like "Snogging, snogging, we caught you snogging." Needless to say, we scramble to our feet and get out of there as fast as we can, giggling like mad.

When we finally reach the end of the maze, we find a gateway that leads to a path up a small hill. We climb up, hand in hand, our feet scrunching through the snow. I look down and I think I see Mr. Fu starting through the maze. But I can't be sure. He's dressed like so many others in padded blue jackets, with caps and glasses. It's started to snow heavily again. We get to the top of the hill and we're panting and our breath is coming out in clouds. We move closer to the little copse of trees at the top of the hill, and soon we are embracing and kissing furiously, tasting the duck in each other's mouths, trying to grope through eight hundred layers of clothing. It is insane. Although we are among the trees, it is hardly a private spot. The trees are small and bare, and not that densely planted either. We can hear the laughing and whooping and shouting of people enjoying themselves on all sides. Mad, mad, mad! I barely know the guy and can't communicate with him to save my life and it's freezing cold and snowing and we're in a public park in China, in the middle of the day, for Christ's sake, and Mr. Fu is probably looking for me and I'm supposed to be representing my country, sort of, and here I am with a street-performer a circus acrobat a snake-swallower a fire-eater a sword-juggler with a Peking opera laugh, and isn't this the most thrilling tryst I've ever had?

He is deftly penetrating my layers with his hand, which, undoing buttons and zips and pulling fabric this way and that, finally reaches my breasts. The shock of the cold air already has my nipples on full alert, and he pulls and pinches them while we continue our game of tonsil hockey. I sling one arm around his neck, my hand weaving into that lustrous mane of his. With the other, I reach into his coat and stroke his crotch. Even through the layers of trousers and long johns, I feel his cock standing up to say *ni hao!* When I pull my hand away, he picks me up and presses my back against a tree. With both my arms around his neck and my legs around his waist, we dry-hump like teenagers by the back door. I am feeling cold and hot and nervous and bold all at once. He puts me down and digs through other layers now and finds me all juicy and pulsating. His fingers are surprisingly warm. With visions of Mr. Fu and security police and guard dogs and yes, how can you not, even Tiananmen in my head, I pull away from his kiss and look all around. Miraculously, though there is still that babble of Chinese voices from every direction, we are alone.

When I look back, I see that Mengzhong has somehow managed to extricate his dick from his trousers and long johns and daks. Amazingly, despite the snow, despite the cold, it is very hard. Impulsively, I kneel down in the snow and swallow the sword of the sword-swallower, charm the snake of the snake-charmer. And he is charmed. I can tell. At one point I'm sure I hear Mr. Fu calling my name, and I panic and lift my head and look around but Mengzhong uses his hands to put my head back onto his cock. I'm very nervous and very turned on. What would happen if we were caught? This is a communist country after all. Bamboo slivers under the fingernails? Thumbscrews? Deportation for me, labor camp for him? The almost unbearable tension and paranoia are, I'm almost ashamed to admit, only adding to the excitement. He draws me up to my feet and kisses me while loosening my belt and tugging my trousers down my thighs. I'm trembling so badly my knees are knocking, but I can't tell whether it's with cold, fear, or desire. By now half my brain's between my legs along with his long, hyperactive fingers, and the other, weaker half is envisioning men in uniform, the shocked faces of little Chinese children, and a horrified Mr. Fu. I am also thinking about my toes, which despite my boots are so cold they are burning, if that makes any sense.

Mengzhong embraces me more tightly now, tenderly kissing the snowflakes off my eyelashes. How do you say "Maybe under the circumstances, darling, we should make this a quickie, besides, I'm freezing my tits off and I'm sure that's an icicle hanging off your balls" in Mandarin? I decide to express, in the universal language, the more readily comprehensible message of "Take me right now." But it suddenly occurs to me that we have a bit of a logistics problem. I mean, my pants (and my long johns, and my panties) are down around my knees, but I can't actually take even one pants leg off without removing my laced-up boots and socks. There's no way I'm going to do that given the fact that we might be sprung at any moment. I think I should be prepared to sprint at the first sign of billy clubs; and besides, I can't just lie in the snow or I'll literally freeze my buns off. Mengzhong's obviously thought this through. He mumbles something in Chinese. (I bet you say that to all the foreign girls.) He turns me around and with one hand on my waist, he gently pushes down on my back until I am bent over in the position that is known in yoga (appropriately, in this case anyway) as the dog posture.

I am grasping the base of the trunk of a slim tree for support, and he wraps himself around me like a pancake around duck and slides smoothly inside, a shallot, no, a giant leek, gliding into the plum sauce. He reaches for my tits with one hand, and my clit with the other, and as he fills me up, my mind dances incongruously with images of snakes and policemen and snowflakes and Mr. Fu and crispy duck skin, and steadying myself with one hand on the ground, I reach back with the other to grasp his hard muscled calf. It is definitely the leg of an athlete, an acrobat. I'm absolutely buzzing with the thrill of it all, and he feels so good inside me. But I'm not sure I'm going to be able to come, not before all those people I am convinced are besieging the hill from all sides now reach our little love spot. Yet I'm sure that Mengzhong is holding back until I come. So I decide to fake it.

I don't want to moan or scream or anything that might really bring on the revolutionary masses so I just grip his legs as hard as I can and arch my back as best I can in this damn position, which doesn't really allow for that, and shake my head from side to side and start to unbalance, and grip him even harder. This seems to convince him because he now starts to slam it into me and finally, with a little groan, slumps over my body. We get our clothes back on pretty quickly, and I lend him my brush and he brushes my hair and I brush his. He takes me in his arms again just as that same group of schoolchildren comes shrieking up the path toward us. We pull apart, but their teacher gives us a sharp look of disapproval anyway—imagine what sort of look it would've been if they'd come along just fifteen minutes earlier. And I'd mentally compared Jake to the Guangdong Acrobatic Troupe! Ha! Jake's just a slacker with a reasonably flexible body and even more flexible morals. No, I shouldn't be so hard on him. That's unfair. Oh, Jake, I do miss you!

Anyway, we bike back to the parking lot where Mr. Fu and Xiao Wang are waiting with the snakes, and Mengzhong gives me a very big smile and reaches out to shake my hand. This, of course, is all we can do under the circumstances, so I clasp it and say *xiexie* ("thank you"); and he laughs and says *xiexie* back and takes his bag of snakes and opens it up to check on them and gives a little sign like, I'm a bit worried about them, shrugs, hops on his bicycle, and takes off; and Mr. Fu scolds me for talking to strangers rarara, and I put on a contrite expression and pretend to take in what he is saying while concentrating on all the sensations still zipping over my skin and through my body. On the way to the airport, I ask Mr. Fu whether *Mengzhong* means anything. "In Your Dreams," he replies. "In my dreams." In my dreams indeed. *Breakfast? Uh, yes, thanks. Yeah, no I suppose I did sleep a bit. And you?* Look at me, with my legs crossed and clamped together and creaming myself. You're such a slut, Julia.

Yes, it was really nice to meet you too, Mike. . . . Oh sorry. Mick. Oh please let my baggage come out nice and early. I wonder if Jake will be there.

(Half an hour later.) *Nothing to declare. . . . Thank you.*

Will he won't he will he won't he will he won't he? Stop obsessing, you dag! Here we go. Look beautiful. Jake Jake Jake. No Jake? No, definitely no Jake. Never mind. Oh my god, there's Philippa! What a hero. Wonder what moved her to come pick me up? I mean, she doesn't even have a car. Philippa! *Thanks for coming, mate! Yeah, it was great. I'll tell you all about it. But what have you been up to? . . . Not much? Oh, well. At least your book is coming along. Yeah, I really hope I can go back soon. I had the most fabulous time.*

CHAPTER NINE

Fireworks

"So, Julia, tell us all about it." Helen was helping Chantal set the table. "Every detail."

Chantal, glancing every so often at a copy of *Vogue Entertaining* she'd left open on the sideboard, shadowed Helen, rearranging, fiddling, calibrating spaces between silverware and plates.

"No worries," replied Julia. "But I want to hear what you've all been up to as well." Chantal noticed Philippa flinch. Odd, that. What had Philippa been doing anyway?

Julia handed round summer cocktails of raspberry purée, lemon juice, Cointreau, and sparkling white wine. "Happy Australia Day, by the way."

"Ta. Happy Australia Day," Helen responded. "May it soon be changed to a more ideologically acceptable date than January twenty-six, the anniversary of white settlement."

"Cheers." Philippa took her drink and plonked herself down in the zebra chair.

Helen returned to her task of setting the table. As she placed the final few pieces of cutlery on the table, she watched out of the corner of her eye as Chantal discreetly repositioned them. Helen was not resentful; she was looking for tips. She had resolved to become more stylish in every aspect of her life. Last Saturday, Chantal had given her an afternoon of retail therapy, helping her alleviate her wardrobe stress by picking out some new clothes and shoes. In the end, of course, it turned out to be more of an update than a makeover. Helen still balked at short skirts and didn't care that stiletto heels were coming back in a big way—there were some principles on which she would not compromise. And she thought that the thumb ring Chantal had urged her to buy made her chubby fingers look even pudgier. (Well, she thought she had chubby fingers. Chantal had just laughed and shook her head. Then again, Chantal, who was an elongated whippet of a thing, could laugh.) Helen had, however, taken Chantal's suggestion about applying a touch of makeup, even if mascara always made her feel like a drag queen and sometimes left greasy stripes on her glasses.

For her part, Chantal had purchased the colorful new plates in the shape of hearts and diamonds that Helen was putting on the table. Reviewing the place settings with satisfaction, Chantal sipped at her cocktail. "This is yummy, Jules," she said, her gimlet eye on Philippa.

Philippa rose suddenly from her perch, as though sensing that she had come under scrutiny. "I'd better get started on my soup."

"Want a hand?" Helen volunteered.

"Uh, maybe," said Philippa. "I do need some grapes peeled."

"I thought you got stunning young men to do that for you."

"How many times do I have to tell you girls that I write erotic stories, I don't live them."

"Right, Phippa, anything you say." Helen chuckled, following her into the kitchen. She hadn't forgotten that lipstick smudge on Philippa's neck the day they'd met at the post office.

The phone rang. Chantal patted her sleek brown hair —she'd become a brunette two days earlier—and waited for three rings to pass. "Never pays to let people think you're sitting by the phone," she explained, picking it up on the fourth. "Hello? Uh, yes, yes, she is. Hold on a tic." Chantal called out, "For you, Phips."

"That's funny." Philippa emerged from the kitchen, frowning. "I didn't tell anyone I was going to be here. Hello? How did you . . . look, can we talk about this later? It's really not conven—What do you mean, gold medal in the Olympic kissing marathon . . ." Philippa took the phone and, with an apologetic grimace, carried it into the hallway. Helen joined the other two in the living room; they exchanged glances. If they concentrated, they could just hear Philippa's voice above the Portishead CD on the player. "What were you doing at Nielsen Park? Who says it was me? Lots of girls wear black jeans and studded leather belts. How would I know whose boot fell in the sea. . . . Really. . . . Can I talk to you later. . . . Don't . . . don't be like that, please. . . ."

"A boy?" Julia queried Chantal in a whisper.

"A girl," Chantal answered under her breath.

"I thought so," nodded Helen, smugly.

"What? Do tell," Julia demanded, tugging on Helen's sleeve. Her silver bracelets jangled.

Chantal shushed them both with an impatient gesture. "Darlings, I'm trying to eavesdrop."

"I'll talk to you later. I'll call you tomorrow. . . . Yeah, I promise. . . . Tomorrow. . . . I dunno, ten-ish? . . . C'mon, don't worry, okay? . . . I'll talk to you then. . . . Yeah. . . . Yeah. . . . Really. . . . Me too. Bye."

They heard the click as Philippa hung up. Julia dipped into the kitchen to whip up some more cocktails. Philippa emerged a minute or two later, looking flushed and bothered; but she walked the gauntlet of their frankly curious stares without explanation. "I'd better get back to that soup," she murmured before anyone had a chance to ask any questions.

"Darling, it sounds like you've got more than soup on the boil," observed Chantal.

"Actually, the soup's not on the boil; it's served cold."

"C'mon Phips, fill us in."

"On what?" Philippa asked innocently.

"What's this about kissing marathons?" Julia smirked, following her to the doorway of the kitchen with her blender of cocktails. "Don't tell me that was the Olympic Committee proposing a new event for the Sydney 2000."

"No," replied Philippa, deadpan. "That was, uh, Richard actually. Oh, ta. Just half a glass this time . . . that's not half. Oh, okay. But if you think you can make me talk by getting me pissed, forget it. Besides, there's nothing to tell." Julia returned to the living room and shrugged in the direction of the others. An incredible banging sound emanated from the kitchen. Everyone jumped. Philippa poked her head out. "Sorry. Have to crush the almonds."

"Almonds? In soup? But wait a minute. Did you say *Richard?* I'm sure that was a girl's voice." Chantal cocked her head incredulously.

"Oh, right, of course. That's just his latest guise. He's writing women's erotica."

Helen and Julia exchanged significant looks. Helen reconsidered her previous assumption that the lipstick came from a woman. Maybe, she thought, it came from a cross-dressing man. In which case, Philippa's sex life was even more interesting than she imagined, and she'd always imagined it was pretty interesting. But *women's erotica?* Was there nothing belonging to women that men were not capable of taking over? Helen recalled the controversy over the politician who opened an envelope marked for Koori women's eyes only. The Kooris feared that the sighting of its contents by a man would bring a curse on their women, causing them to fall ill and possibly even die.

Helen wondered why the curse shouldn't have been directed to the man who opened the envelope.

Chantal arched one perfectly formed, pencil-enhanced eyebrow and expressed their common incredulity. "He's writing women's erotica? That's a bit off, isn't it? Besides, isn't that elbowing into your territory?"

"Erotica is all the rage in publishing at the moment. And cross-dressing is all the rage in everything."

"That's true," Julia concurred. "It's a kind of a *fin-de-siecle,* end-of-millennium sort of thing. Did I tell you girls, by the way, that just before I went to China I got a commission from *Image* to do a photo essay on drag queens? One of my big coups on the China trip was getting a Beijing drag queen to pose for me."

"A Beijing drag queen?" Chantal was immediately fascinated.

"Look, I wouldn't have believed it either, but there you go. Besides, Chinese men tend to have a lot less body hair, and more slender builds than Westerners. They make excellent drag queens. Really beautiful. This guy was stunning."

"For some reason, I never even thought there would be gays in China," Helen admitted. "But I suppose that's silly. Why wouldn't there be? Do you have the pictures here?"

"I'm still developing them. But I'll show you as soon as they're ready. Together with other photos from the trip."

"Come to think of it," said Chantal, "I've always associated China with a kind of gay aesthetic. I remember finding this book with photographs of those, what did they call them, revolutionary operas or something? There were all these really gorgey blokes done up with rouge and lipstick and eyeliner and leaping about in stylized army uniforms. I thought, how utterly, absolutely *camp*. I showed the book to Alexi, and he loved it. In fact, he kept it." Chantal held her glass out to Julia for a refill.

Philippa breathed a secret sigh of relief. This change of topic was most welcome. "So tell us more, Jules," she enthused from the kitchen. "Tell us everything. And speak loudly enough for me to hear in here." Julia happily obliged, saving Mengzhong for last. They were suitably impressed.

"A snake-charmer!" cried Chantal. "How perfectly exotic."

Helen remembered promising Philippa a hand and joined her in the kitchen. Julia followed with an empty blender.

"That's where the blender is!" Philippa exclaimed. "I'm going to need that in a sec."

"Maybe it's time to open up a bottle of wine," Julia said, rinsing it out and handing it to her. "What are you making?" she asked.

"Ajo blanco, an Andalusian white soup, made with garlic and almonds and grapes."

"Garlic and almonds and grapes? Wild."

After Julia had taken a bottle of white from the fridge, Philippa shooed her and Helen out of the kitchen. She decided she didn't need help with the grapes after all. Just as they were exiting the room, however, she thought of something. "Hey, Helen, whatever happened with that letter you were trying to get back? Did you ever find it?"

"What's this, Helen?" Julia demanded.

Helen launched into the story of the lost letter. "It's so weird," she concluded. "Everyone replied to my letters except Bronwyn, a colleague in Melbourne. I was pretty sure then that she'd got the hot one. Very, very embarrassing, but better, I suppose, than my parents or that academic journal. Just to be safe, I sent her an innocent little note asking whether she'd received my letter and if she'd be sending me her paper soon. When Bronwyn wrote back, it was to say she had meant to mail me her paper right after getting my first letter. She apologized for not responding sooner. So it's still a mystery. Sometimes I wonder if I wrote that letter at all or if I just imagined it."

You wrote it all right, Philippa thought.

Philippa preferred to be alone when she cooked. To make the soup, she first took the crushed almonds and poured them into the blender. Then she picked up the bread she had soaking in milk and pinched it between her fingers, letting the milk run over her hands as, mashing the soft pulp, she squeezed out the last drops of liquid. She dropped the bread pulp onto the almonds. Extracting four large cloves of garlic from the head, she lay them on the cutting board and crushed them under the flat end of a large carving knife. They gave in under the pressure with a tiny *phht*. Separating the lacerated and juicy flesh from the skin, she dropped them on top of the bread pulp and almonds. She put her fingertips to her nose. Inhaling, she drew in the strong garlic odor of her fingertips and then licked them, savoring the sharpness. She turned on the blender until all the ingredients turned to paste. She added the olive oil, a few drops at a time, then in a flow. Finally, she added water that she'd been cooling with ice, a touch of salt and white vinegar, and poured the creamy thick mixture into bright green bowls. She tore the skin off several fat and juicy green grapes, cut them in half, scooped out the seeds, and floated them in the white liquid.

It was the first time she'd been able to face grapes since that morning with Jake. After he'd left, she'd suddenly remembered how he'd counted aloud as he'd sucked the grapes out of her. One. Two. Three. It only occurred to her later that there had been four altogether. What had happened to the fourth? She pulled down her pants, bent down, and prodded with a finger. Unbelievable. The thing had lodged just out of reach in the cavity just beyond her cervix. She was able to touch it and roll it around with her finger, but no matter how she tried, she couldn't pry it out. Two days later, it was still there. Red-faced, Philippa fronted up at the Sydney Hospital's Sexual Health Clinic. A nurse, assuring her she'd had to remove far stranger objects from both women and men, managed to extract it with a speculum and a probe. Philippa decided then and there that some things were better left to the realm of fiction. Eat me, indeed.

When at last she emerged with the soup, the girls oohed and aahed and eagerly took their places. Julia poured white wine into each of their glasses as they collectively marveled at Philippa's creation.

"You know," giggled Helen, "maybe I'm just a bit silly from all those cocktails, but this looks suspiciously like semen to me."

"Oh, *nice*," Chantal spluttered. "Thanks for sharing that with us, Helen."

"What's wrong, Chantie," Julia teased. "Don't you swallow?"

"Darling," Chantal replied, dabbing at her lips with a napkin, "I don't even taste. But seriously, it's delicious, Phippa."

"It is," Julia concurred. "Absolutely yummy. Speaking of swallowing, did you hear the one about the boy who had to break up with his vegan girlfriend?"

Now it was Philippa's turn to choke. Helen patted her on the back. "Lethal soup, Philippa," she commented. "If things continue in this vein, we'll never make it to dessert."

Philippa, stifling coughs, signaled that she was all right.

"You sure you're okay Phippa?" Julia looked concerned.

"So what was the story?" Chantal prompted. "About the vegan?"

"Oh right," said Julia. "Well, it seems she wouldn't have oral sex—didn't believe in swallowing animal proteins."

Helen and Chantal chortled. Philippa's voice, on the other hand, disappeared altogether, having apparently followed the ajo blanco down the wrong tube. "Who told you that one?" she finally managed to croak.

"Oh, that boy I'd been seeing, you know, the young one. Jake."

"Jake?" Her voice fled even farther down her esophagus, and the name came out like a tiny squeak. The others burst out laughing.

"It's not that funny a name," Julia protested.

"So, what's the latest news on that front?" Chantal asked.

"Oh, I don't know. It's off, it's over, kaput, end of story. I think."

"Why? And what do you mean, you *think*?" Chantal sucked a peeled grape into her mouth and toyed with it on her tongue, popping it out again between her full lips and then sucking it in again.

"God, stop that Chantal," Julia laughed. "You're making me free-associate. As for Jake, he sort of did the nineties thing before I left, you know, saying he didn't really think he wanted a relationship. All I said to prompt this was, I'll write. It spun him out. I mean, he looked so panicked, you wouldn't believe it. Tell me, is it too much to ask for a little commitment? Like, say, a promise that he'd open and read one or two pieces of mail? Is that really asking too much?"

"But I thought," Helen interrupted, "that the casual nature of it really appealed to you. That you didn't actually want a 'boyfriend' as such. That's what you said when you told me about it, anyway. Did you change your mind?"

"Who knows?" Julia sighed. "Does anyone know what they really want? I mean, casual's fine, and it lasted longer than I expected in the first place. So, like, it's cool. On the other hand, everything seemed to be going so well. And when it's going that well, I really wouldn't mind, to be honest, if they'd just stick around for a year or two. Like till they turned twenty-four or something. Is that really asking for too much? This new generation really is beyond me. Without a second thought, they can make lifetime fashion commitments, to tattoos, to having earring holes all over their faces, but they can't cope with a relationship that lasts more than a few weeks."

"Does Jake have piercings and tats?" Chantal asked.

One eyebrow, one nipple, thought Philippa. And a tattoo of a scorpion on his right shoulder.

"One eyebrow, one nipple," replied Julia. "And a tattoo of a scorpion on his right shoulder." She sighed. "Never mind. The sex was great. Atomic. While it lasted."

Helen frowned, more in perplexity than annoyance. "Sex, sex, sex. Do you think we talk about sex too much?"

"I don't know. I mean, it's not like we're just bimbettes with nothing else on our minds," Julia countered. "We all work pretty hard and spend most of our time pondering serious things like, oh, you know, social issues, and aesthetics, and f-stops; and there's all your academic work, Helen, and—"

"Fashion," Chantal contributed. "My mind is deeply engaged with the style issues of the day."

"I suppose." Helen nodded. She was well aware that she thought about sex even more than she spoke about it. "And, after all, we're all planning to go to that Green rally next Sunday."

"Besides," said Julia, "sex is the eternal mystery. It is our most private experience, yet, unless you're talking about wanking, it's always shared with someone else. Sometimes a stranger. As far as careers and other aspects of our lives, well, they respond pretty well to logical analysis. But sex rarely does. So we're always trying to figure out what it is, what it means."

"Relationships are pretty mysterious too, of course," Helen added. "And they seem to be getting more so, for some strange reason."

"Exactly," Julia enthused. "I don't think that either relationships or sex were less mysterious, say, in our mothers' time. But at least they didn't have to work out the form of things from scratch, and every time at that."

"Quite," Chantal agreed. "It used to be, a boy brings you roses or sings under your balcony, you date, you establish a relationship, then, after a ceremony in which you get to wear the most excellent frock of your life, you have sex. Now it's all, well, bass-ackward. We jump straight into the sex, and then—if we feel like it—we start worrying about the relationship. And frocks don't come into it at all, really."

Philippa had finally regained her voice. "I get to think about sex all the time because I'm writing about it."

"Sounds like a good excuse to me," Julia chortled.

"I don't know about that," commented Chantal. "You've chosen to write about sex. If you were a responsible, socially aware writer, you'd do, I don't know, environmental thrillers or child-care mysteries or something. Then again, we probably wouldn't be so keen to read them. How's it coming along, anyway?"

"Seven chapters down. Five to go."

"You pleased with it so far?"

"Keeps me amused and off the streets."

"Is it all going to be based on real life?" Julia demanded.

Philippa hesitated. She thought guiltily of Jake and had a vision of red velvet. "What's real life?" she countered. No one had an answer.

Surveying the table, she observed, "Well, it looks like everyone's decided to swallow here," and began stacking the bowls. Julia refreshed the wineglasses.

"I suppose I should go and get the main course ready." Chantal rose from her chair, took the bowls and plates, and disappeared into the kitchen.

When she emerged, each plate boasted a tangly pile of black squid-ink pasta topped with a generous spoonful of pesto, dramatically garnished with cherry tomatoes, yellow pear tomatoes, and a leaf of basil. She served up a large mesclun salad in an emerald green bowl with a sprinkling of miniature vegetables and brightly colored flowers. A matching bowl contained the rest of the pasta.

"This is beautiful, Chantal!" For about the twentieth time that evening, Helen wanted simply to *be* Chantal. Helen had no trouble turning out nourishing, tasty dishes but, for some reason, they always turned an unappetizing and uniform brown-gray (curries) or brickred (pasta sauces). She imagined herself preparing the squid-ink pasta dish for her colleague Sam. After they'd finished, she would clear the table, still basking in the warmth of his compliments. He would follow her into the kitchen and stand behind her as she put on the kettle and poured milk into a jug for the coffees. He would fold his arms around her waist and apply his lips to the back of her neck. She'd relax against his body and he'd press himself against her. His hands would move up to her breasts and free them from her new, daringly low-cut blouse. He'd take the creamer of milk from her hand, and spill the cool white liquid slowly down her chest, rubbing it into her breasts and then turning her around to lick it off her skin. Her eyes would be closed and her neck stretched back. Removing her milk-soaked shirt, he would work his way down to her skirt, pull it down, and pour more of the milk over her stomach. He'd lick her tummy and then, rubbing her underwear with his milky hands, start to eat her through her panties, and then those would come off as well. She would open her eyes to gaze out the window of her kitchen, and her unfocused gaze would just register her handsome new neighbor standing at his window, eyes clamped upon her. He'd slowly unzip his fly and take out a dick that looked enormous even at a distance and would spank it until he came all over the window pane. Ajo blanco. She'd reach down now, wanting to pull hard at Sam's thick, salt and pepper hair. Her fingers found his head and curled round the clumps of his lime green pigtails. Lime green pigtails? Sam didn't . . . how did Marc get into her fantasy? Goodness. This was a bit off. She tried hard to reinstate Sam back into the picture, but the image dissolved as the dinner conversation forced its way back into her consciousness.

"For someone who is always claiming not to be much of a cook, Chantal, you've done spectacularly," admired Julia, wiping a spot of pesto off her chin.

"It's all in the shopping, darling," Chantal replied. "I bought the fresh pasta, purchased the pesto. All I did was boil water. And throw two bags of salad ingredients together. I did give the woman at the DJ food hall a bit of a shock though. I wanted to ask for baby vegetables, but my mind was still on a photo shoot we'd done in the afternoon with some local rock stars, and what actually came out of my mouth was, 'A bag of baby animals, please.' You should have seen her face. I think she was about to call the RSPCA. But the dinner was a cinch. Credit card cuisine."

"Too bad relationships aren't that easy," Julia sighed. She hoovered up the last strands of pasta on her plate and took a second helping. "DJ's could have a love and sex hall and you could just rock up with your plastic and say, hmm, could you let me have a look at that twenty-eight-year-old with the baby blues and the three earrings on his left ear who comes with the twelve-month good sex, high amusement, and steady affection value guarantee with an optional yearly renewal (for just a hundred twenty-four dollars a year)? Or, let's see, maybe I'll just take the twenty-two-year-old superspunk special with the cute tattoos and use-by-date of next week. They'd pick them off the shelf, slide their bums over the bar-code reader, and off you'd go." Julia giggled at the thought of what her shopping trolley might look like.

"You know," Chantal began, a little tipsily, "there are places like that. Escort agencies."

"Have you ever—?" Philippa's eyes lit up.

Chantal smiled mysteriously and sucked up some of the squid-ink pasta through still shockingly red lips. Helen wondered how Chantal's lipstick always managed to stay on. Whenever Helen wore lipstick, it always seemed either to feather up into the skin around her lips, or she'd have eaten it off within the hour. Sometimes, she'd look in the mirror after several hours at a party and discover, to her horror, that, as they say in academe, both possibilities had eventuated: while nothing remained on her lips, a bright red aura glowed around the edges of her mouth. But wait, what was Chantal saying?

"Well," —Chantal toyed with a miniature zucchini, plucking at its flower with her fingernails— "sort of."

"Sort of?" Julia leaned forward on the table. "Sort of?"

"Well, yes."

Sharp intakes of breath.

"I was feeling, I suppose, a bit *needy*. I considered my options. I could have called an old lover. But then, that gets so complicated, and you have to do so much talking, and there's no guarantee of sex. I could have gone to a pub or a club and picked someone up. Too dangerous. When I say a bit needy, I mean, really, I was seething. Is this too shocking?"

"I think we all know that feeling," Philippa replied. "Do go on."

"I was flipping through a copy of *Women's Forum* when I noticed the advertisements at the end where they list male escort services, 'sensuous' masseurs, and so on. I chose an ad and picked up the phone. No harm in asking, I thought, but honestly I never imagined that it would go further than that. Well, this man answered the phone, 'Spunkfest, may I help you?'

"Trying to suppress the nervous quiver in my voice, I asked him to explain how it all worked. He told me the prices and stuff, which differed, depending on whether you wanted the 'full service' or just escort or whatever, and then asked what exactly I was looking for.

"This was all getting very concrete." Chantal sipped at her wine and examined a perfectly formed, one-inch-long carrot before popping it into her mouth and chewing thoughtfully.

"C'mon, Chantal, you can't stop there," said Philippa impatiently.

Chantal smiled. "I wasn't planning on stopping."

"I have to go to the loo. Then I'm getting us another bottle of wine. Don't say another word till I get back," said Julia.

The other three sat silently savoring the pungent aroma of the slimy black pasta, letting the pesto sauce create garlicky trails down their throats and exploding the little tomatoes in their mouths while waiting impatiently for Julia to return. "Could you love a man who didn't love food?" Helen broke the silence. "You know, who just ate white-bread sandwiches and refused to go to African restaurants?" A collective shudder went through the table. Most definitely not, they concurred. To revel in food and enjoy eating, they agreed, was to take joy in life itself.

Julia returned with a fresh bottle. She freshened their glasses and sat down. "Okay. Tell us."

"So," Chantal resumed, "I decided to let my fantasies take over. It was just a phone conversation after all. He'd asked what I wanted. Black, I said, thinking fast. Black American. Sailor type. Gorgeous face. Big muscles. Uncircumcised. As large as they come. Into oral, not averse to tongue kissing or a bit of light S&M. With me on top.

"There was a brief silence on the other end of the line. I thought maybe you were only supposed to say something like, 'light body hair, big dick.' I thought maybe I should add, 'or as close to that as possible, you know, a reedy brunette who wouldn't mind being tied up would do.' Well, I then suddenly realized that in the background there was the faint clacking of a keyboard. This was followed by a few electronic beeps and some whirring. 'Hmmm, I believe that Eddie's your man. He's a black American, six foot three, muscled, ten inches when erect, uncut. Would you like to book an appointment?'

"'Uh, sure,' I said. It all felt very unreal. 'How soon would he be available?' The guy said he'd call me back. I began to get the jitters. I decided that I'd say I'd changed my mind. Ten minutes later the phone rang and the sound went through me like an electric shock. I composed myself and answered, my rehearsed response on the tip of my tongue.

"'An hour from now?' I swallowed hard."

"See, Chantal does swallow," Julia chirped, prompting a round of giggles.

"'Yes, that will be fine,' I said. I gave my address and hung up. I went into a blind panic. I tore into my bedroom and straightened it up, jumped in the shower, jumped out again because I suddenly remembered that I'd asked Alexi to stop over after work. I called him to cancel, refusing to tell him why, though he definitely suspected something was up; jumped back into the shower; then dried and powdered myself with scented talc; and got into my best black bra, garter belt, and stockings. Dabbed the patches of white powder off the black bra with a damp towel."

"I hate it when that happens. Especially when you don't notice, and there you are, thinking you're all elegant in black, and there are snail trails of Johnson & Johnson down the side of your pits."

"Shush, Julia, she's just getting to the good part." Philippa had her elbows on the table, her face in her hands, and her full attention on Chantal.

"I realized I was taking ages choosing between the stockings with the lace tops and the ones with the lace-up tops, and I had forgotten to brush my teeth. I flossed and brushed, and then buffed my patent leather stilettos. I brushed my hair and threw on a kimono. I put on some lippy. I sat down and looked at the clock. I got up and changed to a different kimono. There was still twenty minutes to go. I decided to call and cancel—I would pay the guy for showing up, but forget it, I couldn't actually go through with this."

"It's very hard, you know, imagining you so flustered," Helen marveled.

"Oh, darling, I really was. I don't know how those final minutes ticked by. As you've probably guessed, I didn't cancel after all. I poured myself a drink, took two sips, and brushed my teeth again. Finally, after an absolute eternity, the doorbell rang.

"I opened the door to see my fantasy come to life. The most extraordinary thing was, he was even dressed in a sailor's uniform."

"Must be a popular request."

"Yes, I hadn't quite realized how predictable it was. It's a bit of a worry. Next time I'm asking for an astronaut. Or a parking inspector—surely, they can't be popular. Or ET. Anyway, there he stood, grinning at me. 'Howdy,' he drawled, looking me up and down. 'My name's Eddie, and I am most pleased to be making your acquaintance.'

"'Uh, g'day,' I greeted him, cliché to cliché. 'I'm Ramona. C'mon in, big boy.'"

"Ramona?"

"I just didn't want to give him my real name. I thought I'd feel, well, freer that way. Names do tie you down. They come with so much emotional Louis Vuitton that sometimes you can barely stand up under the weight. Much less *tango*. Anyway, I doubt he was really Eddie. He was Eddie my fantasy. As Ramona, I was my fantasy too, don't you see? I offered him a drink. My hands were shaking. Perceiving how nervous I was, he put one hand over mine, looked me in the eyes, and said, 'Ramona, honey-pie, don't be nervous. We ain't gonna do nothing you don't want to be doing. You're the boss lady. And,' he winked, 'I'm made to understand you like it that way.' I blushed. 'You are,' he added, 'one bodacious lady.'

"At this point, he eased his own rather bodacious bod down into the zebra chair. You know how we all sort of just disappear in that chair? He actually filled it up. He looked down at his groin and stretched the cloth of his trousers over what was looking, even through his pants, like the most incredible hard-on I'd ever seen in my life. 'And willya look at that,' he said, shaking his big beautiful head, 'the little fella thinks so too.'

"'Not so little fella,' I replied. I thought to myself, well, Chantie, isn't this what you wanted? I gathered my courage, opened my arms, let my kimono fall open and then crumple onto the floor and my nervousness some-how miraculously dropped away with the rustling silk. I sashayed over to him, and, well, I must say, I did get my money's worth. With interest."

"Oh, come on, Chantie! You can't just leave us with that. We want *details*," cried Julia.

"Details!" echoed Philippa.

"Details!" Helen joined the chorus.

"Oh, you know." Chantal lit a cigarette. "You know what happens next. Kiss kiss, rub rub, lick lick. In and out here, in and out there."

"Don't believe it." Philippa shook her head. "What about the S&M part?"

"It'd be a lot easier, you know, if you girls weren't such attentive listeners."

"C'mon!"

"All right, all right. 'Well,' I said, 'as a matter of fact, I do like being the boss. So you, sailor, will call me mistress from now on. Out of that chair, now, and on your hands and knees at my feet.'"

"Wait a minute." Helen suddenly twigged. "Are you saying you made a *slave* out of a black American man? Jeez, Chantal, isn't that just a bit sus? I mean, when you think of the historical resonances and ideological implications . . . I don't think I could do something like that."

"Helen, remember, we're talking about enacting a fantasy. With his consent. Not real life, darling. As much as I sometimes think an entourage of scantily clad male and female slaves of all stripes and colors would suit me, I would probably die of embarrassment if anyone actually threw themselves at my feet begging for the opportunity to serve. So do you want me to go on, or not?"

"But . . ."

"Oh, Helen, let's save that for later," Julia cooed, refilling Helen's glass and putting a friendly hand on her arm. "Do let her go on. It's getting *most* exciting."

"He dropped to his feet, and put his lips on my shoes. 'May I worship your ankles, mistress?' he pleaded.

"'Have you been a good boy?' I asked."

"Where'd you pick up this dialogue, Chantal?" Philippa interrupted. "You sound like a natural."

"Of course I'm a natural, darling. So he hung his head and said, 'No, mistress, I've been a bad boy. I don't deserve to worship your pulchritudinous pivots, not until I've been properly punished, anyway.' I strode over to the closet and took out a suede lash."

"What were you doing with a suede lash in your closet?" Julia chuckled.

"Oh, right, it was, uh, for a costume party, yes, a bit of a dress-up thing, you know." Chantal hurriedly resumed her narrative. "Anyway, I walked over to behind where he was kneeling. I noticed that he'd lowered his head down onto his arms and stuck his ass into the air. I hooked a finger under the waistband of his pants, and tugged them down, exposing his dark cheeks. He was, of course, wearing no underwear. I couldn't resist running my hand over his bum. He pushed it up into my palm, and I stroked the firm, muscular globes. I ran my hand lightly down the crack, past his anus and over his balls. I heard him expel his breath with a little sigh of pleasure, at which point I drew myself up and let the lash crack down upon that beautiful flesh. He winced, and the buttocks contracted in the most aesthetic manner, all sinews and definition, rippling waves of melted chocolate. I brought it down again, and again, until a roseate glow began to blush through the brown skin, and when I felt it with my hand, it felt hot to the touch.

"'Sit up, sailor,' I ordered him, and he obeyed, rocking back on his heels. 'Does that hurt?'

"'It hurts good, mistress. It hurts real good.'

"'Take off that top, sailor,' I commanded. He took it off very slowly, raising his arms and swaying from side to side as he went, showing off the extraordinary lineaments of his arms and back. I knelt down beside him for a moment, on the carpet, right there, in fact" —Chantal pointed to the patch of white carpet between the zebra chair and the dining room table. Their gazes followed her finger— "and kissed his neck and back. I trailed my fingers after my lips, digging in harder and harder with my nails until I could see the scratches on his skin and he was beginning to writhe under the pain. I stood up then and whipped his back, and his bum too, perched so pertly, as it was, upon his heels. I had put a Cowboy Junkies CD on the player, and I was just sort of swaying back and forth to the music as I lashed him. It was quite hypnotic, really, and exciting, in a rather mad sort of way. To have this incredibly large and male and muscular creature writhing in pleasure-pain on your own living room floor, totally at your command, I mean, what more could a girl want?

"I ordered him to stand up, to turn and face me, and take off his boots and bellbottoms. Before he did this, he dug into the pocket of his trousers and pulled out a handful of condoms, which he tossed onto the carpet. I thought, wow, and counted, one two three four five six seven eight nine. He's certainly come prepared for some action. His ginormous meat whistle, however, had decided to take a bit of a rest. Time for a wake-up call. I flicked it lightly with my lash. Immediately, it perked up and waved at me."

"I love it when men do that," Julia squealed. "It always cracks me up."

"Then what happened?" Philippa demanded impatiently.

"I took his purple-helmeted warrior of love between my fingers and, very, very slowly, lowered my mouth down toward it. As I approached it, I could see that tiny nub of pre-cum pushing its way up to form a perfect pearl on the tip, a dollop of cream on dark plum pudding. I licked it off, and he shuddered.

"'Now sailor darling,' I said, rising, and twisting one of his nipples, hard, as I went, 'I am going to give you your instructions for the rest of the evening. You are going to tear my lingerie off me with your white and pearlies. You are going to worship my cunt as if it were the first you've ever seen, and the last you'll ever see again. You are going to lay me down and ravish me, fucking me good and hard and long as only big strong Yankee sailor boys can. You are going to fuck me so that I feel it all the way up to my eyeballs.'" Chantal lit a cigarette, and blew smoke rings into the air. She seemed lost in thought.

"And?" Philippa, unable to bear the silence, interjected.

"And he did." Chantal smiled. "Two hundred dollars and I had the best rumpy-pumpy of my life. Fireworks! Let's go outside."

"Oh, they really have started." Julia was the first to realize that Chantal was being literal. Grabbing their glasses, they hurried onto Chantal's balcony, which overlooked Woolloomooloo. It was a clear summer's night, and from the balcony they had a good view of the Sydney Harbour Bridge and the top sails of the Opera House. Glittering bursts filled the air over the harbor. The city center, with its narrow ridge of tall buildings, shimmered like a giant cruise ship about to pull out of its moorings.

A spectacular red flare soared high into the air with a great whizzing sound. No sooner had it taken off than it exploded, its sparkling ejaculate dissipating almost as soon as it hit the sky.

"Boy firecracker," observed Julia, "of the worst sort. Gets your attention in a big way, then once it shoots its load, it's gone."

Three soft whistles and now three twinkling jellyfish in gold, violet, and green danced in the air, one after the other, waving their phosphorescent tentacles as they leisurely faded back into a pulsating sky.

"That was beautiful," Philippa commented.

"Girl," Julia nodded. "No doubt about it."

When the fireworks crescendoed with a great, multiply orgasmic explosion that filled the sky with glitter, Julia sighed with appreciation.

Helen was the first to speak. "You know, I still find it a wee bit disturbing, Chantal, this thing about you enacting a mistress–slave fantasy with a black man. I realize that it was consensual, and that he obviously enjoyed it and made money out of it, and that no sexual practice should be considered unduly transgressive if it is mutually agreeable and, oh, I don't know. Do you think I'm overly analytical? Should I get the dessert going?"

Chantal grimaced like a naughty girl caught with her hand in the cookie jar. "It was a bit over the top, wasn't it?" They all sat in silence for a minute or two.

"I'd better put on the kettle." With that, she stood up and strode into the kitchen.

Helen looked guiltily at the others. "Do you think I upset her?" she whispered.

Julia laughed. "Don't worry about it. I'm actually quite sure she made the whole thing up."

"What?" Helen looked surprised.

"You see," said Julia. "I once did a photo essay on sex workers who specialize in bondage and discipline and sado-masochism and they told me they will never act as the bottom for a client. It's simply too dangerous. They sometimes may accede to a request if they know the client very well, but a first time—never. I don't think her sailor boy would have allowed her to do that sort of thing. If there was ever a sailor boy at all, that is."

"Helen, darling," Chantal called from inside. "What's happening with that dessert?"

*I*n Beijing, on the same night, Mr. Fu's wife, Yuemei, put her hands on her hips and studied her husband with a coolness that bordered on contempt. Her trousers and underpants were pulled down to just above her knees. They were standing beside the bed in their tiny bedroom.

He gestured for her, for the third or fourth time, to turn around and bend over.

"Zhe daodi shi weishenme?" she asked, crossly, finally acceding, her palms on the floor. "What the hell is all this about?"

"Bie shuo hua, haobuhao?" he answered, unbuttoning his own pants and pulling out his erect cock. "Can you keep quiet for a minute?"

She grunted as he entered her from behind. He came rather quickly and, withdrawing from her, went to the other room to get them some tissues. Not much fun for her, but she was relieved to be released from the uncomfortable and humiliating position. He'd behaved so oddly since that last job. If she didn't know him so well, she'd suspect him of having had an affair with that, what was she—Austrian?—photographer he'd had to escort around.

"Qi tama guai," she commented under her breath when he returned, shaking her head and grabbing a tissue from him. "Fucking weirdo."

CHAPTER TEN

Googy Egg
on Toast

"She's so cool, Carolyn. She spins me out."

"She's not bad. I think her beige fixation is a bit of a worry. Not much style. And she's got thick legs."

"That's so unfair," he protested, fiddling with his green pigtails. "When did you become a fashion Nazi? I just don't buy into traditional, commercially promoted notions of female beauty. I thought a feminist like you would appreciate that. Anyway, I would describe her legs as voluptuous. Quite luscious actually."

"So you would. You're so goddamn politically correct. Hey, come on, I was only pulling your own luscious leg. Hers aren't *that* thick. And I know what you mean. I like her too. Remember, I was the one who recommended her classes to you. I wonder what this place is like?" She peered inside a doorway. "It's just opened. I think it's the only café in Glebe I haven't been to yet."

"I have. It's excellent. They've got really good vegetarian pita sandwiches with sprouts and tofu and stuff. And it's run by this really together lesbian couple. What? What did I say?"

"Nothing. Sometimes, you know, you just crack me up."

Marc tossed Carolyn a doleful look. They'd finished their first day of classes for the new year, and Marc had just come out of Helen's course. He'd been nervous, but she'd given him a big smile and that had reassured him. He didn't stick around to speak with her, however, because she'd been surrounded by new students. Carolyn, a physics major, had spent a less emotional day grappling with gravitons.

Though late in the day, it was still warm. But the new autumn light was crisp, and the Sydney sky a deep blue. Walking up Glebe Point Road, Marc and Carolyn had passed fellow students schlepping knapsacks full of books, and adorned with tribal regalia: arts students, in their beaded fezzes or long Indian skirts, carried net shopping-bags full of whole-meal loaves and organic peanut butter; law students sported short haircuts and proto-professional wear; and music heads announced their individual tastes on silk-screened T-shirts. Also on the beat were middle-aged crystal healers and aura therapists in vibrant batik turbans, gauntly handsome artists from Latin America with paint splashes on their cotton trousers, and the occasional clot of thick-bodied yobs in red plaid shirts who'd leaked into the neighborhood from some place deeper west. It was as if all the color that was suppressed in Darlinghurst, where black ruled and white accessorized, had crossed the center of town to capture Glebe and its more seriously eccentric sister suburb of Newtown. Glebe and Newtown were candy sprinkles to Darlinghurst's licorice and cream.

Despite the fact that her manner of dress was neither particularly showy nor eccentric, Carolyn attracted admiring looks from both men and women. She was extraordinarily feline, with long sleek legs, a sinuous, sly way of moving, startling jade green eyes and—reinforcing the impression that she was some highly evolved species of pussy cat—ears that were slightly pointed. She had spiky blond hair and a prickly wit to match. "Want to sit here in the window?" she suggested.

"Sure. We can perv on passers-by."

"And they," she said brightly, "can check us out, too." Carolyn plonked her patent leather backpack down on the next stool.

Marc waved to the café owner. "Hi, Jean."

Jean waved back with a big grin. "G'day!"

"How'd you know her name?"

"I asked. I've come here a few times since it opened." Marc tucked his skirt under him on the stool. He was in a particularly androgynous mood today.

Carolyn observed him with barely concealed amusement. "You know, Marc, you're almost too good to be a boy."

"Why do you insist on judging me on the basis of gender stereotypes? If I said something like that to you, you'd be ropable. As you should be. I try my best to use ambigenic language myself."

"Ambi-what?"

"Ambigenic. Means nonsexist."

"Why don't you just say nonsexist then?"

"Because it's negative, you know, it defines things in negative terms. Ambigenic is a positive word for the same quality. Uh, yeah, Jean, thanks. I'll have a latte. And a slice of chocolate mudcake with cream. Ta."

"Same for me. You are *so* cute. Oh, don't look so hurt, Marc. Although that wounded puppy expression of yours is actually quite adorable—your eyes grow very round and buttonlike, and you end up looking like a character out of *Tintin*. Sort of vulnerable and sweet."

"So that's how you think of me, a cartoon."

"Sure," she qualified, "but not just any old cartoon. A classy French cartoon. Things could be worse. I could think of you as Bart Simpson. Or Stimpy. Besides, on some level, you must think of yourself as a cartoon or you wouldn't wear your hair like that." Marc's hands flew up to his pigtails and his mouth opened in an affronted O that exactly matched the round circles of his eyes. Carolyn burst out laughing. "That only makes it worse. So, back to what you were telling me—are you saying you have a crush on Madam Teacher?"

"A bit worse than that. But I don't know if I want to tell you now, Carr."

"Don't be such a child." She pointed out the window with her chin. "I think that boy standing outside with the guitar is looking at you."

Marc looked up. "Oh it's Jake!" He waved him inside.

"Marc. How ya goin', mate?"

"No complaints. Jake, Carolyn. Carolyn, Jake. That gig was sick, man," Marc said admiringly. "You were so tight. The crowd totally went off."

"Oh yeah? Sometimes it's hard to tell. I mean, sure, we could sense it and I think that's why we were really cooking. You never know from gig to gig whether that's going to happen, or whether anyone's gonna come at all. It gets sorta depressing when you look out at the audience and there's, like, one completely blotto dude about to pass out on the bar; two or three punters standing toward the back of the room with their arms folded on their chests, real icy-like; and a small pack of groupies who've come for the next band standing over to one side, chewing gum, and talking all the way through your set. It's always nice to see a familiar, friendly, happy-vibe-giving face like yours beaming away out there."

"Oh, I reckon you had plenty of happy-vibe givers in the audience on Saturday. It was packed." Marc indicated the stool next to him. "Join us for a cuppa?"

"No, can't. Got a rehearsal."

"Too bad. By the way, why are you wearing two different shoes?"

Jake shrugged. "Long story. My personal life's been a bit full-on lately. Tell you about it some other time."

"When's your next gig then?"

"Next weekend. Ever heard of Bram Vam? Punk poet and cult hero of the early '80s?"

Marc frowned. "Doesn't really ring a bell. Then again, I was only a little kid back then. Why?"

"And you call yourself an alterna-type," Jake tsk-tsked and then laughed. "Actually, I only know about him cuz he's my cousin. He's been away from Sydney for about ten years. Even though he's really old, like in his forties or something, he's pretty cool. The reason he's back is cuz there's been this new interest in his books and stuff, and his publisher thinks it's time for a comeback. So, like, he's gonna do this next gig with us. See how it goes."

"Cool. I'll try to make it." Marc sounded enthusiastic. He liked the idea of supporting old people, especially when they were doing cool things. He was against ageism as well as sexism.

"Catch ya."

"See ya." Marc and Carolyn watched Jake lope down the street, dreads bouncing like springs.

"Marc, that guy is a babe! Why didn't you introduce me earlier?"

"Sorry, Carr, but I thought you only went for women."

"I'm not that dogmatic," she shrugged. "Whatever's fresh and in season."

"Anyway," he continued, a tad vindictively, "you're not his type. Too young."

"What do you mean? I'm twenty-one. How old's he?"

Jean returned with their coffees and retreated to the counter, from which discreet vantage point she continued her interested inspection of Carolyn.

"Twenty-two. What I mean is, he's into older women."

"What is this young men and older women thing? A plague? Did you catch it from him?" Shaking her head, she took a bite of her cake. "Yum." She chewed thoughtfully. "Have you ever thought about it though? What are we younger women supposed to do while you lot are off pursuing your mother substitutes? And what do you have against pert breasts and taut thighs anyway?"

"Will you stop being so ageist? Two is not a plague. Besides, thirty-two is hardly a mother substitute for a twenty-two-year-old. Anyway, you know, you're going to be thirty-two someday too. And, I might remind you, your girlfriend is thirty-two. I didn't think you had anything against *her* body."

"What girlfriend?" Carolyn snapped. "That's over. I caught her sucking face with a *guy,* in a public park no less." Carolyn's lower lip quivered. She looked away from Marc. "At least I think it was a guy. I didn't really get a good look." Something had been bothering her ever since Jake had taken his leave, but she couldn't put her finger on it. "Some stupid gangly creature with lots of hair. It was dark. But I'd recognize her anywhere." Lots of hair. Jake? No, couldn't have been. Or could it? He was a very sexy boy. How could she!

Seeing distress darken her features, Marc put down his latte and threw a nonsexually harassing arm around her shoulder. "Oh, Carr, I'm sorry. When did that happen? Why didn't you tell me?"

She shrugged off his arm. "Well, didn't have a chance, did I? Did I hear you say, and what's new with you, Carolyn?" she asked snippily. He looked so hurt that she was filled with regret. It wasn't his fault. She was seeing Philippa later. She'd ask her outright: was it Jake? And then she'd watch her reaction. Carolyn reached over and patted Marc on the hand. "Oh, don't mind me," she sighed. "I'm just a big crabby apple at the moment. I don't really want to talk about it anyway. I want to hear all about you and Madam Professor."

He gave her a searching look.

"Really, I do. Every detail."

"It was all a bit traumatic, really. I'm sure I told you I asked her to go out for coffee with me last week, didn't I?"

"Yeah, but you never told me how it went."

"Well, it was funny. She actually seemed sort of shy at first. And I was really nervous, though I tried to hide it. Then we got talking, and I was asking her all about how she'd come to teach at the uni, and she asked me how I'd come to take courses in women's studies. So that was all going really well. Like, I was beginning to feel like she was seeing me, you know, not just as a student, but, like . . ." He laughed, embarrassed.

"A *man*?" Carolyn teased.

"No, yeah, oh, you know what I mean."

"I do. A man."

"Anyway, I worked up enough courage to ask her out, like, really out. You know, for a Saturday night or something. I was terrified she'd say no, and I'd be so humiliated that I'd have to drop out of her course."

"You mean, your male pride couldn't handle the rejection?" Carolyn smirked.

"No, I don't have that kind of male pride. Be fair. Anyway, tell me women don't angst out when they want to ask someone out?"

"Yeah, yeah, yeah. Go on. Get to the good part."

"God, Carr, sometimes I wonder about you. Do you really think I suffer from a male pride problem? I mean, be honest. If you think I do, I'll—"

"You'll what?" she challenged, trying to look stern.

"I'll, you know, try to reform. I'll enroll in another sensitivity workshop or something."

"Marc."

"Yeah?"

"Spare me your workshops and get on with the story."

Marc sighed. "Well, I thought I'd ask her to go and see Jake's band. Tell me honestly, do you really think I'm hung up on male pride?"

"Oh, will you stop? I regret saying anything."

"All right, all right. We were out, right? Things were going really well. We went to the Sando a bit early to have a drink, and it was amazing how we just clicked. There wasn't any of that awkwardness of the first, uh, date? God, what a funny word . . ." Marc's voice trailed off. He looked around the café to make sure no one he knew was there, and lowered his voice. "You know," he ventured after a long pause, "that I was a virgin, don't you, Carr?"

Carolyn's eyes widened, and her jaw dropped. "What do you mean *was*?"

Marc suddenly felt embarrassed. Maybe he shouldn't be telling anyone this. Helen was his teacher, after all. And that book had come out causing a huge stir about a teacher who'd merely put a hand on the breast of one of his students. Marc had taken a very dim view of the whole affair. Of course, this was different. Or was it? He didn't want Helen to get into any trouble. Helen. Helen. He had a vision of the softness of her full breasts and sexy tummy, of his hands parting her thighs. His tongue worried a tiny piece of mudcake that had taken up lodgings next to a molar.

"What do you mean *was*?" Carolyn repeated. "Did you really do the thing with her, or what?"

"Jeez, you're crude sometimes, Carr."

"Who made the first move?"

"Uh, I suppose she did."

"So who made the first move?"

"Uh, I suppose he did."

Chantal leaned forward, one elbow on the bar, her beaked nose extended toward Helen as if she were an eagle who'd just spotted a small furry creature with the words *midafternoon snack* tattooed on its forehead. "Well? Do go on, darling. You know how I hate suspense."

Without taking her eyes off Helen, Chantal ferreted in the bowl of nuts for a cashew, which she sucked up between russet lips, russet being the new color for autumn. Russet looked particularly good on her now that she was a brunette.

Helen rotated her glass and studied the swirling malty liquid. She noticed how she'd managed to get her own lipstick on nearly every part of the rim. How did Chantal manage to make just one single, perfectly formed smudge? She looked around the lower Oxford Street pub to make sure that no one she knew was there. It was late afternoon. Not many people were in the pub. A couple of less-than-super model types who'd tripped over their platform shoes coming into the place sat smoking cigarettes, sucking up red drinks through black straws and giggling in the bartender's direction. An intense young man animatedly recounted some story to a beautiful woman his age. She appeared utterly uninterested, her eyes scanning the room with a rude restlessness. A roughhead in a flannel shirt sat a few stools down from them, brazenly studying Chantal from her perfectly coifed head to her shiny patent toes.

Chantal, meanwhile, was studying Helen. She adored her friend. She wasn't, however, altogether sold on her taste in men. Rambo with a garnishing of nuns and David Letterman she could understand. But truckies? And now baby feminists with lime green pigtails?

Then again, at least Helen had the guts to get out there and jump in the fray. Chantal certainly didn't lack for offers, and often from the very sort of urbane cowboys she most fancied. But she was simply not overly keen to take them up. And she'd made up the slave story, as Julia had suspected. For some reason that she couldn't quite fathom, the longer the period of her sexual abstinence continued, the easier it seemed. The others never quite believed her when she told them, so she'd given up trying to convince them. Besides, it was more fun telling stories.

Helen's voice recalled Chantal to the present. "We went to this pub, right? So, of course, the first awkward thing we have to face is, who pays for the beers? I mean, the obvious thing is, I shout this round, you shout the next. But I had this feeling, like, I'm older and I'm working and financially secure. You're a student and poor. So I should pay. On the other hand, what exactly were the roles we were playing? Teacher and student? Woman and man? Just friends? Besides, automatically assuming I should pay would patronize him in the way women have traditionally been patronized—and subsequently disempowered—by men, right? If he paid for me, then, of course, there's the old problem about men paying for women. Of course, we could've each paid for our own, but that would have been, I don't know, so terribly *un-Australian* or something. Anyway, when the beers came, he pulled out his wallet and said, 'I'll get this round, you can get the next,' so that took care of that conundrum."

"Do you think," Chantal suggested gently, "that you might have a tendency to overanalyze situations?"

"I don't know." Helen frowned. "Maybe I do. It's probably something of a professional hazard, analyzing the power plays within every situation, particularly those involving gender politics. I suppose now that you mention it. . . . Do you really think it's a problem?"

"Not particularly," Chantal hadn't intended to interrupt the flow of the story. "What happened next? But first, what pub were you in, what were you wearing, what was he wearing, etcetera? You know, darling, I'm a visual sort of person, I need these details."

"The Sando, in Newtown."

"Don't think I've ever been," mused Chantal. "What's it like?"

"The core crowd is pretty young and crusty, so there's lots of torn clothing and T-shirts and dreads and blue hair and people getting up to dance on the bar, that kind of thing. I was wearing that long black crinkly skirt that I bought with you and that low-cut maroon top. He had on his baggy black jeans and a Luscious Jackson T-shirt. He had tied his pigtails with small green bows."

"I know Luscious Jackson," Chantal said. "We featured them in a round-up on women in rock called 'Girl-sounds.'"

"That's right," Helen enthused. "He'd actually read that piece."

"He reads *Pulse*?" Chantal asked, surprised.

"I told you he wasn't your typical boy," Helen replied smugly. "It came up in the conversation. We just got talking about all sorts of things—somehow we went from the position of women in the rock industry, to land rights, to the way the Communist revolution failed the women of Cuba, stuff like that."

Chantal smiled and blew a smoke ring. "Sometimes, Helen darling, you are such a cack."

"What do you mean?" Helen looked hurt.

"Don't take it the wrong way. It's just the things you talk about with your young men."

"Man. Singular."

"Sorry, I interrupted. Do go on."

"Well, I really was getting off on his enthusiasm for everything. And how seriously he took issues that, well, I take seriously. I was just feeling really amazed at how easy it was to talk to him, and how much we had in common. You know, despite the, uh, age difference."

"Which is, exactly?"

"Eleven years."

"What's eleven years between friends? Julia doesn't let that sort of thing bother *her*."

"Yes, but I'm not Julia. She looks twenty-five."

"Helen, darling, you're not going to have another crisis about your looks, are you? First of all, I can't afford another shopping expedition this week, and second of all, you've just seduced what sounds to me like a very dishy young man. So just get on with the story."

"'Seduced.' Jesus Christ. What have I done?" Helen suddenly whimpered. "He's my student. I could lose my job."

"No use crying over spilt seed." Chantal shrugged. "Besides, didn't he make the first move?"

"Yes, I suppose," Helen paused.

"How'd it happen? But hold on a tic." Chantal signaled to the woman behind the bar. "Could I've another one of these?" she said, holding up her glass. "And another Coopers for my friend."

The rough-head in flannel saw his opportunity. "'T's on me," he blurted out with a leer he considered his most winning smile.

"Thanks, but no." Chantal smiled minimally in his direction, then addressed the woman at the bar in firm tones. "It's on *me*."

"No worries," nodded the woman.

The man suddenly got up and left. As he walked away, he spat out the word *bitch* under his breath.

Chantal rolled her eyes at Helen. "You're better off with the young and innocent ones, darling," she commented. "They haven't yet been molested by life. Sweeter on the tongue and gentler on the mind. But do go on."

"Well, his friend's band finally came on, and by then it was really crowded, and we were sort of pushed up close together. You know, funny thing, I thought I saw Philippa across the room at one point, but it was pretty hazy with smoke; and then the woman I thought was her disappeared, and I figured it was just someone who looked like her. Must ask her if she was there. Don't see why she would be. The Sando isn't her sort of haunt, I wouldn't think. Anyway, Marc was standing directly behind me—he said I should stand in front because I was shorter and he could see over me. At one point, the movement of the crowd pushed him dead up against me. We were on our third beer, and when it happened again, I, uh, well, I leaned back on him."

"Nothing wrong with that," Chantal approved, blowing a smoke ring.

"I wasn't sure if I was imagining it or not, but he seemed to, you know, have an, uh, erection."

"*I* got a stiffy, Carr. Right in the middle of the Sando. The second she leaned against me. I was so embarrassed. I wasn't sure if she was aware of it or not. I was completely convinced, of course, that everyone in the whole room could tell. And I was terrified that I was going to, you know—"

"Shoot?"

Marc blushed. "Carr!"

"Well, isn't that what you meant?"

"Yeah, I suppose. But there have to be other ways of putting it. I hate that one. It's so, I dunno, masculist or something. I think we should get rid of gun metaphors for sex."

"We should get rid of guns, period. And just keep the metaphors. I rather like them myself." Carolyn smiled. "Not being a dogmatic kind of feminist like you."

"I'm not dogmatic! Do you think I'm dogmatic? God, one minute I've got a male pride problem, the next I'm a dogmatic feminist."

"And that's why you're such a cutie, Marc. You're a mass of contradictions."

Marc decided not to consider the implications of that. "Anyway, she took half a step forward and started to dance. I stood behind her, completely mesmerized by the sight of her hips swaying. And her back. I really like the little lumps of flesh that swell up just underneath her bra and push out against her shirt, as if all that voluptuousness refuses to be contained."

"You're weird, Marc."

"I told you that when you insisted on being friends with me, Carr. Now you're stuck."

"Yeah, so I noticed. What kind of music does Jake's band play anyway?"

"Surfie metal. With a touch of funk."

"Right. Maybe he's not for me after all. I'm more of an acid jazz kinda girl. So then what happened?"

"We just kind of bopped around in place and after a while I felt his hands alight, very gently, on my shoulders. We danced like that, both facing the band. I was thinking, where is this going? And then again, I knew. Of course, I knew. To be honest, I had a pretty good idea where it might go when he asked me out.

"Just then, the band blew an amp and had to break while they rustled up another one. I wasn't sure what to do. Should I move away? My conscience was chucking a wobbly: He's only twenty-one! He's your student! Lecturers have been crucified for lesser crimes than the one you are about to commit! Meanwhile, his hands were slipping down my arms, very slowly, coming to rest on mine. I'm not quite sure who made the first move, but soon we were standing very close together, and he definitely had a hard on now, if he didn't have one before. My heart was beating like a schoolgirl's. I twined my fingers into his and we stood there, not talking, not even looking at each other for the eternity it seemed to take for the band to find another amp."

Helen gazed off to the side.

"And then?" prompted Chantal.

Helen sighed. "And then, well, we just sort of went to his place and did it, didn't we?"

"Oh come on, you can't leave it there, after all that buildup. Was it good?"

Helen scratched her nose as she thought about how to answer that one. "Yes, it was. It was good," she replied, carefully. "But it must never happen again. I really like Marc, and he's terribly cute, but it just doesn't feel right. I can't do it again, Chantie. I can't sleep with a student."

Just as Chantal was about to press for more details, a tall forty-something man approached them. He was wearing a simple black T-shirt with jeans over his lean but taut body. His thick salt-and-pepper hair topped pleasant if unremarkable features. With an apologetic air, he tapped

Helen on the shoulder. She hadn't seen him coming, and she jumped.

"G'day, Helen," he addressed her shyly. "Hope I'm not interrupting."

"Oh! Sam! G'day. What are you up to?" Had he heard what she was saying? She felt a cold sweat irrigate her palms.

"Going to meet a mate of mine just up the street for a drink and then we're heading off for dinner. I spotted you in here as I was walking by." Sam smiled at Chantal. "I'm Sam. A colleague of Helen's at the uni."

"Oh, God, I'm sorry, how rude of me. Sam, Chantal. Chantal, Sam." Helen began to relax. He didn't seem to have overheard after all.

"Nice to meet you, Chantal," Sam said.

"Likewise," answered Chantal. "I've heard Helen speak of you."

"Really?" Sam glanced at Helen, a hopeful expression flickering across his features. "Not all bad things, I hope?"

When Helen invited him to join them for a drink, he said he really should get to the other pub to meet his friend. He was already running late. "But, uh, if you're not doing anything special," he suggested warmly, "you two are welcome to join us."

"So, finally, we walked out and down King Street. I was half bent over, I was feeling so self-conscious about my hard on. Amazingly, she didn't seem to notice. Thankfully, it soon calmed down. Must've been the chill in the air. Anyway, somehow we ended up back at my place."

"Did you tell her you were a virgin?"

"Not so loud, Carr! Jeez!" Marc's eyes darted anxiously around the room. If anyone had heard, they gave no indication. He frowned down at his plate. "Not really."

"What do you mean, not really?"

"Uh, not until, you know, not before, like . . ."

Carolyn leaned forward and ran her hand over the Velcro surface of his scalp and gave one of the pigtails a playful tug. She smiled. "You know, Marc, I think you're actually embarrassed."

"Piss off, Carr," he pouted.

"I'm only joking. It's just that you're so cute. I can't resist teasing you."

"Cute? There's that word again. Is that anything for a boy my age to be?" He put his head in his hands. "Oh, Carr, what am I going to do? Do you think she'll see me, you know, outside class again? How will I be able to last out the semester?"

"Don't you think," Carolyn commented, shaking her head, "that you should have thought of that a bit earlier?"

What exactly, Philippa wondered, staring into her computer screen, do you lose when you lose your virginity to someone? Can it ever be considered merely to have been misplaced? And where does it go, when you lose it? Down the back of the sofa with the small change, stale lollies, and that key you've been looking for all afternoon? And what does the other person gain, exactly, when you lose your virginity to them?

What exactly did happen that night?

She gazed out her window. There was that man across the way again. He must have rented the flat. She'd seen the lights on there a number of times now. He was looking away from her, though she was sure he had been spying on her just moments before. She studied him, sure she'd seen him somewhere else before. Finally, it twigged. He worked in the local supermarket. Of course.

She'd deal with him later.

But it was time to get back to Helen and Marc, whom we last saw walking through Newtown to Marc's flat.

$\mathcal{I}$nside Marc's place, they were suddenly awkward. Helen looked around. They'd passed through a foyer and into the living room. It was furnished with thirdhand sofas and chairs. A Greenpeace poster, the Aboriginal flag, and assorted posters for bands were stuck to the wall with Scotch Tape and tacks. The room was strewn with books and papers and CDs.

On the floor, close by where they were standing, was a coffee cup in which white mold floated on the remnants of an ancient brown liquid. Marc carefully nudged the saucer with his foot until it and the cup disappeared under the hem of the sofa. He hoped Helen hadn't noticed. She had of course; women notice everything.

"Do you live by yourself?" she asked.

"No, there are three others," he explained. "But they've gone away for the weekend. So it's just me." Indicating the general mess, he laughed nervously. "We're not really the greatest of housekeepers." She shrugged. He beckoned her into the kitchen. "Uh, do you want a cup of tea or something?"

"That'd be nice." Helen nodded. When he turned on the light, she tried not to flinch at the sight of half a dozen cockroaches scurrying for their little safe house in the bottom of the toaster. She pulled up a chair and sat down. Marc filled up the kettle. As he moved to put it on the stove, he walked close by where Helen was sitting. Impulsively, she raised her hand and lightly stroked his back. He put the kettle down with a heavy hand; it clattered on the stove. Forgetting to turn it on, he returned to sit down in another chair, kitty-corner to hers. He could feel his cock rising once more to the occasion. Down boy, down, he commanded it vainly. Their knees were almost touching. She had a funny tight little smile on her face and was staring at her hands, which rested in her lap.

"Helen," he began. She looked up and into his eyes.

The stern Ms. Analytical with her tight bun and severe suits began to make disapproving noises inside Helen's brain. Don't even think it, she warned her. You've gone quite far enough, young lady. Just then, the leggy bombshell who was her chief rival stormed over and decked her. With Ms. Analytical out for the count, Helen leaned across the corner of the table separating them and placed a little kiss on Marc's lips. He blinked. Half rising out of his seat, he pushed his mouth against hers so hard she could feel her teeth pressing against her lip. She sensed the down of his light stubble against her skin; it almost tickled. While keeping up the pressure on her lips, he put his arms around her and tried to pull her closer, but the corner of the table stood between them. Helen opened her mouth a little bit, and he immediately responded, unhinging his jaws completely, as though trying to swallow her up. I haven't been kissed like this since I was a teenager, Helen thought with a touch of nostalgia.

Without breaking contact, she levered herself up and negotiated the corner of the table. He pulled her to him while sitting back down. It was, however, a less than polished maneuver. The smooth soles of her new shoes slid on the linoleum and she came in for a rather clumsy landing on his lap. "Oof," he cried, despite himself.

"Am I too heavy?" she whispered, embarrassed. Self-consciously, she redistributed her weight as best she could over his lean thighs while holding onto his neck.

"Not at all," he whispered back, hugging and kissing her with a mad urgency that quite excited her. "You know, I've had a, I've, you know, you're just. . . ." Marc sighed at his sudden inability to articulate. He felt like nearly all his blood had left his brain on a southern migration.

Something about the eager, almost clumsy way he was holding her, stroking her back, and putting his hands through her hair as they kissed told Helen he wasn't very experienced, and she found this oddly thrilling. If the truckie had been a taste of full-on, all-Australian meat pie, Marc was more like googy egg on toast, nothing too complicated or heavy, just the sort of warm, comfortable thing you'd be happy waking up to. As his tongue searched out hers again, the thought suddenly crossed her mind: Could the yolk be still intact? He was what—twenty, twenty-one? Didn't they all do it by the time they were fifteen these days? Lifting up the back of his T-shirt, she put her hand on his skin. It felt warm and almost impossibly smooth and silky. She slowly brought her hand around to caress the sleek, flat surface of his stomach and sweetly underdeveloped chest, upon which grew only a few stray hairs, a wee cluster in the center and several more around each nipple. She leaned down to kiss the delicate peaches of his areolas. She could feel his heart beat. He took her hand and lowered it to the bulge in his pants.

"Would you make love to me?" he croaked.

There was something touching about the combination of the formality of the request and the crack in his voice.

"Yes."

She stood up and held out her hand. He wasn't sure if he could stand up straight, but somehow, his arms around her the whole way, he managed to lead her to his bedroom, and they sank down onto his musty futon, side by side. Blushing, he took a condom out from the bedside table (he'd bought a pack that afternoon, just in case) and put it down on the bed. The act made him shy again and he pressed his face against hers and she felt its hot flush. He put his hand on her breast and, when she lay back on the bed, scrambled on top of her. Just as abruptly, he rolled off. He tore madly at her clothes, and then at his own, indecisive, wanting to stroke her and be stroked, to kiss and be kissed. They now both had their shirts off, and one of Helen's breasts had escaped its lace bindings. Her skirt was above her waist, their shoes were off and she was working on his belt buckle when her rational self lifted her head off the floor. Ms. Analytical's hair was disheveled, and her head spun. She made one last attempt to remind Helen of her ethical responsibilities. Just at that moment, along came Longlegs with a gag and masking tape. Jeez, you can be such a dill said Longlegs as she stuck in the gag and sealed her rival's lips. You haven't got a hope. It's only a matter of a couple of centimeters now.

She tugged at his trousers and freed his stiff and straining cock from his briefs. It was bent slightly to the left. The phrase "tummy banana" jumped into her mind and, to hide the smile that had simultaneously leapt to her lips, she leaned over and kissed it. Licking the glans, she tongued the head playfully, briefly flicking at the vein before moving down to his balls. She noticed with a pang of tenderness how they still hung in their sack tight and close to his body. She sucked on them one at a time and tickled the area between his balls and anus with one hand while pulling on his cock with the other. When she took the length of it into her mouth and throat, Marc flopped backward onto the bed, utterly helpless, paralyzed, his entire consciousness, all of his senses, concentrated in the close, warm, wet, kinetic tunnel of her mouth. He had become the living embodiment of a principle he had so often denounced: phallocentricity.

Something of this seeped vaguely into his mind, to the extent that his mind was still relevant to the experience. The few brain cells still on active duty began screaming instructions at him like a drill sergeant: Don't just lie there taking it! Do something! To her! Find the clitoris! Give foreplay lots of time! Pay attention to her nipples! Take it slow and build up the rhythm! Whatever you do, don't come too fast! But his rioting hormones surged out of control and broke down the barricades of sexual etiquette. Squirming out of Helen's grasp, he clawed off her underpants and spread her legs with his hands, rubbing blindly at the wet crevice he found there. Without further ado, he rolled on top and entered her. A zillion images flooded into his head: of mascarpone, of Sharon Stone, of steaming cannelloni, of lingerie, of Elle Macpherson, of stallions, of stamens, of Mal Meninga on a run, of Madonna on a gondola, of cocker spaniels, Mick Jagger's lips, of ET, of wet T-shirt contests, of mangos, of his father swinging a golf club, of a platypus wriggling its way down a muddy river. Much to his horror, Beavis and Butthead provided the soundtrack, laughing: *hehheh hehheh hehheh*. His cock had traveled at last to that mysterious place he had long imagined but never known, traversing a terrain both foreign and familiar that was somehow traversing it at the same time. And it was Helen down there! His teacher! His obsession! This all had something to do with her! Suddenly, his balls tightened and the top of his head came off like the cap on a volcano. He spasmed, groaning, and collapsed with an abruptly clear mind upon the soft mound of Helen's still writhing and sweaty body.

The whole event had lasted approximately nine minutes, including the five minutes that Helen had spent going down on Marc.

Helen's realization that Marc had been a virgin tempered her disappointment. She found his innocent ineptness touching. She put her arms around him fondly and kissed the flushed cheek which lay astride her mouth.

Marc, however, was in turmoil. As his cock withered inside her, his brain snapped back into gear. Here was this woman he worshiped, whom in his fantasies he had pleasured in infinite ways, and he hadn't managed to make her come even once. He had meant to relish her like a banquet, and instead he'd scoffed her like fast food. He rolled off her in his shame. He got out of bed and began to throw on his clothes.

Helen sat up, surprised. "What are you—"

"No! No!" Marc cut her off. He waved his hands about his head and stamped his feet on the floor. "I can't talk now!" he cried. He had so much to think about. He ran out of the house before the astonished Helen had the chance to say another word.

Pacing the streets of Newtown, one pigtail still tied up, the other laying flat on his head like a broken wing, Marc recoiled from the sight of groups of people his age, pissed or stoned, boys' arms around girls, girls kissing boys, girls kissing girls, everyone laughing or shouting. They could have been from another planet. He went over the events of the evening a hundred times. He wanted to weep, though out of desperation or joy or embarrassment over his melodramatic departure he wasn't sure. My God, he'd even forgotten the condom. For hours, he wandered.

After he left, Helen lay in his bed anxious and fretting until the alcohol and the emotional intensity of the evening took their toll, and she dozed off.

When he finally returned, panicked that she might have gotten up and gone, he was much relieved to see the full contour of her body under the duvet. One of her feet stuck out from the coverings. He stood in the doorway, gazing at her sleeping form and a happy calm settled on his mind. He went to pull the duvet over the stray foot. Its perfect beauty made his heart beat. Kicking off his boots, he quietly undressed and slipped back under the covers. Feeling for the curve of her body, he spooned it with his own.

Through her dreamy haze, Helen sensed his presence and hugged his arms close to her chest. Soon, she was feeling sexy again. She rolled over and, snuggling up against him, she kissed his forehead, nose, and chin. She could feel something stirring below.

Marc had half expected her to have fled by the time he returned. He certainly didn't expect to be given a second chance. Not after that disappointing premiere performance, anyway. This time, he was going to do it right. He would not gobble his food. He would be a good student. He paid attention as his teacher showed him how to savor a kiss, and then, with her hand on his, how to tease and explore her pleasure zones. When she made to go down on him, however, he stopped her. That was a bit too exciting, and he needed to keep his wits about him this time.

Trying to ignore the urgency of his loins, he explored her breasts and belly, kissing her madly as he went. He parted her legs and stared. It was a fascinating and yet somewhat scary sight. All that hair! Did they all have so much hair down there? And were there always so many uneven folds and tucks? What was in there anyway? For some reason, his overeducated brain threw up the term *vagina dentata,* and he felt his prick suddenly begin to deflate. No! This couldn't be happening! This was the classic unreconstructed male antifantasy: the fear of being castrated by a cunt! He'd written a paper on it last term! He knew it was just a pernicious myth. Why was it haunting him now? Chomp chomp. Chomp chomp. Stop it, Marc! His panic mounting, he tried to focus on what he was doing. Right. The clitoris! He was going to stroke it, and kiss it and lick it until she came. Now, which bit would the clitoris be? He studied the options and made a reasonable guess. Judging from Helen's satisfied moans he assumed he'd passed with honors. The smell of her cunt, which he found slightly overwhelming at first, began to thrill him. He was getting hard again. Had she come? How can you tell? Oh well. That would have to do. If he didn't stick it up her *right this second* he was going to explode. He scrambled on top, poked himself inside, remembered the condom, pulled out and, somehow, with Helen's help (he really couldn't recall how it all happened) got it on, entered her again, and several thrusts down the warm wet track, blew like a whale.

The next morning, he tried to apologize. Helen put her finger to his lips. She was Understanding personified.

Marc was in love.

CHAPTER ELEVEN

Ergonomic

Allow me to introduce myself. My name is, well, you can call me Argus. How should I describe myself? "SWM, 38, powerfully built, paraphiliac (inspectionalist, to be specific), looking for . . ." No, make that just looking. If I were a food, I'd be fried eggs, black-eyed peas, lemon tartlets, and certain varieties of sushi. If I were a game, I'd be marbles. Do you get it? All right, I'll spell it out: I am a voyeur.

I can see some of you mouthing the word *pervert* or *sleazebag* (yes, I can see you, too, readers!) but please, hear me out. The women I enjoy watching are perfectly safe. I look but I never touch. That's a matter of principle and pride with me. Besides, I would never allow any harm to come to my pets—and I think of them as pets, in the nicest possible sense of the word. If, for instance, I ever saw someone sneak into one of the flats belonging to "my women" and try to rape her or nick her television set, I'd be over there in a second. I'd break the bastard's neck between my fingers before he could say boo. That's not an idle boast. I am a master of Zen do kai and of other more esoteric, but no less lethal, forms of martial arts as well. I like reading: George Bataille is a personal favorite. *Me too, thought Philippa.*

I am not what you'd call a very social sort of person. I don't go to parties, or barbies, or cafés, or clubs, or pubs, or dinner parties, or brunches. I don't, in fact, have any friends as such. Of course, there's Ahmed. Each day when I purchase my daily supply of milk, corn flakes, steak, and artichokes from the corner store, Ahmed, the owner, always asks how I am. I always reply "Fine, Ahmed. How are you?" He will answer, in turn, "Not bad—for a Tuesday" (or Wednesday, or Thursday, or whatever day it is) and always I laugh as if hearing this little joke for the first time. Then I pay him my money and leave. Does Ahmed count as a friend?

I also have a lady friend I meet once a week. We have a little arrangement, you might say. But that's another story. It's the first story, I might add.

Have you noticed the number of times I say *I* ("eye")? Do you think it's a coincidence?

You might wonder what I do. I'm a guard at . . . well, does it really matter if it's the art gallery or the Pussy-cat Lounge or the State Bank or Bondi beach or government offices or the Hellfire Club? If you're very observant, you've already worked it out. If not, never mind. Suffice it to say: I keep watch over things. I enjoy that. When I'm not doing my paid job of guarding, I assign myself other tasks, which I take no less seriously. The task I have assigned myself most recently is keeping watch over Philippa. You might think of me as her guardian angel.

The reason I know Philippa's name is because one day I saw her come out of her building with a council recycling box. She put it down on the pavement and caught a bus into town. I hurried outside and, under the pretense that I was interested in the previous Saturday's *Good Weekend,* picked through the more personal scraps of paper. I found a number of envelopes, all addressed to Philippa Berry. I also found a few pale but intriguing segments of what looked like erotic fiction, printed out on a printer badly in need of a ribbon change: "tracing little circles on her clitoris," "sensation of that massive rod sliding in," "she slides the head of a large dildo into the," that kind of thing. There were also three small bottles of Coopers Ale, a scrap of red velvet, an empty box of Panadols, and a newsletter from Greenpeace. I kept the scrap of velvet. They don't really recycle velvet, do they?

I already know a lot about Philippa. *It's not surprising, Philippa chuckled.* Our buildings nearly abut. My flat is on a slightly higher plane than hers. Physically speaking. I wouldn't presume to make any such judgments on moral or metaphysical grounds. From my bathroom window I can spy into her kitchen; my bedroom gives me a vantage point into her living room cum study. If you knew Philippa like I know Philippa, you would understand that these are crucial centers of activity. I do regret not being able to see into her bedroom, of course; but I don't mind using my imagination. I don't always, if you'll pardon my crudity, have to see the gleet on the sheet.

Besides, Philippa puts on quite a good show in her kitchen and study. She sometimes feels her nipples in the middle of a stir-fry, or touches herself when she's writing. I had guessed she was writing erotica before I found those scraps in the recycling bin from the way she sometimes seems overwhelmed by what she's tapping into her keyboard. I love the slow, resigned way she unbuckles her belt, unzips her jeans, and slips her hand in. She holds onto the back of her ergonomic stool with her other hand and closes her eyes and leans back and just goes for it. It's a riveting sight. I try to come at the same time as she does. Simultaneous orgasm is such a beautiful thing, don't you think?

That stool is the sexiest piece of furniture I have ever seen. It doesn't look like much—one downsloping red cushion for her ass and an upsloping one for her knees and lower legs and a few black bars holding it all together. It spends nearly all day caressed by Philippa's buttocks and limbs. Sometimes, she wiggles around to get more com-

fortable on it or straightens her back, lifting her ass and pushing her pussy down on the seat, and I think, please, let me come back in my next life as an ergonomic stool.

If she has her window open and so do I and the wind is right, I may occasionally catch snatches of conversation she has on the phone or when someone visits her. Sometimes I know she has visitors from the activity in the kitchen—she's preparing more food than usual or maybe someone's in there talking to her. There's a younger girl who's often there, who has beautiful green eyes and short blond hair, not my type really, too thin. She does seem to be on fairly intimate terms with Philippa, however, if you get my meaning. I've seen them engage in a bit of suck face over the salad making, and there's always something going on with fingers and breasts and pussy, but they save the really good stuff for the bedroom. That's what I assume, anyway, because I only get the appetizers in the kitchen, and they rarely go into her study. What I'm trying to say is that Philippa is a lesbian, and that interests me a lot. Or I thought she was a lesbian, anyway. I'm a little confused after what I spied with my little eye earlier this evening.

Of course, there was that episode when I was just checking out the flat before renting it, but I didn't really, you understand, *know* Philippa at the time. Besides, I could hardly see the woman involved for all those revolting—what do they call those things?—dreadlocks, that's right, dreadlocks on the guy. Never mind. I later came to assume it was someone else, maybe a friend of hers, who'd borrowed the flat. I don't think my Philippa would ever do it with someone who had dreadlocks. No, not her type at all.

It's funny how suddenly summer just sort of slips into autumn and autumn slides into winter. It's chilly enough to wear a sweater in the daytime now, and the days are as short as they'll ever be. That suits me just fine, because once it's dark, if someone has her lights on, and yours are off, you can pretty much gaze away to your heart's content, and my heart is rarely content unless I've done a lot of gazing, believe me.

I had just got home from work. I was about to switch on the lights when I noticed that Philippa was in her study with that girl. Or I thought it was that girl, anyway. Sitting on the ergonomic stool was a gamine creature with short blond hair and very red lipstick, a neat black sweater, an aqua miniskirt, and black stockings. She'd kicked off her shoes. Her legs were a bit on the muscular side, but her feet! Perfection itself! The exquisite arch and shapeliness of her feet exceeded in beauty even my darling Philippa's own pulchritudinous pedals.

Allow me a slight digression here. As I mentioned above, I am actually involved with a woman at work. Well, she's not a colleague exactly. But you could say we are having a bit of a regular thing at my workplace. She is beautiful, and she understands me perfectly. She knows I am sinful and punishes me for it, which is good, but I have always been deeply disappointed by her feet. They remind me of nothing more than cod, and I detest cod. I do love to worship a good pair of feet.

Anyway, I was so deeply fascinated by this woman's feet that it took me a while to realize that she was reading what Philippa had written on her computer. Possibly some of that erotic fiction. Philippa paced, in and out of view, until her reader, without taking eyes off the screen, beckoned to her with a graceful curl of the hand. Philippa stood just behind her to the right, reading over her shoulder. Because of the peculiarities of the view, while the stool and its occupant were perfectly framed for my delectation, I could see Philippa only from the waist down. I saw her friend's hand reach out to embrace her knees, and then glide absentmindedly up and down her legs, as though basting them. Philippa sidled up a bit closer. I could see the other hand of her friend on the keyboard, scrolling. Then, much to my delight, the hand on her legs started to travel up the inside of her thighs. Oh, that's right. I forgot to mention this. Most uncharacteristically, Philippa was wearing a skirt today. A short black pleated skirt—a schoolgirl's skirt. And stockings—real stockings, the kind you wear with a garter belt. I saw that when her friend's hand lifted up the skirt. Her thighs were a pure vanilla against the licorice lace tops of her stockings. They made my heart race. Anyway, then the hand moved right up between her legs, and I don't know exactly what it was doing but it must have been good, because Philippa appeared to go a bit wobbly at the knees. Then the hand pulled her panties down her legs. She stepped out of them, and then returned to be fiddled with some more. Now I'm not really an expert on this sort of thing, but I think it's possible, judging from the fact that the hand seemed to go higher and higher and Philippa's body seemed to be expressing something on the border between pain and ecstasy, to assume that she was being fisted. I watched that elbow move up and down like a piston. Very interesting indeed.

I should make it clear that throughout, her visitor continued to read what was on the screen. Never once did she take her eyes off it, even when she slowly pulled her hand out from between Philippa's legs and licked her fingers, one by one. When the hand returned to embrace her around the waist, Philippa swiveled around, threw her right leg over and perched on her friend's lap, kept from sliding off (the stool slopes down, don't forget) by a strong arm around her waist. She hung her head over her friend's shoulder, snuggled up, closed her eyes, and began to wriggle around in her lap. After a while, her friend, still scrolling, still reading, got Philippa to lift her hips up while she pulled off her own undies and lifted the miniskirt, only to reveal—and this is where things get a little weird, if you ask me—what must have been a thick, stiff, eight- or nine-inch cock! Where'd that come from? Philippa wove her fingers through her friend's blond hair and—here, I received my second shock of the evening—it came off! It was a wig, which she tossed off to one side. The head underneath was closely shaved, and now, I could see clearly, was definitely that of a man.

Philippa then raised her own skirt and sat down on this guy's erect dick very slowly, pulling up and nearly off it, and then down a bit more, and then up and down, engulfing it bit by bit until she was seated again. Now, she fucked him, fucked him hard. She fucked him in a vertical fury, as a matter of fact, and believe you me, I was in a bit of a vertical fury myself by this time. Occasionally she broke the rhythm to sit right down on that swollen porridge pump of his and, with her hips, stir him like oatmeal.

He was still trying to keep up the pretext of reading, but I fear it had become a bit of a charade by now. Philippa noticed his eyes drifting from the screen, and in a half-strangled, extremely sexy voice, cried out, "Scroll! Scroll! Don't stop!" I could see him straining to concentrate, one hand still working the scroll button. She glanced over her shoulder at the keyboard. "You're almost there!" she gasped. "You're at the climax! Keep going! Don't stop! Just a little more!" Just then, he bucked upward so powerfully that she nearly fell over and his love boat almost slipped its mooring. His upper body arched back to the floor, where he supported it with his hands, and his top lip curled up over his teeth. "Aaaaaargh," he groaned, "aaaaaaah." "Sorry?" I heard Phillipa ask. "Nonverbal," he explained. After about a minute, during which time neither moved, he slowly righted himself and, holding the panting Philippa close to him, with half-closed eyes read for about a minute longer. "The end!" he shouted.

At this, she threw her hands into the air. "The end!" she exclaimed, laughing hysterically. "The end!"

It was as good for me as it was for them.

The end.

Amen.

"Fuck off Argus, Adam, whatever your name is," snapped Philippa, closing the blinds with a sharp crack. "It is most definitely not the end yet. Remember, this is *my* story. I don't mind you watching but piss off out of the narrative, all right? Just piss off!"

She sat back down on her stool, still fuming. The *nerve* of some characters. Trying to end the novel there. She shook her head. You let them into one story and they think they can rule your book. Such a sleazebag. All that guardian angel bullshit. And that crap about masturbating on the ergonomic stool. In his *dreams*. Mengzhong! He didn't even bother with the condom. Men. You just can't trust them.

Ahem. Now, where were we?

Actually, it's true. I have finished my novel. Richard, my writing teacher, he of the wild costumes and exquisite feet, seemed to like it. And yes, it's also true that it was as he was reading the final chapters that we finally consummated what had turned out to be, after all, a secret and smoldering *mutual* passion. But that's as far as it went. Never mind. He told me that evening that he had just finished his book of women's erotica too. Since then, he's cleared the frocks out of his closet and stocked up on denim shirts with fringes and cowboy boots. He's learned to play the guitar, to do the boot-scoot, and to speak with an American accent. He's grown a mustache (it took him a while after all that waxing), and departed for San Francisco to investigate the gay country scene there. I got one postcard from him. He's having a ball. So to speak.

I was sorry to see him go. He was great, reading every chapter as I wrote it, giving me loads of good advice. I just wish he'd shown me his. After all, I'd shown him mine. Never mind. He always claimed he didn't want to influence me.

So, I've sent the manuscript to a few publishers, but so far (it's been four months) there are no takers. I know that's what you're supposed to expect with a first novel, but still, it is a bit discouraging. Never mind. I'll persist.

I bet you're wondering what's happened to everyone else in the meantime.

At Chantal's urging, she and Helen did join Sam and his mate for dinner that night. Serendipity struck: That evening turned out to be the start of something beautiful. Not for Helen, but Chantal. At first, she thought Sam's mate, Damien, had to be gay: He was attractive, stylish, and had a fabulous sense of humor. He was a furniture designer and shared her passion for style in all things; when he commented that the sight of a beautifully proportioned toaster could make him swoon, she knew exactly what he was talking about. He was even a faithful reader of *Pulse*. Later, he dropped an apparently casual but in fact pointed reference into the conversation about his ex, "a gorgeous woman who is still my best friend." He wasn't gay after all! She realized that she'd finally met her living ideal: the heterosexual gay man.

Two days later, on a Friday, Chantal arrived at her office only to be informed by the secretary that the publisher wanted to see her immediately. She knocked on his door with some trepidation. What he told her, however, was that the editor-in-chief had handed in her resignation, and he wanted to promote Chantal to the position. She thanked him, walked into her office, closed the door, took off her heels, jumped up and down a few times on the carpet while waving her hands in the air, put her shoes back on, sat down at her desk, freshened her lipstick, and rang up Damien. She invited him to join her for some champagne that evening. They had another bottle over breakfast the following morning and have been inseparable ever since. She confides that if she'd known sex could be that good she'd have made more of an effort to get some over the years.

Bram has been enjoying a comeback. He has a huge following among the "alternative" crowd in Newtown and Glebe. He and Chantal have become friends. They meet for coffee occasionally. He's been too embarrassed ever to drink in her presence again.

As for Helen and Sam, the Chantal and Damien thing certainly made them a lot closer. They see quite a bit of each other. Sam is rather keen on Helen, and as we know, Helen's been rather keen on Sam for a while now. But the little fling with Marc and the experience with the truckie really threw her, and she reckons she's got to sort out her head before she gets involved with anyone else. So, she and Sam are in a kind of relationship without sex—quite a nineties sort of thing to do, when you think about it.

I think Julia secretly continues to mourn for Jake, but she's always quick to bounce back and since him (and Mengzhong) there's been a twenty-three-year-old Thai kick-boxing champion, a twenty-eight-year-old Rastafarian from Brighton, and a young bushie from Bourke. She's currently seeing a twenty-five-year-old artist from Guatemala. She always puts on this big casual act, like, it doesn't really matter if these flings don't last longer than a few weeks, or a month, or whatever; but I think, underneath, she really does want a more steady relationship. Just the other night, we were having another one of our veg-out evenings. There was this wildlife documentary on the tube, and when the narrator said something like "After mating, animals automatically turn their thoughts to nesting," Chantal commented that it was probably just the females that turned their thoughts to nesting. The males were probably off looking for some more mating action. Julia burst into tears. We all looked at her, quite shocked. She quickly wiped her eyes and mumbled something about "PMS, don't mind me," so we thought it best to leave that subject alone.

As for me, well, you know I don't have a real sex life. I've told you before—I'm mistress of the V-words: voyeurism and vicariousness. I'm most deeply into the F-word: fantasy, of course.

None of us girls have been afflicted by gamomania or biological clock watching. Not yet, anyway.

As for the rest, well, Marc has started to see a girl his age, but he still secretly dreams of Helen. The truckie is now constantly on the lookout for women with motor trouble, but while he's fixed a lot of engines, he's never had a second offer. Not like that one, anyway. There's been a renewed vigor to Mr. Fu and his wife's sex life. Mengzhong haunts the restaurants and bars in Peking where the foreign girls hang out and has discovered Julia's not the only Western girl whom he can charm with his snake. As for Jake, well, Helen was right. I was at that gig at the Sando. I'd gone to tell Jake I didn't want to see him again. Not long after that, he met Ava; and they've been living together for several months now. I hear that they have the most extraordinary grocery bills.

Philippa hit the "save" button. Wouldn't it be nice if every-thing really did resolve itself in such a tidy manner, she thought. Fat chance, she murmured to herself, leaning back on her ergonomic stool and stretching. She'd have to get ready soon. She was meeting Jake in just an hour.

CHAPTER TWELVE

Eat Me

Ellen was the first to arrive at Café DaVida. Although it was a late winter's morning, the tables outside the popular café were already chock-a-block with people reading the weekend papers, dogs and children at their feet. The table between the cake display and the window, the one she wanted, the only one with a bit of real space between it and the rest, was taken. The other window table was free, however, and she parked her coat on the back of a chair to stake her claim and went up to the counter to order a cappuccino. She briefly considered ordering some tsurros as well. As tempting as they were, she decided she didn't really need the oily pastries. She was trying to watch her weight—in a sensible, nonbulimic, nonanorexic kind of way, of course. Ellen was what her grandmother called *zaftig,* Yiddish for "healthy." She had thick curly brown hair, intense dark eyes, and strong features that would have looked out of place on a more waifish figure anyway. She cut a striking figure in the ethnic-inspired clothes she favored—swirls of colorful fabrics from Africa, Indonesia, Latin America.

Looking around at the cheesy reproductions of famous oil paintings, breathing in the comforting aroma of freshly ground coffee, she tried to collect her thoughts.

Several days earlier Ellen had dropped into the campus bookstore for a browse, as was her wont. As she lectured in English and Australian literature, she liked keeping up with new writing. Erotica was a special interest. When she spotted *Eat Me* among the new releases, her heart skipped a beat. Wasn't that the title that her writer friend Philippa had chosen for her own novel? Last she'd heard, Philippa still hadn't found a publisher. Besides, as Ellen examined the cover, she discovered that this one was by someone with the revolting name— pseudonym, surely—of Dick Pulse. What a regrettable coincidence! When she flipped it open, she was stunned.

The first chapter was almost word for word exactly the same as the story Philippa had read to them nearly a year earlier when she first started on the book. How bizarre! Although the girls had asked several times, Philippa never read them anything else from the book. She had always seemed a bit shy about it.

What really made Ellen's heart race, though, was what she saw in the next chapter. Art hadn't just imitated life, it had swallowed it whole and spat it out again. Horrified, she thought she'd better get a copy and take it home to read. She spent all afternoon and evening reading it. Then she'd called Jody and Camilla. They were just as astonished as her, but agreed they shouldn't say a word to Philippa before they'd all had a chance to read the book and discuss things among themselves.

"Ellen! Sorry I'm late!" Jody bounded into the café, chucked her gym bag under the table, and sang out "a latte please" to the handsome Spanish waiter who always seemed to appear, as though by magic, when Jody walked through the door. Her long black hair was up in a ponytail and she wore a classic black-and-white herringbone coat, her latest op-shop prize, over a lime green turtleneck, black leather hot pants, purple opaque pantyhose, and blue Docs. Her neat olive features were flushed with physical exertion and the cold.

"You're not late," Ellen reassured her. "I was early. Just come from the gym?"

"Yes," Jody replied, "You know, it's funny, but I was thinking today while I was working out about the way men make so much noise when they're exercising. They huff and they puff and they *phooo* and they *aaaarrgh*. The women, on the other hand, manage to do all their routines with just simple, healthy exhaling and inhaling, none of that *Sturm und Drang* of the male jocks. And yet in bed it's just the opposite. Unless they're into talking dirty, and that's another thing altogether, men usually just stay unnaturally silent until the moment of orgasm, when all that macho self-control breaks down and they let go with a wee little *phut*. Some guys just grimace or bite their lips or press a hand against the side of their face. Women, on the other hand, will shout and moan and pant and gasp and squeal in bed without the least bit of inhibition. Now why do you think that's so?"

"I reckon," Ellen ventured, "that it has a lot to do with expectations, performance anxiety, and peer pressure. Men fake it more often in the gym, and women fake it more often in bed."

"And what are you two talking about?" Camilla laughed as she moored her bag on the back of a third chair and, shuffling off her own coat, settled elegantly into the seat, each long slender limb automatically finding its most aesthetically appropriate position. "Before I forget, copies of the latest issue for you both." She hauled two copies of *Pose* out of her bag and handed them over.

"Cool," Jody cooed, flipping through the pages. She stopped at one and, screwing up her face in an expression of disgust, pointed at one of the pictures. "I can't believe that style's coming back in! I was so pleased to see it go the last time."

"Never mind." Camilla shrugged. "It'll be gone by the next season. And then a year or two later, if I know you, you'll be scouring the op shops for one."

"I'm not that much of a fashion victim, am I?" Jody looked horrified.

Camilla cocked one perfectly tweezed eyebrow and gave Jody's outfit the once over. "I don't know, darling. You tell me."

"Takes one to know one," Jody replied, reaching out to ruffle Camilla's new blond crewcut.

They were still laughing when the waiter set their coffees in front of them. "I'm really a musician, you know," he explained unprompted to Jody, lowering heavy eyelids over black bedroom eyes and rolling his r's on *really*. Jody smiled wanly at him.

"I wish he hadn't said that," she whispered when he retreated to the counter. "I mean, you can fantasize about them being artists or whatever, but they shouldn't just tell you like that. Spoils the mystery."

"Speaking of mysteries." Ellen tapped her copy of *Eat Me,* which she'd placed on the table, and which they'd all managed to avoid eyeballing until then.

The others pulled faces. "How could she have done that to us?" Jody moaned. "I mean, really, it's not like she even made much of an attempt to disguise our identities."

"The disguise is so thin," Camilla concurred, "it could be Kate Moss."

"Hold on a tic," Ellen cautioned. "Are we absolutely sure it was her? After all, she tells us she's still looking for a publisher. And the name on the book is Dick Pulse, not Philippa Berry. The biographical note reveals almost nothing, just that he's a Sydney writer."

"Yes, but, isn't it pretty obvious?" Jody protested. "Tell me you don't see yourself in Helen. And us in Julia and

Chantal. And, of course, there's Pippa herself, totally cognito. Anyway, if you hadn't been disturbed by all these coincidences too, we wouldn't be sitting here."

"Absolutely true. But let's think about it. Would Philippa represent me as that confused, ideologically speaking? I mean, I don't feel that confused. I don't think I come off as that confused to others. Personally, I don't see any contradiction between being a feminist and a sentient human being, full of irrational and unpredictable desires and whims. But then again, maybe that's why I teach literature, not women's studies as such. And I've certainly never deflowered a student. Mike, who had orange, not green pigtails, turned out to be gay, remember? I'm Jewish, not Catholic. And" —Ellen sounded a bit huffy now— "I never, ever wear beige."

"And I'm a vegetarian. I would never eat duck." Jody pouted. "What really gets me, though, is that Josh, 'Jake,' whatever his name is, slept with Philippa too."

"Jody, darling, didn't I warn you that slacker gigolo was bad news?" Camilla shook her head. "What I can't work out is, how did she know about my jumping up and down in my office when I got the promotion? I'm sure no one saw. How embarrassing. Not to mention dragging that miserable Trent skeleton out of the closet. I thought I'd exorcised him from my life around the same time I chucked out all those goth togs. And I don't think Jonathan would have been highly amused by Trent/Bram lizarding across our bed to perform the Technicolor yawn. Bloody hell. Where does she get these tawdry ideas?"

"That's just it!" cried Ellen. "I don't think it was Philippa. Look, you know her writing teacher, Richard?"

"Do you think she really did it with him on her ergonomic stool?" Jody giggled.

"Maybe," Camilla said. "Maybe not. But I think I see what Ellen's getting at. Perhaps, darling, Pippa's been pipped to the post."

"What?" Jody didn't get it.

"Consider the facts," Camilla said. "As far as we know, he's the only one who's seen the whole manuscript, right?"

"Yeah, but—" Jody demurred.

"But what?" Ellen cut in. "He's supposed to be writing women's erotica too, remember? Philippa told us that ages ago."

"Chapter nine to be specific." Camilla nodded. "I mean, in fictional terms."

"So, don't you get it?" Ellen pushed on. "Philippa wasn't letting us see any more of the manuscript possibly because she was so obviously basing so much of it on us. To give her the benefit of a doubt, let's assume she was going to rework the material as she went, making it more fictional. But she was also showing her early drafts to Richard, who basically just ripped off the material and elaborated on it. Dick Pulse—Richard. Get it? She was feeding off our experiences, and he was feeding off her writing. 'Eat me,' indeed! Isn't it as plain as day?"

"Do you think Philippa has seen it yet?" Jody wondered. "If your theory is right, and she's been ripped off that badly, she should be spitting snakes."

"The other thing, of course, is that it's just a little, uh, tame, don't you think?" Camilla poked the tip of her tsurros into her latte and then fellated the long pastry for Jody

and Ellen's benefit. The Spanish waiter immediately shifted the focus of his attention from Jody to Camilla.

"Yes, Madonna." giggled Ellen. "Seriously. Maybe
that's our fault. Philippa should find some friends with
raging sex lives if she's going to get most of her material
from them. My sex life is totally Australian—long periods
of severe drought followed by flash floods."

"And I've been with Jonathan for two years now. All
very predictable, really. Nothing much to draw from me."

Jody laughed. "Well, at least I'm keeping up my end of
things. She—he—Dick Pulse got that right. I do wish,
however, that I didn't have such an unerring instinct for
finding the wombats among men."

"Wombats?" Ellen looked puzzled.

"Yeah, you know, the kind that eats bush and leaves."

"Old joke," commented Camilla. "And," she added
kindly, "just as fresh as the day it was born. But to get back
to what I was saying about it all being, well, rather weak.
Like take the scene where Helen deflowers Marc. If I were
going to write a deflowering fantasy, it would have to be
a bit more out there."

"Definitely," Jody concurred.

"Like what?" asked Ellen curiously.

"Oh, say," Camilla inhaled and blew a smoke ring as she
pondered the issue, "I'd do all five of the boys in that really
young rock group tinstool—all at once and on stage."

"You think they're virgins? Can someone really be a
rock star and a virgin in this day and age?" Ellen sounded
incredulous.

"Assuming. They're only fourteen or something. But
you see my point, though, don't you?"

"I suppose so," Ellen considered. "But what sort of sexual fantasies were you thinking of, Jody?"

"Here's one of my favorites," Jody offered. "You travel to the American West. You're some place where they've still got cowboys. You're on a horse—horses are so sexy, and this is the sexiest one of all, a big creamy Palomino called, oh, Shilo or something—and you're galloping over the proverbial plain."

"I hope you're not wearing an equestrian helmet, darling," Camilla interjected. "I know it's dangerous but your hair should be flowing free."

"Of course," Jody reassured her. "You don't have to wear helmets in fantasies."

"Yes," Ellen agreed. "That's exactly why they're so wonderful. No one gets hurt. But we're interrupting. Do go on."

"You're in jodhpurs and you've got a red-checked shirt on with a cute little bandanna around your neck. In the distance, over by some amazing rock formations like the ones in *Thelma and Louise*, you spot him. At first, all you see is a cloud of dust, and you hear the pounding of hooves, and before you know it, this man is galloping right next to you on a huge Appaloosa. Even at this speed, you can see that he's got cheekbones to die for. He looks like one of those models in that issue of *Vogue for Men* when they did that special on the cowboy look. You know, designer stubble, piercing baby blues, tousled hair, square shoulders, leather chaps, nothing but a g-string underneath."

"Ouch," said Ellen. "Isn't he going to get saddle sore?"

"Ellen, didn't you just say no one gets hurt in fantasies? He's bare-assed, and that's that. Anyway, he leans over and says, 'Goin' my way?' and you say, 'Sure thing, cowboy. Show me your way.'"

"You are such a tart, darling," Camilla said admiringly.

"So he lifts his cowboy hat into the air, goes 'Yee-ha!' and leads you and Shilo, at a full gallop, to this gorgeous little sheltered watering hole. You dismount and tether the horses. You feed and brush them down while he builds a fire. Shilo gently nuzzles your neck, licking off the sweat, and his horse, whose name is Buck ('so that he don't'), snuffles your ass and cunt. The smell of the carrot sticks that you keep there as a special treat is driving him wild."

"This reminds me," interrupted Camilla, "of my favorite line from *The Sound of Music*."

"Which is that?" asked Ellen.

"You know, close to the beginning, when Sister Maria has gone off to sing that the hills are alive etcetera and the other nuns are looking all over for her. One asks, 'Have you tried the barn? You know how much she adores the animals.'"

Jody, who'd taken advantage of the break to sip at her coffee, spluttered with laughter. Wiping her mouth with a tissue proffered by Ellen, she continued. "You kiss both of the horses on their soft lips and bury your face in Shilo's thick mane, breathing in the sweet grassy smell of his sweaty neck before joining Buck—that's the cowboy's name too ('cuz I do')—round the fire. The sun is setting in a rather spectacular manner. As he shifts closer to you, he suddenly jumps up, jutting his firm round buttocks out in your direction and twisting his head round to look down at them.

"'Doggone nettles,' he says."

"I thought no one got hurt?" Ellen objected.

Jody ignored her. "'I'll get that,' you say. 'Kneel, cowboy.' He does. You lean over, running your hands over the warm, firm, hairless flesh. You kiss each cheek. His ass smells enticingly like saddle leather. You pull out the nettle with your teeth. Your fingers, meanwhile, have worked their way under the strap of the g-string and are pulling it down. His cute little pucker-kiss of an asshole comes into view, looking for all the world like it's just there for your delectation. You extend your tongue and lick the sweet, tangy little entrance. He groans. Moving your attention down to his balls, which are gigantic (you can't see the rest of his riding tackle yet, but you've got all night, and the next few weeks if necessary), you fondle them and then take the whole saddlebag into your mouth to suck on the balls one at a time. He has come down on all fours by now, and spread his legs apart in the prairie grass, that pert ass pointed high into the clear starry sky.

"You ease him out of his shirt, so that he's wearing only his chaps, his hat, and his boots. You wrangle off your own clothes, till you're dressed just in your boots and bandanna. Reaching for your crop, you straddle his muscular back, which he arches up underneath you. You slide your wet pussy up and down his withers. He arches his neck like a stallion, and you suddenly let the crop down on his rump. He bucks like his name; but you cling on to his mane; and it's rodeo time until, exhausted and laughing, he rolls you over underneath him and starts lapping like a thirsty steed at your trough and rubbing your nipples with the flat of his hands like a farrier filing a hoof. By now, of course, you've noticed that he's hung like a—need I say it?"

"Oh, say it, Jody, say it for us," cooed Camilla. "C'mon darling."

Jody laughed. "Like a *horse*. Satisfied?"

"I would be," purred Camilla, "under those circumstances."

"Now, where were we? Ah yes, he's moved round so that he's kneeling over your head and his pulsing percy is dangling over your mouth like a pink carrot. You stick your tongue straight up and lick it. You can't really concentrate on giving him good head, though, because he's gentling you right to the edge with his tongue and his fingers and you resolve to make it up to him next round. But you like to have it dangling there, its raw meaty smell, mixed with the horsy, sweaty smell of both your bodies, filling your nostrils. You come suddenly with a shudder and a moan and you feel yourself flooding into his mouth."

The two men at the next table had given up all pretense of conversation. They couldn't have stood up to leave if they'd wanted to, of course. They were, you might say, inconvenienced.

"He sucks at you greedily, and keeps you coming till you're begging for mercy. Then he positions himself over you, pulls your legs over his shoulders and asks, 'Ready to go for a ride with Buck?' Once you're in the saddle he starts out at a walk; and you're really into the easy, swinging gait of it, when he switches to a trot, and that's getting a little exciting. So you're rising in rhythm with his flanks; and you press your legs into his sides; and he breaks into a canter, thrusting with a long *one* and short two three, *one* two three, *one* two three; and you're loping along with the wind in your hair. And then you urge him into a hand gallop; and finally, you're both going flat out. He's bolting now, out of control, and you're into it. You see the fence at the same time, and with a great leap, you're over it together, and he's screaming '*Wooo-yi*' and you're just screaming; and when you come to, panting, you're amazed to discover that somehow, you've ended up side saddle and you've lost a boot somewhere along the way. 'Oh, cowboy,' you sigh."

"You used to be a member of a pony club, Jody," Camilla said admiringly. "I can tell. But then what happens, darling? Do you become a professional rodeo rider, or what?"

"Nah," Jody considered. "He's not actually very intelligent. As you're lying next to the camp fire he asks where you're from, and you say Australia. He goes, 'Ain't that left of Hawaii?' You say it is. You ask if he'll call, and he says, 'Wow. The phone bills'd be astrological.'"

Camilla sighed. "I hate it when you realize you've just slept with a guy who's so stupid he has to wear Velcro strips across his runners so he doesn't embarrass himself trying to tie his shoelaces. They can be the biggest spunks and great in bed; but the second they open their mouths, you want to dive for cover. I never know quite what to do. They're always the postcoital talkative ones, too. The rocket scientists just roll over and go to sleep. Then they use all their powers of articulation the following morning to explain why, although it was great, it could never happen again."

"You said 'dive for cover,' Camilla," Jody remarked. "Well, that's exactly what I've always done. Dive *under* the covers, actually. When a guy starts saying something so dumb it's painful, you just wriggle on down and start tonguing his balls or something. It shuts them up every time and keeps them doing what you had them there to do in the first place."

"Oooh, you're a hard woman, Jody Raphael!"

The two men at the next table paid and left, worried expressions on their faces.

"So what else is going to happen in this book of ours? *Eat Me, the Sequel? Daughter of Eat Me?*" Jody challenged the others.

"Well," Ellen began, taking the bait. "You go to England next. You're running a little short of cash; and since your grandfather was English, you get to work there. So you're perusing the employment section of the newspaper when you see something that catches your eye: 'School mistress wanted. Must be a good disciplinarian. Full figure a plus. Discretion crucial. No experience necessary.' You call the number. Next thing you know you're being asked all sorts of questions. There's a meeting with a fellow in a well-tailored suit, who asks you even more questions. Finally, he makes an offer of heaps of money but insists on an oath of secrecy. You're intrigued. You accept.

"You're driven across London to Tory headquarters. You're taken into a dressing room. A seamstress does a few quick alterations to a stern black suit while a hairdresser gives you the severe coiffure of the classical schoolmarm. You are given a pair of clear, tortoiseshell glasses, a cat-o'-nine-tails, a cane, and a whip. The only slightly out of character elements to your new look are the black fishnet stockings, stilettos, and bright red lipstick. Also, your matronly suit is worn open and low at the neck, your new push-up bra ensuring that your cleavage is more than visible.

"Finally, you are taken into a room where, despite the fact you've been prepared for this, you gasp under your breath because you recognize the entire Tory cabinet. The reason they've hired you is that they've decided the Conservative Party can't stand any more scandal. They've decided to try to meet all of their needs within a controlled environment. Very controlled. They stand up at your approach, awkwardly, like schoolboys, and chorus, 'Good afternoon.' You flourish your cat-o'-nine-tails and remind them, in a menacing tone, 'Good afternoon, headmistress.' They all correct themselves except one, an elderly gentleman with a florid expression and a club tie, and you order him to the front of the room. 'Take down your trousers, elite scum,' you say. 'Yes, headmistress,' he replies, trembling. He pulls down his trousers. You motion for him to lie across the chair there. He obeys. As your lash licks his fat pink ass, the flesh quivers and reddens under its patchy matting of fur. You realize just how much these men need to be punished. You are really enjoying this now. You take up the cane.

"After a while you dismiss him. He looks disappointed to be going back to his seat. You look around the room. You look directly at the prime minister. 'Have you been a good boy?' you ask.

"'Uh, yes,' he answers, nervously. He thought he was just here to observe.

"'I don't think so,' you retort. 'Come here and pull down those pants.'

"He frowns and hesitates. Looking around for support, he encounters a roomful of stiff upper lips."

"Wouldn't be the only things that are stiff in that room, I'd think," Camilla murmured.

"Oh, for sure," agreed Ellen. "Anyway, he makes his way, with obvious trepidation, to the front of the room. You motion again, disdainfully, for him to pull down his pants. As he nervously unbuckles his belt, you lightly tap the cane into the palm of your hand. 'Hurry up, you foul piece of privileged lowlife,' you snarl. His little dick is standing at attention. You sneer dismissively at it. He lies, red-faced, over the chair.

"'This,' you say, with a mighty *whack,* 'is for your bloody arrogance toward us "colonials" and this'—*whack* —'is for the way the Conservative Party's policies have widened the gap between rich and poor in this country!' He jumps with each blow. 'This'—*whack*—'is for Ireland!' A big red welt forms upon his flabby, lame buns. 'This'— *whack, whack*—'is for selling out Hong Kong!' Another two marks appear. You decide you will make the pattern of the Union Jack upon his flesh. *Whack, whack.* You're really getting into this. You decide there are some men who can never be punished enough for their sins, and well, you're just happy to be able to do the deed. Quite thrilling, really. Especially when you've got the rich and powerful over a barrel. Literally. Well, a chair. Anyway, you've got a reasonable picture of the Union Jack glowing on his sallow flesh. Tears are forming in his eyes. At this point, you administer an enema. Right up the ass, and hard."

"Don't forget to punish them for their dress sense too," Camilla interrupted.

"Of course," said Ellen. "I think I'll make them wear nylon panty hose on their heads for that one. Do you think I should give them any tickle with the slap?"

"Definitely not." Camilla shook her head.

"Snuff the Tories!" enthused Jody, whose father came from Argentina and mother from Ireland.

"That American congressman, the spokesman for the American right, of course, is there as their special guest," Ellen continued. "And you say that you are going to give him a golden shower to welcome him. He seems quite excited by this, until you tell him to open his mouth."

"Good one," Camilla approved.

Ellen sat back in her seat, pleased with herself.

"You need to have some time by yourself after this," Jody inserted. "So you take the Chunnel to Paris. Yes. It's springtime, natch, and you find this absolutely wonderful little café, one with history and gorgeous waiters and waitresses and a great view of the passing trade. You've just been to the post office, and you discover that your mother has sent you a packet of TimTams. They're stowed in your large leather purse. You order *un bol* of café au lait, and it's delivered to your table, steaming hot, in a canary yellow bowl. You take a TimTam out of its packet. You sniff it, and the sweet aroma of chocolate fills your nostrils. The chocolate begins to melt under your warm fingers. Carefully, you nibble a small hole through the chocolate and into the underlying cookie in the center of one end and then make a similar indentation in the middle of the other end."

"I think I know where this is going." Ellen sighed appreciatively.

"You brush your hair back with your free hand, lower your eyelids to half mast, and wrap your red lips around the upper end of the TimTam. Slowly—very slowly—you lower the other end down to where it is just skimming the surface of the coffee. Timing and concentration are crucial. You suck in hard and fast. The coffee shoots up through the TimTam, collecting chocolate as it goes, and fills your mouth with a sweet rich mocha. You pull again, but now the cookie is melting under your fingers, and a more viscous surge of chocolate and coffee coats your tongue and throat. You can feel that the TimTam is on the verge of implosion. Just before it collapses, you shove the whole thing into your mouth. It's all chocolate and coffee and softened cookie, and you shiver slightly as it fills your mouth, and slippy-slides down to your stomach. You tongue the chocolate jism off your fingers and savor the sensation."

"Darling"—Camilla chuckled—"that was a truly heavenly fantasy. I never realized a cookie could come."

"You haven't lived." Jody smiled. "And, of course, anyone who witnesses a girl give head to a TimTam immediately lays themselves down at her feet and offers their services as a love slave."

"Of course," Ellen mused. "Why didn't I think of that? Maybe that's my problem. I've always done TimTam straws in private."

"It strikes me as a very private sort of thing," Camilla commented.

The Spanish waiter frowned. TimTams? What the hell were these TimTams? As an immigrant, he reflected mournfully, there were always some cultural references that caught you out. He snapped out of his puzzled reverie when Ellen motioned to him for some tsurros.

Camilla leaned forward. "As hard as it is to imagine, you eventually weary of Paris and decide to head south to the Riviera. You rock into Cannes just at the time of the film festival. All the hotels and limos and things were booked out ages ago by all the actors and directors and others who are no more glamorous but a bit better organized than you. You head down to the beach to figure out your next move. You slip into your bikini, throw your stylish carryall down beside you on the blanket, and are soaking up a few rays—you don't get melanoma from sunbathing in fantasies, by the way—when this French man approaches and says, '*Pardonez-moi, mademoiselle. Vous êtes tres belle. Voulez-vous jouer en film?*' Or something like that. You look up. He is fortyish, handsome in a sleazy kind of way. You're thinking, right. Wall-to-wall starlets, and this guy asks me to be in a film. You tell him you're more interested in finding a room. He says he can arrange it. His name is Jean. You shrug, throw on a sundress, and follow him to a waiting limo. The limo takes you to a film set. You step out of the limo, and a pack of paparazzi strain at the barricades set up between where you are let off and the set. You pose and smile for them. You decide you could live with superstardom. The set consists of a very large swimming pool made out to look like the ocean, complete with a sandy beach. On the water bob blow-up rafts, some in the shape of a woman's tits, others like vulvas with slits in the middle, and still others like erect penises and balls. You realize that you've been invited to star in a porn film. You're about to turn around and walk out when Jean leads over your co-stars: a dead ringer for Christopher Lambert and a woman who looks like Catherine Deneuve. You'll stay."

"Of course you will," affirmed Jody.

"Chris and Cazza approach you with dazzling smiles. The cameras roll and soon two mouths are roaming over your body and four hands are stripping you. They are already naked. Your self-consciousness dissolves under their caressing fingers. Murmuring seductively in French, Cazza drops to her knees in front of you and begins to lick you out while Chris caresses your breasts and kisses you full on the mouth. She puts a finger up your ass and Chris sticks his tongue in your ear. You're so turned on that you don't even notice at first that she's picking you up on her shoulders, still burrowing away with her tongue and fingers. Chris has got your shoulders and arms and head. They carry you to the pool and lay you on one of the vulva air mattresses. Your ass hangs down through the slit, and while Cazza paddles over to you on the inflatable dick, Chris takes a dive and, swimming to just underneath your ass, demonstrates his remarkable lung power, among other things. There are underwater cameras, of course, to track all the submarine movements."

"I take it that in fantasy, just as no one ever really gets hurt, there's no chance that your parents or professional colleagues or future fiancé will ever come across a porn film you star in," Jody said.

"None at all," Camilla affirmed. "Unless you want them to. Which is an option, you know."

"Is there a plot to the film?" Ellen was curious.

"Yes, of course, darling. It's supposed to be a kind of *Madame Bovary* meets *The Story of O* in the nineties at Cannes, but there's not much dialogue, so it's not terribly obvious. Anyway, you've tumbled off the float and are holding on to the side of the pool with your elbows. Chris is bonking you and Cazza, who's somehow come up with a strap-on dildo, is fucking him up the ass at the same time while paddling water. You are tongue kissing her over his shoulder, and it's all impressively athletic, and, natch, you look absolutely marvelous throughout. Your lipstick doesn't come off with all the kissing, and your mascara doesn't run in the pool."

"Yours doesn't," observed Ellen. "Mine would. Which is why I, uh, you move on to dry land after that one. You spend some time in Katmandu, making friends by showing them the videotape of your porn film from Cannes. Then you trek to the Tibetan border. You want to hitch to Shigatse. Once over the border, a Chinese army truck picks you up. It turns out they're not going all the way to Shigatse after all, and they drop you off by the roadside somewhere in the middle of absolutely nowhere. You try to follow a side road but it peters out to a horse track. You are beginning to despair. Your backpack is starting to dig into your shoulders. Suddenly, you hear the pounding of hooves, and you turn to see a Khampa tribesman galloping toward you.

"He has on the Tibetan coat, the chuba, which he wears in the traditional way, off the shoulder. His bare muscular right arm is holding the reins, and he is swinging his whip wildly with his left and singing. His boots are made of red and blue and green felt; and through his long, thick black hair are woven countless red threads. In a dazzling display of horsemanship, he circles you once and comes to a perfect stop right by your side."

"How do you know all this stuff about Tibet?" quizzed Jody.

"Adventure Holidays Package," Ellen replied. "I studied the brochures. Then the Chinese started clamping down on Tibet again, so I just booked a flight to Bali. Anyway, he says something in Tibetan, and you observe that he has the classic handsome Tibetan features: the high, prominent cheekbones; lively narrow eyes; thin lips; and reddish brown skin with a coating of mountain dust. A jagged scar marks the right half of his forehead and cuts through his thick eyebrow. When he gestures to you to hop up behind him, you don't think twice.

"He takes off at a gallop, and you're holding on tight, and he's laughing, and you're laughing, and the sky is the most brilliant blue you've ever seen in your life, and the yak-butter-and-sweat smell of his chuba is almost overwhelming. He takes one of your hands with his left and feels how smooth it is compared to his own callused mitt and laughs again and takes it and moves it down to the waist of the chuba, tied up with a red sash, and you feel something hard and long, which he places in your hand. Carefully—you're feeling more balanced on this flying horse now—you close your hand around it. Ha! I know what you girls are thinking! But he's showing you his dagger, of course. It's encased in an exquisite sheath crafted of silver and wood. You admire it, and then reach around to give it back to him. Your hand slips down to his woolen breeches, and he catches it and holds it against his muscular thigh, which you can feel working against the horse's sweating girth. The smells, the mystery of this man and the rocking of the horse's spine against your clit are combining to make you quite horny."

"Did everyone go to pony club except me?" Camilla asked with a touch of regret.

"You didn't miss much," Jody assured her, "though I did have my first orgasm while cantering bareback. Then I fell off. I've associated sex with danger ever since. But hold on a tic, Ellen. Isn't this just an exotic twist on my cowboy story?"

Ellen laughed. "Isn't every fantasy just a variation on a theme anyway? So, finally, you see in the distance a round tent made of compressed yak hair, and you pull up in front of the tent. He hops off and helps you down, and his warm, tough hand holds yours a second longer than necessary. He leads you inside and, lighting a fire of yak dung, makes tea from a fragrant brick, which he strains into a brass churn, and mixes with pungent yak butter. He offers this to you in a wooden bowl, and then, with his fingers still smelling of sweat, horse, and leather, pinches up some barley meal, dips it in his tea and rolls the tsampa into a ball, which he places in your mouth. You lick his fingers. Soon he has put aside your bowl of tea, and he is kneading your breasts like tsampa and laying you down on furs, to make vigorous love to you, again and again, until the night comes and it grows cold and he pulls more furs over you both and takes you again. You sense he was made in the precise mold of your insides; no man has ever fitted so perfectly before, filling you in all the right ways. You adore his lean, muscular dark body, the tautness of it, with its brown nipples and sparse body hair, and you love that strong spurt of his seed when he comes." Ellen paused and frowned. "Although, I suppose, you really ought to have been using condoms."

"Oh, Ellen, it's just a fantasy," Jody protested. "I didn't have to wear an equestrian helmet, remember?"

"Yes, but, I don't know, I think it's important to valorize safe sex practices even in fantasy." Ellen glanced over at Camilla, whose features betrayed a slight hint of impatience. "Oh, never mind. At the first light of dawn, you reach for him but he's not there. You pull your clothes around you and walk outside, where you find him curled up with a sheep. You're not sure what to make of this, but when he beckons you over, you go and the two of you lie with the sheep, enjoying its warmth, and then make love next to the animal, under the fading stars and by the light of the rising sun. He is tender and ardent, and for nearly a month you stay there, getting used to the oily tea and the smell of the yak butter and the taste of the tsampa and the surprising sexuality of the sheep. Every day you make love so many times you lose track. But after a while, you begin to crave a wash, and some fruit, and clean clothes, and conversation. Besides, the short Himalayan summer is coming to an end. With regret, you take your leave."

"How poignant," Camilla commented.

"Well then," Jody said, picking up the thread, "after a few detours, you end up smack in the middle of Tokyo. Traffic, suits, neon, department stores, noodle shops, and more people moving down the pavement in front of you at any moment than you saw your entire time in Nepal and Tibet. You are feeling a bit dazed. You finger the heavy silver necklace given to you by your Tibetan lover. As you are crossing the road, a man in a suit takes your elbow. You look at him curiously, not sure how to react. He is speaking to you in Japanese but you make out the word *coffee*. You think coffee might be a nice idea. You allow him to steer you past several nice, warm, and cozy coffeeshops, to which you gesture, and into a back alley and a rather sleazy-looking place. You are feeling a bit more wary now. You've just noticed that the man is missing two fingers. It is seeping into your travel-lagged brain that he is probably a yakuza gangster. You will have your coffee and bolt. The waitress brings over your coffee and nods to the man. This strikes you as strange, and as you drink your coffee you suddenly recall stories about yakuza involvement in white slavery. As the drug in the coffee begins to take effect, you dimly perceive the yakuza pulling out of his briefcase a videotape of *La Belle Aussie Slut à la Plage,* the porn flick you made at Cannes. That's the last thing you remember before coming to.

"Your head is spinning and your eyes are heavy. Bit by bit you become conscious of the fact that you are lying down, naked, on a long, low table, around which kneel two dozen Japanese men in traditional dress. You are trying to comprehend what has happened when it occurs to you that there are small, cold things placed all over your body. You strain to pick up your head. Before dizziness forces it back on the table, you manage to see that you have been made into a tray for all manner of sushi and sashimi. Your pubic hair has been shaved, as has the hair underneath your armpits, and something about the tightness of the skin on your face tells you that you've been made up quite heavily with what you guess is the white paint of the geisha girl. Your pubic mound is covered with something warm—you realize later that it is rice. There is something pushed up into your vagina—a baby octopus?—and something else—a strip of eel?—up your anus. Something is burning your labia and clitoris and nipples—you realize it must be hot wasabi mustard, and your sex is becoming engorged and embarrassingly, frantically needy, your nipples painfully hard.

"The men, who are quite handsome and dressed like something out of a Kurosawa epic, all brocades, half-shaved heads, and triangularity, are nodding and exclaiming with delight; and after they've admired you for a while one says, '*Itedakimas!*' (Bon Appetit!), and the others chorus it. One raises a pair of bamboo chopsticks to pluck a morsel of raw tuna from your navel. After he swallows it down, encouraged by the others, he bends down and plants a wet kiss on your bellybutton. Now it's a free-for-all. Some of the men dispense with chopsticks altogether and just put their mouths to your body and keep their lips on you as they take the raw seafood into their mouths. It's a feeding frenzy. The men are moving around your body now, taking mouthfuls of rice from your pubis and licks of wasabi from your vulva. Your entire body is being nibbled and licked and kissed and touched and rubbed and stroked by these men, one of whom slowly devours the octopus from your vagina, and then another, lifting and parting the cheeks of your ass with both hands, eats out the eel. Just as this is happening, you see one of them part the folds of his robe and direct his own straight, shiny eel into your mouth. Hungrily, you suck him off, and he has no sooner spasmed and withdrawn when the next is poking his dark red tuna between your lips. You sense another man straddle the narrow table by your hips and suddenly, with a great thrust, he enters you from below. There is just a tiny little piece of octopus still in your cunt and it's tickling you inside, stuck fortuitously next to your g-spot, like one of those extra knobs on the fancier dildos. You come within minutes, but he's still going strong, and you come again, and again. Two men are biting your nipples and yet another is manipulating your clitoris. Someone is sucking your toes, someone else has your hand in his mouth, and yet another is slapping his cock against your thigh. You feel another cock—or is it two?—pushing through your hair, humping your head, rubbing your forehead. The cold sashimi has all been devoured, or pushed off to the tatami, and now your skin tingles with smeared wasabi and you are suddenly cresting and writhing and pumping, and this just sets all of them off at once, and they're coming inside you and coming all over you, your face, your body, your legs and arms, and of course there's one in each hand and you have come so much and so strongly that you're beginning to lose consciousness. You fade out just as they're stroking your skin with their hands, rubbing in the cum like body cream. Your eyes close.

"When you come to, you're lying in a bubble bath in a luxury hotel. There's a silver platter by the marble bathtub on which sits your passport, your purse, a bottle of warm sake, and a beautiful black lacquer box, which you open to find a lavish Japanese supper inside. You take up the chopsticks, pincer a slab of sashimi, dip it in the wasabi and soy, and then put it into your mouth, savoring the taste and wondering if it were all a dream. The skin behind your ear tingles. You reach up to scratch it and find a tiny trace of wasabi there."

Camilla realized she was squeezing her thighs together. Then again, so were the women at all the adjacent tables.

"That's a hard act to follow," Ellen commented, after a long pause. "Maybe we should just take our heroine home and give her a rest."

"Good idea," Camilla nodded. She gasped, "Ohmygod, darlings, I can't believe it." The others followed the direction of her gaze. Trent was standing there, staring at Camilla as if he couldn't be quite sure that it was her. Camilla ventured a tight little smile.

"Truth is stranger . . ." whispered Jody, fascinated.

Trent stepped into the café, but before he reached their table, two twenty-year-old girls in pale makeup and brickred lipstick jumped up and threw themselves in front of him. He blinked at them. "You're Trent Bent!" one exclaimed. The other was biting her lip and looking up at him coyly through heavily lined eyelids.

"Uh, yes"—He grimaced, looking over at Camilla apologetically—"I suppose I am."

"You're our idol," declared the more forward of the pair. The other giggled and nodded, her eyes wide and upon him.

Camilla looked on, half in horror and half in amusement. Trent had aged badly, rather like Bram in *Eat Me,* she suddenly realized. Had Philippa seen him and not told her?

"Thanks, really, but I . . ." He strained out a smile and looked down at his arm, upon which a young female hand had taken a firm grip.

Camilla shook her head and a great wide smile broke out across her ever-luscious lips. "Nice to see you again, Trent," she said. She pulled a card out of her purse and handed it over to him. "Call me sometime if you want to go for a coffee. That's my office number. I'm usually there."

"I'd, uh, like that," stumbled Trent, as the girls pulled him firmly down onto a seat at their table. "Really. I'll call you."

Camilla turned to the others and winked. "The more things change . . ." she commented under her breath.

"What a morning!" Jody laughed.

Ellen glanced at her watch. "I've actually got to go soon," she said regretfully. "I've got a goddess workshop at one."

"And I've promised to visit Jonathan's folks with him. Not exactly a fantasy afternoon, but there you go. Reality bites." Camilla shrugged. "What are you up to this weekend, Jody?"

"I've got a hot date." She winked, grinning. "With a cool young man. I'm interviewing for Josh's replacement."

"You," Ellen said, shaking her head and smiling, "really are a bad girl."

"Next thing you know you'll be wanting to spank me," Jody offered provocatively.

"Anytime," Ellen said. "And you know I mean it."

"So, what are we going to do about the book?" Camilla pressed.

"I say," Jody proposed, "we don't say a word about it unless Philippa brings it up."

"Agreed." nodded Ellen.

"*D'accord*," said Camilla.

CHAPTER THIRTEEN

Just Desserts

Philippa handed the weekend papers to Cara. She sat down next to her on the sofa. They were wearing matching silk robes. Cara narrowed her cat eyes as she looked through the papers.

Philippa got up again and paced.

"Sit down," Cara said. "You'll drive me crazy."

She sat down.

When Cara found what she was looking for, she threw the rest of the pile carelessly on the floor. She read silently and without expression.

Philippa curled herself into a ball and put her hands over her face. "Well?" she peeped after a while.

"You want me to read it to you?"

"Please."

"Brace yourself."

"Braced."

"'Indigestible Prose from the Smelly Deli.'"

The ball that was Philippa grew smaller.

"'*Eat Me* is a stale collection of erotica cooked up in the filthy oven of one Dick Pulse's fetid imagination. It is a veritable gorgonzola of a book, its stench as overpowering as its narrative is underwhelming. Like the vegan mentioned in chapter two, this reviewer couldn't bring herself to swallow.'" Cara looked over at Philippa, and laughed. "Only joking, dearheart. Now sit up straight and listen to what they really said."

Philippa raised her eyes, in which tiny, pearl-like tears had begun to well. "You mean?" She sniffled hopefully.

"You're being a very silly little girl, now, aren't you? I think you should kneel for your sins. In front of me. That's it."

Philippa knelt.

Cara held the paper up to her. The headline of the review read, "Spicy and Delicious, an Erotic Feast." Philippa grinned despite herself and then, flushing, hung her head as Cara read aloud the rest of the article.

"See," said Cara, folding the newspaper and placing it safely on the table next to the sofa, "I told you that you shouldn't have taken it so much to heart that the girls haven't said a word. I'm sure, as I've told you a hundred times, that they haven't worked it out that Dick Pulse is your pen name. Maybe they haven't even seen the book. You should just tell them, you silly creature." Cara shook her head. She reached over to the table and picked up the open box of Belgian chocolates. Studying its contents, she chose one in a conch shape. "Now what does this remind you of?" she asked, holding the shell briefly between her legs before popping it into her mouth.

Philippa smiled. "You know," she said shyly, "you haven't told me what *you* thought of the book."

"You want to know my honest opinion?"

"Of course."

"Well, it was all right." Cara shrugged. "Oh, don't look so disappointed. You know me, the mistress of understatement. I liked it, I did. Really. There were a number of places where I laughed out loud. And natch, chapter five was my favorite. That was a particularly clever bit of cross-dressing, I thought." Sitting very straight, she penetrated Philippa with her green-eyed gaze. "Of course, the sex in most of the other chapters was a bit too, oh, vanilla for my taste. And, if you don't mind my saying so, a bit too straight as well. Really, Philippa. Hairy necks and phalluses don't exactly put my knickers in a twist, as you know."

"What hairy necks?"

"Oh, don't be so literal. You know what I mean. Men."

"Oh."

"Also I don't see why you had to fuck boys in the novel yourself. You don't really fuck boys, do you?" Cara asked in an ominous tone of voice.

"Course not," Philippa replied. "It was a narrative convenience. You know, to create a little more tension."

Cara's eyes drilled into her. "You describe hetero sex as though you know it very well, however." She sniffed.

"I'm a novelist," objected Philippa. "I read a lot and I've got a good imagination." And, she thought to herself, there has been the odd boy on the side. Not that Cara's ever going to find out about that.

"Hmm," Cara replied, not entirely convinced but unwilling to press her on this point. "I've got to go home soon. I've got heaps of course work to do this weekend. For my women's literature class with Ellen, in fact. So, are we going to sit here jabbering all day, slave, or are you going to eat me?"

"Yes, mistress." Philippa obediently bent down and pressed her lips to Cara's knees.